Scripted LOVE

KAREN FRANCES

Dedication

This book is for anyone who has
ever wanted to help someone else.
You can make a difference.

Contents

Chapter 1

MY HEART STUTTERS AS I struggle to draw in a breath.

Bloody hell.

If I could turn the clock back, so help me God, I would turn back five years and ensure this man was never in my life. It seems every time I pull myself together, allow myself to be happy, he appears in some form, back to turn my world upside down.

Why now?

I don't think I've hated before, but, right here, right now, I hate him.

But I can't turn back the clock and he's here, larger than life and staring at me. I blink rapidly, hoping my eyes are playing tricks, but I know they're not when I hear his smug chuckle. *Donovan Bell.* The man I hoped and prayed I would never set eyes upon again. He's here in my living room, but why? Has he come here to torment me further? Jonathon and my dad had someone keeping tabs on him. He shouldn't be here. He's not allowed to be near me. As far as I was concerned, he had been keeping a low profile in London with Katherine Hunter.

I gasp, holding my chest as my heart races, feeling as though it could explode at any moment. My eyes dart around the room, looking for an exit, but he's blocking the way. Even if I could get past him, my body is too weak to run. He'd catch me.

"Are you not pleased to see me?"

I pull my blanket around my cold body and shiver. *If only I wasn't feeling so weak.* "What do you want?"

He takes a step closer, kneeling down on the floor beside me. He reaches out and moves a strand of my hair. I wince from his touch, but he doesn't seem to notice my reaction. If he did, he's not interested in how he makes my skin crawl.

"I've come home. We have things to discuss and it looks as though I'm back at the right time, to take care of you. Oh, Ella. You look awful."

Home. This isn't his home. It's mine.

Confusion fills the air around me and I want to scream. To tell him to leave. Leave me alone. My head is pounding and my body is sore. He moves his hand across my cheek, sweeping his thumb across my skin. The small, intimate touch takes me completely by surprise. Wave after wave of fear washes over me. A deep churning in the pit of my stomach has me wanting to be sick. My heart pounds so loudly that I'm scared it's going to pop out of my chest. Pains shoot down my legs.

I can't breathe.

I'm going crazy.

I'm losing control.

Why today?

"Ella!"

His voice does nothing to soothe me. The arms that wrap around me don't comfort me in any way. Tears blind me and I try to push him away, but he's too strong. He holds me tight. I close my eyes, not wanting to see him. I wish I could switch off my sense of smell. The familiar aftershave that I couldn't stand wafts under my nose, turning my stomach more.

He can't be here. With me. I don't want him here. Not holding me. His arms aren't the ones I want.

I want Connor.

Connor should be the one holding me.

I need him.

Donovan pulls me closer, rocking me in his arms, and I don't have the energy to pull away. He kisses the top of my head and tears run faster down my face. I will them to stop and I fight to find my strength again. Strength to tell him I don't want him here.

Keeping my eyes closed, I try to bring my breathing back under control, but it's hard. There was a time in my life when Donovan was my world. Now, he's a part of my past that I'd rather forget about.

Questions spin around in my head, but right now, alone with him, I don't want to hear his excuses or anything else he has to say. When we have that conversation, I need to be one-hundred-percent focused, and today, I'm not.

"There, there. I'm here. I'll look after you. What has happened to my beautiful girl? Who has done this to you?"

His question is laughable because he's the one who has done this to me. In this moment, all the confidence I've had over the last few weeks has been stripped away by his presence.

"I don't need looking after. I'm capable of doing that on my own."

"That's not what I hear. You've had *my* friend looking after you, sleeping in my bed. You, my darling Ella, aren't capable of making decisions for yourself. If you were, you wouldn't be making bad decisions over and over. He's not the man you need. You need me. Connor Andrews is just another bad decision on your part. You'll see that soon enough."

He has some fucking nerve. The only bad decision I've made in my life is Donovan Bell. I don't need him and I certainly don't want him. Not now, not ever.

I open my eyes. My tears finally stop and my breathing is calmer. "Why are you really here?" I ask, freeing myself from his hold.

"Because I love you."

I can't hide the small laugh that escapes my mouth. "You don't love me. The only person you love is yourself."

"Don't be like that. It doesn't suit you, sounding so spiteful. I came back home for you. That must prove something to you."

I have no answer. He's still playing games; that's why he's here. I don't have the energy to argue with him. If I felt like myself it would be so easy to argue with him, to stand up for myself. But I just don't have the strength.

Julie will be here soon. She'll help me get rid of him, although she might take great pleasure in slapping him hard across the face first. He must be mad if he thinks he can just come waltzing back in here and I'll welcome him with open arms.

Yes, that's it. He has a screw loose.

"Donovan, go away. I don't want you here," I say, finally getting to my feet and walking—albeit unsteadily—towards the window, still with the cover wrapped around my shivery body.

I stare out to the driveway, looking for someone, anyone, to be there. But there's no one. It's damp and grey outside, much like my mood, and it has just started raining again. I watch as large raindrops fall quickly outside. *How did he get here? There's no car in the drive.*

"Ella, you don't mean that. I need you."

"What is it this time? Do you need more money? Don't you think you've taken enough from me already?" I'm trying to rein in my anger, but I can't.

"No, it's not like that. I just need you. I want you. I miss and love you more than you could ever know." He stands and takes a small step toward me, and my whole body shudders as he closes the distance between us. Reaching out his hand, he strokes my face. I flinch and push his hand away.

"Ella, don't be like that." He's only inches away from me. "Why have you been avoiding me? All those messages I sent and you never replied to a single one of them. Why is that? Is it because you're so pre-occupied with Connor?"

"You're not supposed to be here."

"Oh, yes. About that. Did you really think an injunction was going to keep me away from you?"

Yes. I had hoped so.

"Connor will be back soon," I say, trying to sound confident.

He takes another step closer to me and I feel his icy breath against my skin. "I know he won't be back soon because your daddy hasn't been the only one keeping tabs. I've been doing that too. And I know for a fact Connor is looking at apartments most of the day, so it looks like it's just you and me for a while."

"Leave!"

"I'm not going anywhere, so why don't you just lie back down and I'll take care of you. We can catch up. You can bring me up to speed on everything going on in your life."

He can't stay here. I take a step to the side, but he grabs my already aching shoulders, digging his fingers in, stopping me from turning away.

Where the hell is my phone?

I glance around the room, not wanting him to see what I'm searching for. I see it on the couch. *I need to get to it.* "You're hurting me."

"Am I? You know, you've hurt me these past few weeks. Connor fucking Andrews. It had to be him. Why couldn't it have been someone else? Seeing you out with my best friend has hurt me in more ways than you'll ever know. You've no idea the thoughts that have been in my head about the two of you together. Does he make you feel as good as I do?"

I'm not going to answer his last question because I sense my answer will anger him, so I choose to ignore it and focus on my own hurt and anger.

"I've hurt you?" I shout, finding a little strength. "You left me broke. Not only that, but I find out you cheated on me two years ago. So explain to me how any of this fucked up situation is my fault, because I can't see it. All I see is a man who disgusts me with his recent behaviour. You've followed me, watched me, tried to frighten and intimidate me."

He laughs loudly, still gripping my body, "And it's worked. Just look at your pathetic panic attack. You, Ella, are a weak woman, but you're *my* woman."

I'm trying not to be the woman he described, but I know, at the moment, I am. If being frightened by him being here makes me weak, then so be it.

Donovan pulls me closer to him and leans his head forward. No. He can't kiss me. Tears fill my eyes. I want Connor. I don't want this, not with him.

"I love you," he says softly as his lips meet mine. I gasp and shove him as hard as I can, knocking him off balance slightly, but not long enough for me to rush past him.

I lift my hand to slap him, but he grabs my wrist, laughing at me. His grip is tight, but I try to pull away from him. He's strong; stronger than me. I look into his eyes and all I see is darkness glaring back at me. There's no sparkle as he stares blankly through me. The man holding me isn't the man I spent five years of my life with. I'm now more certain than ever that he's involved in drugs or something. Because the Donovan I thought I knew would never have hurt me. The man before me is a complete stranger. I have no idea what he's capable of and that single thought terrifies me.

I wriggle against him. "Please let go of me."

"If you stop fighting against me, I might just consider it. Come on. Let's sit down. I need to have you in my arms."

My stomach churns at his words. Still holding me, he ushers me back to the couch and I reluctantly sit down. My phone is now under my leg. *Please don't ring.* He joins me on the couch, wrapping his arm around my shoulder, allowing his fingers to trail down towards my breast. I close my eyes, hoping and praying he stops, because I'm tired, and all I want to do is sleep.

"You're sick, Ella. Just try and sleep." If it was anyone else saying that to me, maybe I would, but not him. My skin is crawling from his touch and I feel as though I'm going to throw up. "Why don't I go and make us a cup of tea? I presume everything is where it should be."

"That would be nice, and yes." He kisses me on the head and leaves the room. When I hear him in the kitchen, I grab my phone and type out two quick messages, one to Connor and the other to my brother.

I need you. Donovan is here.

Callum, I need help. Donovan is here.

Then I put it on silent and slide it between the cushions, hoping Connor or Callum sees my message soon. I lie down with my feet up, pulling the cover around my body, and close my eyes. Hopefully, if I keep them closed, he'll stay away from me when he comes back into the room.

My phone vibrates beneath me and I fight the urge to check it. And when I hear Donovan's footsteps crossing the floor, I've never been so relieved that I didn't pick up my phone to check who was messaging me.

"Ella, honey. I've made you tea."

I wriggle on the couch, pretending he's disturbing me. "Thank you," I say weakly, pretending I'm grateful, which I'm most definitely not. I'll be grateful when he leaves my house.

He lifts my head and I feel his body sink into the couch before he rests my head in his lap. Oh, no. I cringe at the contact and a lonely tear rolls from my eye and falls onto his trousers. My whole body trembles as he touches me and I'm desperate for him to leave. He must know how I feel about him. I wonder how long

I'll have to lie here and pretend I'm sleeping before help arrives.

Why the hell did I not think to change all the locks and numbers to the gate?

Chapter 2

A CAR SKIDDING TO A stop on the gravel of my driveway grabs not only my attention, but Donovan's. He jumps from the couch, my head falling onto the seat, and rushes over to the window.

"Shit!"

I want to smile when I see he's concerned, but I don't. Instead, I find myself wondering if it's Connor or Callum.

"What the hell have you done?" Donovan shouts, storming toward me at the same time as another car comes to a screeching halt outside.

He grabs me by my shoulders, pulling my aching body off the couch. I hear the slight rasp of the material of my top ripping. "Stand up, you stupid, stupid bitch!" He spits the words at me. I do as he says because I know that, any second now, someone is going to come barging into the house to help. "Did you call them?"

"No." Well, it's not a lie.

"Why couldn't you just leave us alone? Why involve others in our tiff? We would be okay without any interference. We could've got through this alone, but, oh no, Ella . . ."

Tears pool in my eyes. A tiff. He's funny. There's no way in hell we could work through what he's done. I fight against his hold, but his grip tightens. The noise of my front door banging against the wall makes me jump.

"Let go of me!" I scream, letting whoever has come in know where I am.

"You bitch." There's so much anger in his eyes. Donovan slaps me across the face. Heat spreads quickly across it, and the pain . . .

"Let her fucking go!" It's Callum's voice that echoes around me. I'm not facing my brother, but I'm glad it's him. Donovan pulls me tighter to him, his nails digging into my skin. Two sets of footsteps rush toward us and I close my eyes.

Taking a deep breath, I open my eyes and finally pull out of Donovan's hold. My vision is slightly blurry, but I make out Connor as he grabs him, throwing the first punch. Callum takes me in his arms and I bury my head against him and allow my tears to fall. I can't watch them fight. I don't want Connor to get hurt because of me.

"Ella, I've got you. Everything is going to be okay now. It's okay." Callum's voice is offering me no comfort as I break down in his arms.

"You fucking bastard!" The sound of crashing and shouting fills the room. I turn my head. Fists fly. Everything is out of focus except for the two men. Donovan takes a step back from an angry Connor. He bangs his legs on the table and falls backward, crashing on top of it and breaking the table in two. Connor leans over him and punches him in the face, bursting his nose. Blood slowly trickles down Donovan's face.

"Connor, stop. He's not worth it!" Callum shouts. Connor's eyes dart to me and I see his concern and sadness, but for the first time since I've known him, there's anger and frustration. He nods. Donovan lies on the floor, breathing heavily and wiping the blood from his face, and almost laughing. We all look at him. He thinks this is funny? It all seems like a huge joke. What the hell is wrong with him? Or should I ask him what drugs he's on?

But it's not a joke to me. Far from it. This is my life he's turning upside down. Playing with my emotions, yet again.

Connor takes a step toward me and I don't hesitate in leaving my brother's arms and walking straight into Connor's. He holds me softly yet securely, kissing me repeatedly on my head. "I'm sorry I wasn't here for you," he whispers. This isn't his fault and I don't want him to think it is. Blame can only go to Donovan.

"Don't you two look fucking cosy?" Donovan mumbles, getting back to his feet. "My *friend*, she's not yours. She'll always be mine. You, you're not worthy of her love and never will be. We've all made mistakes in the past. I'm here to rectify mine."

Past and mistakes. These words play over in my head and I ask myself what mistakes Connor has made. Because I think that's what Donovan has implied.

"I think you'll find Ella belongs to no one. She's more than capable of deciding who she wants in her life. What did you hope to achieve by coming here today? Did you really think you could bully your way back into her life?"

Donovan stumbles across the living room and makes himself comfortable on a chair. I swear all he needs is a damn cigar hanging from his mouth. There's something odd about him. It's the way he's sitting there without a care in the world. His eyes are glazed, pupils dilated. "I came home."

"This isn't your home! Never has been! What is it you want?" I scream at him.

"You. Only you, Ella." I wonder if he says the same thing to Katherine Hunter during their intimate moments together. Does she know he's here today? I bet she doesn't. Why would he tell his new love interest he was going to see his ex?

Connor takes a large intake of breath and I feel his fist clench tightly as he holds me. Donovan's words and intense stare are making me dizzy, or maybe that's how I was feeling before he showed up. I'm tired and my poor body is hurting more than it already was. I glance at my shoulders and deep red and purple marks are already there. My top is ripped. I want to go for a bath, get changed out of these clothes, and just lie down in my bed, close my eyes, and forget all about today.

But somehow, I don't think today is a day I'll forget about easily.

"You can't have me. I don't want you, Donovan. Please just get out of my house."

I hear the clip-clop of shoes walking across the floor. I lift my head and Julie is standing in the doorway, her eyes roaming the damage in my living room before they settle on Donovan, who is sitting calmly, as though he's entitled to be here.

"What the fuck? I was going to ask why the cars were abandoned outside with doors open, but I now see why."

"You look good, Julie," Donovan says as she struts into the room.

Her eyes cast over me, making sure I'm okay. I give her a slight nod because, in this moment, in Connor's arms, I'm okay.

"So do you. Blood red suits you." How she says it with a straight face, I'll never know. All I want to do is laugh. "Still causing trouble I see. What is it with you? Why can't you just leave Ella alone? Not happy that she's moved on and is finally getting on with her own life with someone who loves her?"

"You never could keep your nose out of our business," he says. "What's wrong, Julie? Were you jealous? Did you want me all to yourself?"

Julie laughs loudly but takes several steps toward him. "God, do me a favour. Me, want you? No," she says before she looks outside. I hear sirens then see blue flashing lights.

Thank God. That means Donovan will be removed from my house and I don't have to look at him with the silly, smug grin that's on his face any longer. Although, why he's looking so smug, I have no idea. Something tells me today won't be the last I hear from him.

"Hello?" a loud voice calls out.

"We're in the first room," Callum tells them. Either my brother or Connor must've called them on the way over after I sent my message.

Donovan stands as two officers enter the room. "You'll be looking for me," he says, holding out his wrists, waiting for them to cuff him. I watch him for a moment as Connor rubs my back in circular motions. *What the hell is he playing at?*

The officers look at each other then one walks toward Donovan.

I turn and look at Julie, and I know straight away she's thinking the same thing when she shrugs her shoulders.

"Miss McGregor." An officer calls my name.

"Sorry," I say, looking at him.

"Is there another room where I can speak to you?" I nod and take a step, but Connor keeps hold of me. "Sorry. I'd like to speak to Miss McGregor alone."

Connor kisses and releases me and I walk away with the officer out of the room. I hear Connor cursing as I leave, along with that bloody awful laugh from Donovan.

Yeah, he's still up to something.

I'm almost in the kitchen when dizziness and nausea sweep through me. I stumble in the kitchen and the officer catches me. "Miss, sit down." He helps me to the chair. I sit down and rest my head on my arms on top of the counter. "Miss . . ."

"Please, it's just Ella," I say weakly.

"Okay, Ella. What's wrong? Are you injured?"

"I'm tired and cold. Other than the bruising on my shoulders and arms, I don't think there's anything else." I shiver.

"I'll go and get you a cover." I hear his footsteps leaving and I close my eyes. I just want to rest. I need my bed. I want to forget about today.

"She has the flu. That's why I was coming here today, to look after and keep her company," Julie says. I lift my head slightly and she's there with the officer. I smile weakly at her. "Can you not just take him away and come back for a statement? After all, he's handing himself over to you."

"Julie, he's up to something," I say, sitting up.

"You're probably right, but we have no idea what it is yet and I just want him gone. I want him as far away from you as possible before the officers have to arrest me." She might be smirking, but the lowering of her tone with her last statement tells me she's deadly serious.

"I have a few questions, Ella, and then we can come back at a later date." I agree to a few questions and Julie stays with me. It doesn't take long and the officer is very nice. Julie gives him my backstory with Donovan. Well, the most recent history. The officer is sympathetic and understanding of the whole situation. When he's finished asking questions, he leaves. I hear voices in the hallway but I don't pay attention.

"I want a bath," I say.

"Ella, honey, you're shivering with the cold. I don't think that's a good idea. Why don't we just get you upstairs, tuck you into bed, and I'll bring you up a hot drink? And I think I'll call your doctor to come and check you over."

"Fine," I huff, but I don't need a doctor. Sleep is all I need, and then I'm sure I'll be fine. She helps me to my feet. I'm still unsteady but I know that's more to do with the flu rather than everything that has happened today. Connor and Callum come into the kitchen. Callum is on his phone, no doubt to our dad, but I don't listen to what he's saying. My focus is on the man before me. The pained expression on his face has my chest aching. Julie hands me a tissue and I wipe my nose. I cross my arms, holding onto my shoulders and wince from the pain.

"Ella!" I walk instinctively toward him as my name falls from his lips. He's hurting because I'm hurt. He looks as lost as I feel. Then I see his bloodstained hands. "Babe, come on. Everything is fine. I'll take you upstairs, and if you want a bath, I'll stay with you."

Julie doesn't argue with him. I nod and leave the kitchen with Connor's arm around me, holding me steady as we walk up the stairs to his bedroom.

He sits me down on the bed and I watch as he enters the bathroom. The sound of running water pleases me. I'm hoping the hot water and warm hands that will hold me close soothe my aching body.

But I'm not sure they will.

Chapter 3

I'VE HEARD THEIR MUFFLED VOICES throughout the night. Callum's, Julie's, and even my dad's. They've all been here. Checking up on me, along with Connor, making sure I'm okay, but it's Connor who has been beside me. He's the one who has looked after me since he brought me up the stairs yesterday. The only time he's left my side is to go to the bathroom.

"How is she?" It's my dad's concerned voice I hear. I woke up a few minutes ago but I wasn't yet ready to open my eyes and face the day. I'm still not sure I want to be awake; that's why I've lay here silent and still. But I know I need to face everyone.

"Her temperature is slowly coming down, but she's been so restless," Connor replies. He held me in his arms when I woke during the night after having a vivid dream. It was as though my mind was on repeat, playing over the day's events.

"I'm not surprised. A lot happened here yesterday. Has she said anything about what happened before you and Callum got here?"

"No."

There's not much for me to tell them. I'm so mad with myself for not being able to stand up to Donovan when he first appeared. I was weak.

I turn over and open my eyes. Connor takes my hand in his and I hold his gaze. He looks exhausted. He needs some sleep too and I tried to tell him that during the night. "Hey. How are you feeling?" he asks.

"Tired, but a little better than yesterday. Hi, Dad."

"Hi, sweetheart. Do you want to talk about yesterday?"

"What do you want me to say? He scared me. Has Donovan been charged with anything?" I ask, rubbing my cheek. I already know it's bruised. It's marked, like my shoulders; I saw it in the bathroom when I went for a bath.

"I've not heard from Jonathon yet."

"Ella, can I get you anything?" Connor asks, staring into my eyes. I'm still cold but my body doesn't ache so much today. "Painkillers?"

"No, I'm okay just now. You shouldn't be here. Are you not supposed to be looking at more apartments today?"

"I've cancelled all plans for today to stay here and look after you."

"You do know you didn't have to do that?"

"Yes, I know, but I want to be here with you."

I sigh. "Fine," I mutter before coughing. God, my head hurts when I cough. It feels as though it's rattling about. "Who else is here?" I ask, thinking how quiet the house is.

"Callum is on his way over. He's been with Trevor all morning. I told Julie to go home last night. She has work today, but she said she'd be here tonight to see you."

"Why has Callum been with Trevor all morning?" I ask, although I already have a horrible feeling yesterday's events have made today's news. Connor and Dad share a knowing look. "It's fine. I've already guessed. I'm today's headlines."

"Sorry, sweetheart. We're not sure how the story was leaked so quickly, but it will be dealt with. What did Donovan want? What did he say to you?"

I shift in the bed, sitting up. Connor starts fussing and props the pillows behind me. "It was all very strange. I had expected him to be . . . I don't know. He was different, kept telling me he loved me and that he had come home to me. Made me tea. That's when I sent the text messages. But he hurt me. At times, he seemed so calm and collected. As though it was the most natural thing in the world for him to turn up here. Then he would lash out. There's still something wrong."

"What do you mean?" Dad asks.

"He's still playing some sort of game. He didn't discuss the money, but I get the feeling he's looking for more and hiding stuff."

"Well, you're right that he's hiding stuff. Sweetheart, he owes millions to different people, and as I've said before, from what I've been told, some of them are very unsavoury characters. Not people I want my daughter to be associated with."

Millions. How can he run up that amount of debt? "Dad, you don't have to worry about that. I don't want to get mixed up with whoever he owes money to." Loud drilling and banging stops my words. I pause for a moment and listen. "What's going on?"

"I'm changing all the locks and the security system at the gate."

"Okay." That's something I should've taken care of months ago when he first left me.

"Sweetheart, if you feel up to it, why don't you go and grab a shower then come downstairs and have something to eat?"

I suppose I could do with a shower. After all, I've been sweating most of the night. I must stink. "Shower, yes. Food, no. I don't feel up to eating."

"Fine." Dad huffs before leaving the room.

"You've had us all worried," Connor says, moving his position so he's sitting on the bed, facing me.

"Connor, I'm fine. It's only the flu."

"That's not what I mean and you know it. Truthfully, tell me, how did you feel yesterday?"

"I was scared. I was scared that if I put up a fight, he would hurt me more. Yes, I argued with him, but then I just gave in. My body felt so weak yesterday. All I wanted to do was sleep, and I thought if I just tried to ignore him and pretend to sleep, you or Callum would arrive."

He moves closer, wrapping his arms around me, and I rest my head on his shoulder. "Ella, you did the right thing. I know it might not seem like it, but you did. Now, do you want me to stay here and help you shower?"

"No, because I can't have you."

I lift my head to see his reaction. He's smiling brightly at me. "You always have me." His words are my undoing as my tears fall and he holds me close.

"WHAT THE FUCK do I pay you for?" My dad's voice is hardly ever raised, so to hear him shouting above the noise of all the drilling and banging is somewhat alien to me. I know why he has workmen here today, I agree with it, but I wish it wasn't today when I still don't feel like myself. Now that I'm up and moving about, my head is still banging, and the noise really isn't helping. "You had better sort this because, so help me God, if he comes near my daughter one more time, I'll kill him. And that's not a threat, it's a promise."

I enter the living room and Dad is pacing the floor, his phone tight to his ear. Connor is sitting on the couch, leaning forward, his head in his hands. My brother stands by the bay windows, watching Dad closely.

Connor lifts his head and offers me a smile then holds out his hand. I take it and he pulls me down onto his knees and wraps his arms around my back, holding me close to him. He rocks me nervously as we wait for my dad to end his call. But I'm sure we all know what's just happened.

Donovan Bell must have been released from custody.

Dad ends his call. His eyes glare straight ahead and his brows are knitted tightly together. He inhales deeply before turning his attention to me. "I'm sorry, sweetheart. There was nothing I could do. Donovan has been charged but he's been released."

"It's not your fault, or Jonathon's."

"Maybe not, but it feels like it is." Nothing I say is going to make my dad feel any better. I'm not a parent so I can only imagine how he's feeling; helpless is the one word that comes to mind. "Callum, why don't you tell your sister what's happening? Bring her up to speed on the media."

Callum walks away from the window and sits down, crossing one leg over the other. "Well, there are various stories running and they're all so far-fetched, but in your world, maybe not so much so." I want to laugh at his honest statement. Nothing in the showbiz world would surprise me anymore. "Sis, I do think you need to issue a written statement about yesterday. I'm sure one of the nationals will be more than happy to print your side of the story."

"Okay. Trevor can organise this." I know if there are any problems with the PR side of things that he couldn't handle on his own, he would bring in an outside party.

"Perfect. Now, one of the stories running is about Connor finding you and that arsehole in a compromising position. That's why a fight broke out."

"We were never in a compromising position, although he did try to kiss me." I don't know why I say it, but I do.

"He what?" Connor shouts, and I rub my ear.

"Connor, please. I still have a sore head."

"Sorry. But the thought of him forcing himself on you . . . I'm going to fucking kill him."

"Look, can we not dwell on this? Because, if I do, I'll end up making myself ill and I don't want him having the upper hand with me. I don't want him to control my life. Not again."

With my last words, I feel my dad and Callum watching me, but my focus is on Connor. He nods, reluctantly agreeing with me. He understands. I've accepted that Donovan had been controlling parts of my life these last few years, even though I didn't realise it at the time.

"Is there anything else I need to know?" I ask, not wanting to be surprised with anything else later on.

"At the moment, no, but you know as well as I do that can change at any time," Dad reminds me. "I'm going to check and see how much longer it's going to take the guys replacing the locks. The gate code and new security is already in place, and there's a new camera there too. It's all hooked up to the intercom. You'll be able to see who is at the gate."

"Thank you," I say as he leaves the room. Callum is watching me and Connor with a strange look that I can't place. "What is it?"

"Even after yesterday, and I know you're still not feeling a hundred percent, you still look happy. Looking at you with Connor has me thinking about what you were like before with Donovan, and you never looked this happy and content."

"I am happy, and even he can't take that feeling away from me." Connor's grip tightens and I lean further into his arms. He kisses my cheek.

"Connor, I think of you as family, but if you hurt my sister, I'll hunt you down, because she doesn't deserve it."

"You won't have to hunt me down. There's no way I'm hurting her or letting her go from my life."

"The guys are finished," Dad says, re-entering the room. "Callum, come on. We'll let your sister rest." My brother laughs and I feel my face redden at what he's thinking.

"Head. Gutter," I say. Everyone laughs. I attempt to stand up but Connor holds me.

"Don't even think about getting up to see us out," says Dad. "I'll give you a call tonight and see how you are. Take care of my girl," Dad tells Connor.

"Of course." Dad and Callum leave, and suddenly the house seems very quiet without them and all the noise of the drilling and banging. "Are you okay?"

"Yes, just a bit tired."

"Come and lie down here."

I look at where he's sitting and wanting me to lie down and I freeze, my heart hammering in my chest. "I c . . . can't. Please don't make me." My lips tremble as I speak and my eyes cloud over.

"Ella, what's wrong?"

"He sat here, with me lying on the couch and my head resting against his lap."

"Let's go upstairs. I want you to relax, and hopefully we'll both get some sleep."

"Okay," I say quietly.

Chapter 4

THIS IS GETTING RIDICULOUS. CONNOR has cancelled every-thing he's meant to have done the last few days. We've both been cooped up here, and I'm sick of looking at the inside of this house. I love that he wants to be here and take care of me, but I'm almost over the flu. With the exception of a runny nose and bit of a cough, I feel okay.

"Morning," I say, climbing back into bed and snuggling up beside him. Resting my head on his bare chest, I lay my hand on his well-defined stomach.

"Good morning. You look better. How are you feeling?"

"Much better," I say, tracing my fingers lightly against his skin. "What are your plans today?"

"I don't have any other than looking after you."

"Interesting." I place a soft kiss above his heart. "Well, why don't you take me away from here for the day?" I need to get out before I drive not just myself insane, but Connor too. Yesterday, I know my temper was simmering away, and it's not Connor's fault. I was snappy with him on more than one occasion.

"Where do you want to go?"

"Anywhere, as long as we get out and get some fresh air." Because I need it. It might help with the flat mood I've been in for the last few days.

"I'm sure that can be arranged. But I know what I'd like to do first if you're feeling better," he whispers, running his fingers through my hair. God, I want that too, so badly. Desire fills me. I crave him. "I need you."

"I'm yours for the taking," I murmur, lifting my head. I press my lips to his. I see the excitement in his eyes as he takes in what I've just said. This kiss is tender, slow, and thoughtful. He's being too gentle with me, but I'll allow him this moment because it's what we both need after everything. Connor lets out a low moan as his hands glide softly up and down my back.

We share an undeniable connection. It's one I'm struggling to explain to myself. There's a bond holding us together, and I don't think I ever want it to get broken. As the thought enters my mind, it scares me, yet excites me. What I have with Connor is completely different to the feelings I've had for anyone else.

He's all my hopes and dreams.

He's my future. *I hope*.

My heart feels light when I'm with him. Connor has brought me back to life and I want to share my life with him until I'm old and grey.

He flips me onto my back, hovering above me, breaking our connection. His eyes are filled with so much emotion as he gazes lovingly at me. My heart skips a beat. Nothing else exists in the world except the two of us.

Connor's strong hand grazes against my cheek. My eyes fill with unshed tears as I see his deepest feelings. The depth of his love for me. This man before me would walk to the end of the Earth and back again if I asked him too.

"Ella, tell me you're mine? Forever."

And in this moment, I am. "I'm yours forever and always." I lift my hand and run my thumb along his lips, savouring the feeling against my skin. "Only yours."

He lowers his face to mine and our lips meet. I lose myself to him. My hands roam his back, taking in every muscle and how perfectly they move. His erection presses against my core and I need him to take me.

I trail my fingers down his back until they reach his boxers. Slowly, I hook them under the waistband and lower them. His free erection presses against me and I want it deep inside me. His lips leave mine and I stare at him. He drops his gaze down my body and my eyes follow to see my erect nipples press hard against my vest top. He sits back and tenderly, ever so tenderly, trails his hands down my body.

It feels so good.

"You are so beautiful," he says, leaning forward and kissing my shoulders where they're bruised. I'm safe. Yes, I saw another side to Connor when he lashed out at Donovan, but I understand why he did it; he wanted to protect me. His rage was raw and frightening, but with me, he's himself.

He looks up and our eyes meet. I hold his gaze, ensuring he sees the desperation I feel for him. Every fibre of me wants him. Of this, I'm certain.

He pulls at my small shorts and I wriggle, helping him remove them. He casts his eyes over my vest and I don't wait for him to take it off. I pull it over my head and discard it to the floor. I'm lying beneath him, naked and exposed, my breaths coming quicker as he starts a slow trail, caressing me. My back bows when his mouth reaches my nipple, arching and pushing my breasts toward him, begging him silently for more.

But he stops and I groan.

Slowly, his fingers start moving again, only this time south, bypassing my stomach and slowly lowering to my thigh. My whole body tenses in anticipation of what's next.

Again, he stops, and this time the pause has me crying out his name. "Connor, please!" He smiles that cheeky boy grin that I know so well before slipping his fingers between my thighs.

I close my eyes. My back arches further, pushing my hips closer to him, to where I want him. He pushes two fingers deep inside me. My muscles tighten around him, holding him firmly where he belongs. My pleasure starts to build already as his fingers explore and massage me deeply. "Oh, dear God." I sigh.

The sensation builds within. "Don't come," he tells me. *But I want to.* His attention is completely devoted to me as he pumps his fingers into me. I grab hold of the bed sheets, gripping them tightly. There's no way he can keep doing this and expect me not to come.

"Please," I whimper.

"Not yet," he says, and his words offer me no reassurance or comfort. He rubs his thumb over and over my clitoris, ensuring he's pushing me close. My burning need rises and I'm so close.

He inhales and exhales deeply.

He stops.

I watch.

I wait.

He grins and removes his fingers and I whine. Just another few minutes and I would have been done.

His chest meets mine, his arms bending at his elbows by my side. His face edges closer to mine. I feel him, but he should be deep inside, not waiting and watching. Connor's eyes stay on mine and I know he wants us to keep our eyes open for the moment two become one.

Taking a deep breath in an attempt to control my breathing, I nod.

Connor lifts himself from his elbows onto his hands and angles his hips, gliding effortlessly inside me, filling and stretching me. I moan with a sigh, wrapping my legs around his waist, pulling him closer to me.

Needing him.

Wanting him.

Loving him.

A lonely tear slips down my face as I think about my last thought. I never believed it was possible to love so much, so quickly. Connor lifts his hand and wipes away my tear. "I know," he says. I throw my arms around his shoulders, pulling him closer to me. "From this moment on, I'm never letting you go. I'm yours. Always have been and always will be."

His words hit me. They should frighten me so early in our relationship, but they don't. They excite me. I'm now looking forward, and I don't want to take slow, small steps.

Starting now. I push against him, urging him to hurry up and move instead of gazing into my eyes. He dips his hips and pushes deeper, both of us gasping for breath. When he's inside, he pulls back before pushing deep, filling me completely. He grinds hard and slow.

I'm done for.

Unable to keep my eyes open, I allow them to close as intoxicating sensations flood my veins. I grip his shoulders and I don't ever want to let him go. In this moment, everything has completely changed for me, and I know he realized it when he looked into the depths of my eyes.

With the rhythm he's set, neither of us will be able to hold back. Our moans of pleasure fill the air around us. Our bodies move together in perfect harmony.

It's perfect.

I feel him swell within me and I know he won't last much longer. I've been holding my own release back since he told me not to come. His mouth crashes against mine, kissing me firmly. I whimper and start clawing at his back, my slow-building orgasm now powering forward.

"I'm right there with you," he says into my mouth, pushing forward and rubbing me in all the right places.

His lips leave mine and I open my eyes, seeing everything we share in his gaze. "Connor!" His name falls from my lips and he roars loudly before a long, satisfied sigh falls from his.

My body shakes violently beneath him as I bask in the warmth spreading through me. His body falls to mine and he quickly rolls us both onto our sides.

"I'll love you forever," he says softly. I open my mouth to speak but he silences me with a kiss. "No words are needed from you. I already know."

Chapter 5

"ARE YOU READY?" I CALL out as I stand impatiently by the front door. I don't know where we're going, he just told me to make sure I was wrapped up. He doesn't want me ill again. It was really cute and thoughtful of him.

So, I've done what I'm told, and that's not like me. I'm wearing jeans and a T-shirt because it's nice outside, but I have a heavy knit cardigan that I'm taking, just in case the weather changes, because this is Scotland and we can get four seasons in one day.

Wherever we're going, I'm just looking forward to spending more time with my man, because in the next few weeks, our schedules are going to be hectic. When I start filming, we won't see much of each other until he's on set with me.

"I'm more than ready for a day with my girl," he says, slipping his hands around my waist. I'm standing with my back to him, flicking through today's mail that sits on the sideboard. I presume Connor collected it whilst I was having my shower.

I lean back against him and enjoy the feeling of his mouth against my neck as he trails sweet kisses around it. *Heavenly.* "If you don't stop that, we'll be going nowhere."

"Spoilsport. I'm not sure I've had my fill of you today."

His words go straight to . . . well, I'm standing here pressing my legs together. "If you're very good today, I'll make it up to you tonight when we're home." I pause and stare at the envelope in my hand, putting the other letters back on the sideboard. My whole body tenses. This was hand delivered and has my name printed on the front. It has to be from Donovan. Who else would be hand delivering mail to me?

"Ella, what's wrong?"

I turn in his arms and I'm met with his confusion. "Can you open this?" I say in what I hope is a controlled tone. He releases his hold and takes the envelope from me.

I watch as he opens it carefully and removes a letter. His eyes scan it before he looks at me. A deep sadness washes over him briefly before being replaced with anger. There's a tightness around his eyes and he's shaking his head in disbelief. "Do you want to know?" I nod and take the biggest breath I can. "Your man owes me, and if he doesn't pay up, I'll be personally coming to collect his debt from you."

"What the fuck? Who is it from?"

"It's not signed. Ella, please. I don't want you to get angry and upset over this. Fuck, I'm angry enough for the both of us. Why the hell did I not think to look through the mail when I collected it?" He pulls me tightly in his arms and I feel the tension in his body.

"What do I do?" I ask.

"We'll go on a detour today. Pick where you want to go. Your dad's, or straight to Jonathon's office?"

"My dad's." It's the closest to here and I want to see him.

"Okay. I'm driving." I don't argue with him because I'm probably not in the right frame of mind to be driving, even the short distance to my dad's. We leave the house and Connor sets the alarm. It's funny, a few months ago, I never really set the alarm. I was always forgetting, but now it seems too important.

I get into the passenger side of my car, avoiding looking at Connor, because I know if I do, I will put a fake smile on my face and pretend everything is okay. But it's not okay. It's far from it.

Whoever Donovan owes money to knows where I live. That means he's been giving out my address. But what does it have to do with me? Doesn't that person not realise we're not together anymore?

"Ella."

"I'm fine," I say, trying to convince not only Connor, but myself. He sighs as the engine roars to life and we drive away from my home. A home that was always my safe place. A home I thought I'd stay in forever. Now, though, I'm not so sure. Doubts are lingering in my head. I have so many happy memories, but those seem so distant now with everything that's going on in my life.

Why is it that one person can cause so much damage and hurt?

I stare out the window and watch the scenery change. My car is speeding along the long country road that takes me toward my childhood home. A home that isn't tainted by my past mistakes. It's a home that was and will always provide me with happy memories.

Connor was right about the weather. It does look as though it's going to change. Trees are swaying as the wind picks up and the clouds are darkening. It looks as though a storm is brewing in the distance. A bit like my life. A storm is brewing and there's not a thing I can do to stop it.

My car stops, but the engine is still running. We're at the gates to my dad's estate. I watch as Connor punches in the code and the gates open. We drive until we're in front of the house.

I'm already opening the car door before Connor has even put my car into park. As soon as I get out, I stop and take in the beautiful house before me. It's an incredible, faultless home with a truly arts and crafts era feel to it. The porch is amazing with its archway matching the original brickwork.

The double wooden front door opens and my dad stares at me. I know he must be wondering what I'm doing here.

"Hi, sweetheart. What a wonderful and unexpected surprise," he says as I walk toward him on auto-pilot. I wrap my arms around him. "Hey, my girl. What's wrong?" I don't cry, but I don't let him go. "Connor, what's wrong?"

"Someone hand delivered mail today, saying that if Donovan didn't pay up, they'd be calling by in person to collect his debt."

"Ella, we'll sort this out," Dad says, but his voice doesn't convince me. When I was little, I used to think my dad could solve all my problems. Now, though, I'm not so sure.

"Okay," I reply, taking a step back from his hold. "I'm sure it will all work out, but can we let Jonathon know about this? Maybe he can find out who is behind this note."

"Of course we can. Are you staying for a bit? I'm sure I can make us all some lunch."

I turn and look at Connor. He shrugs, letting me decide. "Yes, we'll stay for lunch, but I'll cook." I laugh.

"Come on inside then."

I don't mind cooking. It will give me something to do to keep my mind off things.

Dad turns and walks inside. I wait for a moment with Connor. "Is that okay with you?"

"Yes, of course, it is. I'm happy to do whatever you want today, and if being here is what you need, then we'll spend the day here."

"Thank you," I say, pressing a kiss to his lips.

"You can thank me later." He takes my hand and we enter. I pause in the great hallway. When I was younger, I hated the fact that it was all wood. Wood on the walls and floor, but now I'm older, I truly appreciate the period style inside my family home. The old oak beams on the ceiling are exquisite. The best part of the hallway is the grand oak staircase that leads to the bedrooms. Many a time, as kids, Callum and I would chase each other up and down, usually causing our mum to shout at us to stop it.

We find my dad in the kitchen; he's already having a look

through the fridge. "Leave it," I say. "You two can talk. I'll do some lunch." I don't look at Connor or my dad, but I see them from the corner of my eye, exchanging glances. I know they both want me to talk, but I'm not sure what to say to them. "Go on. Go and sit in the sun room." If they're in there, I can't hear whatever they say about me, and right now, I'm sure that's for the best.

"Okay, sweetheart. But, whatever you're making, can you make extra? Your brother should be coming over." I nod as they leave me alone.

This kitchen is still full of my mum. It's very modern and practical. This is where she could be found most days when I was growing up. I was allowed to help her with cooking from a very young age. She was always cooking and baking, and there was nothing better than clearing the bowl after she was making cakes.

It's funny the memories that stay with you.

I find everything I need to make toasted club sandwiches and go about it. Everything is exactly where it should be. Footsteps carry through the hallway and I turn to see my brother watching me.

"It's strange seeing you there cooking. It's taken me back. I wish she was still here with us," he says softly, walking toward me.

"Me too."

"Connor called me and told me about the note. He also said you've not said much about it."

"What is there to say?" I reply, turning back to what I'm doing.

"Ella, if you're scared, you don't have to pretend. Not with any of us."

"Yes, it freaked me out when Connor read it to me, but there's nothing I can do about it."

"Jonathon has already been sent a copy of the note and wants you to inform the police."

"What good is that going to do?" I shout at him. "Fuck, they even let Donovan go!"

"Ella, turn around." I shake my head. He's standing right

behind me. "For pity's sake, just turn around." He pulls my hand and spins me around to face him. "I won't have my sister being tormented because of that bastard."

"Callum, I'm not sure there's anything anyone can do about it. I'm trying not to let it get to me, but it's hard. I need to stay focused on all the good and exciting things going on in the next few weeks."

"Are you sure?"

"Yes. Now, if you're in the kitchen, you can help. Why don't you make some tea?" He kisses me on the tip of my nose before turning and switching the kettle on. My phone beeps; I have a message. I hope it's from someone I want to speak to. Alex.

> *Trevor has been in touch about trying to arrange a meeting. I know it's short notice but what about tonight at the hotel? Bring Connor. Libby will also be there.*

> *Me: What time?*

> *Alex: If we say 6pm it gives us time for dinner and plenty of time to discuss how you got on when you met the charity.*

> *Me: Perfect.*

I'm smiling to myself as I put the sandwiches on plates. "There, that's more like it. What has you smiling?" Callum asks.

"Alex has just texted. He wants me to meet him and Libby tonight at Stewart House."

"Great. I'm sure between you, you'll come up with great ideas for fundraising."

"I hope so."

I take the sandwiches and Callum carries a tray with a pot of tea and cups and we go and join Dad and Connor in the sunroom. They are both deep in conversation when we enter, but stop, and Connor can't hide this smile. I'm sure that's because I'm smiling.

"That's better," he says as I join him on the sofa.

"This looks delicious," Dad says, picking up a sandwich.

Talk is light as we eat lunch, which is just what I need. The note is still in my head, but I'm trying not to think too much about it. Although, I should organise with Trevor to release a statement distancing myself further from Donovan in the hope that whoever he owes money to will realise I'm not interested in what is going on in his life.

"Connor, before I forget, Alex texted me about us going to Stewart House tonight. Is that okay? We could leave from here later."

"Yes, that sounds good."

When we finish, Callum and Connor clear everything away, leaving me alone with my dad. "Ella, I don't want you to keep things bottled up. I'm here for you. Surely you know that."

"I do, Dad. I just don't want to worry about it. Callum says Jonathon is looking into the note and wants me to go to the police."

"Yes, he does. There's not a lot the police can do at the moment, but at least it would be on record should you get any more." He has a point. I never thought about that.

"Dad, do you know what Donovan is mixed up in?"

I watch as my dad struggles with his thoughts. He sits forward on his chair and stares out of the window into the garden. "Yes."

"Well?"

"Drugs. He's been dealing and taking . . ."

"Is it that bad?"

"Yes. Trevor and I will do whatever it takes to ensure your name stops being linked with Donovan. I know it's not what you'd like to do, but you and Connor need to be seen together more."

I sigh heavily, understanding what he's saying. It's not what I want to hear, because at the moment, I want Connor all to myself. I never wanted our relationship to be making news headlines.

"Ella, I've spoken to Connor and he's in agreement with me on this. We would all do anything for you and I know how much he loves you. Even your mum knew you two would end up together."

I smile. I can imagine Betty, Trevor's wife, and my dear old mum sitting around the kitchen table, discussing me. I laugh. I really was the last to know how Connor felt about me.

"Okay. I'm more than happy to be out and about with Connor, you know that. I'd just rather we had privacy."

"I know, but like me, you chose this career and you won't get much privacy here in Scotland. How about when things settle down and get back to normal, you and Connor go on a holiday?"

"Maybe."

Connor and Callum enter the sunroom just as it starts raining. A loud clap of thunder startles me as Connor sits beside me and wraps his arm around my shoulders. I snuggle into him and watch the rain fall heavily outside. I can hear the three of them talking but I'm not paying attention. Whatever they're talking about, Connor can fill me in later as we drive out to Loch Lomond and Stewart House.

Chapter 6

I'VE ALWAYS LOVED THE SCENERY on the drive out to Loch Lomond. The storm we had earlier cleared after a few hours, leaving behind a glorious afternoon. The sun has been shining brightly, but it's not too warm.

Connor has given up trying to hold a conversation with me as he drives. It's not that I'm in a mood or anything. I'm just trying to think about everything Alex and I need to discuss. I know he's the right man to help me. I also spoke to my dad about me going to help the homeless on the streets. He's not overly thrilled about the idea, especially given current circumstances, but he said he will join me if I do decide to do that. Connor also offered to help.

Of course, I'd love their help but part of me thinks this is something I need to do on my own.

I turn and smile at Connor when he takes the right turning into Stewart Estate. I've been here a few times over the years with my parents and Callum. The hotel might not be as big as some of the hotels in the city, but it has an amazing reputation. Libby is doing a great job; she has put Stewart Hotel firmly on the map.

We drive a few hundred yards and I can't help but smile as the scenery changes. The Loch is right before us and it looks incredible. All I want is for Connor to stop the car so we can go for a stroll.

He pulls up in front of the hotel and we get out. Connor hands the keys over to the doorman. As they talk, I walk over to the wall that surrounds the main building and look out over the Loch. We really do have some of the best scenery in the world right here on our doorstep.

"It's stunning, isn't it?" I would recognise that accent anywhere. I turn and find Alex standing beside me.

"Hey. Yes, it is. How are you?" Connor joins us and greets Alex with a warm handshake.

"I'm good. What about you? I heard about Donovan."

"I'm okay," I say quietly, turning back to look over the calm water.

"Is she really okay?" I hear Alex ask Connor. "We didn't have to do this."

"She needs this. I'm hoping it helps as a distraction."

"A distraction to what?"

I turn around. "To the fact my ex is an arsehole who is mixed up in drugs and God knows what else. And I seem to be getting dragged into his awful world."

"Babe."

"Connor, I'm fine." I take a deep breath. "Now, Alex, where is your gorgeous wife? Because I'm not sure it's good for my reputation to be seen with a married man."

We all laugh, although Connor shakes his head with a frown before taking my hand. "She's just finishing off a few things in her office and then she'll join us."

We let Alex lead the way inside, and as soon as we're in the reception area, I can't help but stop and admire the beautiful room. I love everything about it. It looks as though it's had a re-vamp since the last time I was here.

"Come on. Stop dreaming," Connor says, tugging my hand. It's hard not to.

Alex leads us through the hotel and I suddenly feel

underdressed for dinner in my jeans and t-shirt. I relax a little when he takes us into the bar and grabs a table in the corner by the windows overlooking the Loch.

"Can I get you both a drink?" Alex asks.

"Can I have some water and . . . no. That's all."

"I'll take water. I'm driving us home," Connor says.

"Ella, Libby will have some Prosecco if you want that?"

Connor beats me in answering, "Yes, she'll have that." Alex smiles, leaving our table. "What?" Connor asks.

"Nothing. Nothing at all."

He slides into the seat beside me and takes my hand in his. "Everything will be fine. I promise." I know he means what he says, but I'm struggling. I've not had a panic attack because I've been trying to keep it at bay and I'm sure Connor knows this.

"I hope so," I say, turning my attention back outside. It's not hard to understand why people from all over the world fall in love with this beautiful setting. Connor is rubbing his thumb against the back of my hand, and I'm not sure if it's that or looking outside at the water splashing against the pebbled shoreline that has a calming effect on me.

"Here we go," Alex says, placing our drinks on the table as Libby approaches us.

"Hi, everyone." She runs her fingers through her hair before Alex kisses her briefly.

"Hi, Libby. Great to see you again," I say as she sits opposite me.

"Are you okay?" Alex asks Libby, his voice full of concern, reminding me of Connor's voice earlier today when he was making sure I was okay.

"Yes. I've had to sort out a few problems, but it's all fine now. Never mind that. We should order food and then talk." Libby turns her attention to me. "Alex has told me you've already met with the charity."

"Yes, I have, and what they do and are trying to achieve is nothing short of remarkable. I'm doing a commercial to highlight the charity, but I'm really keen to help out, not just financially, but hands on."

"Wow, I can already tell how passionate you are about this. Why don't we order and you can tell us what has made you so passionate about this cause," Alex says, picking up the menu.

The menu is full of family favourites and traditional meals. We order from the waiter who also ensures we have enough drinks.

"Okay, Ella. Tell us your story," Libby says, leaning back in her seat.

"Okay." I start at the beginning and tell them about Donovan and what he did and how badly I handled it at first on my own. Connor keeps my hand in his, squeezing gently to encourage me to keep going when it gets too much for me. I tell them that if it wasn't for the support of my family, I'm not sure what position I would be in. Which makes me talk about others who find themselves in similar circumstances.

"Ella, I had no idea the extent of what you've been through. I have heard some bits in the news . . ."

"Alex, let me stop you. I don't want you to feel sorry for me, because I do enough of that for myself. But, I also know I'm still incredibly lucky given my position. That is why I want to help others."

"Well, after hearing your story, I'm more than happy to help you in any capacity I can."

"Thank you. That means a lot to me and I'm sure the charity will be over the moon too. My dad wants to do his bit as well. I really believe that people shouldn't be living on the streets, regardless of their background. More emotional support is needed to those in less fortunate positions."

"Never mind a Grammy award. I vote Ella McGregor for our next PM," says Libby with a huge smile.

"I don't have the energy or the brains to run our country."

"Oh, I don't know about that," she says with a warm smile. "You have enough passion to do the job."

We continue talking about various events that can be organised to raise much-needed funds and awareness for the charity. "I've got it," Alex exclaims. We all pause and look at him, waiting to hear what he has to say. "We all know Jess and Fletcher do a lot for charity, and his football club now hosts a yearly charity football match between two clubs. I know Peter extremely well. Why don't we put it to him about doing a star studded-match at the end of this season? Players versus celebrities. I'm sure you and I have enough connections between us to form a team. All money raised could be split between the women's charity that Jess supports and the one you've chosen. It makes perfect sense. And I know you and Jess will be working alongside each other at different times."

"Do you think the club would go for it?" I ask, hopeful.

"There's only one way to find out. I'll call Peter in the morning and put it to him. As soon as I know anything, I'll call you."

The waiter appears at our tables with our food and we all tuck in. The conversation still flows freely. Libby asks Connor lots of questions about, not just his career, but about us as a couple. He is very honest and open with her considering he's only met her once before. My heart swells with his honesty.

My phone buzzes from my bag. I consider ignoring it, but decide against it. Pulling it from my bag, I see it's a text message. My house alarm is going off. What the hell?

"Ella, what's wrong," Connor asks, his voice full of concern as I dial Callum's number.

"The house alarm is going off. Callum, where are you?"

"Just heading home, but I'm dropping Dad off first," my brother tells me.

"Good. Can you swing past my house? The alarm is going off."

"Sure. Are you still at Stewart House?"

"Yes. It would take me a good forty minutes to get back."

"Okay. I'll talk to you soon."

I end the call and leave my phone on the table. Something is wrong. I know it is. The only time the alarms have gone off is when it's been tested.

"Ella, is everything okay?" asks Libby.

"I'm not sure. I don't have a good feeling about this."

Connor squeezes my hand, but it doesn't offer me the reassurance I need. "Are you nervous because of the note this morning?"

"Maybe," I reply, facing him.

"What note? Ella, is there something you aren't you telling us? If I can help, I want to," Alex says softly, his voice full of concern. Connor tells him about the note that was hand delivered today and how my dad wants me to be seen out more with Connor to put distance between me and Donovan.

Libby and Alex exchange glances whilst he holds her hand tightly. A silent conversation is exchanged between them before Libby nods her head slightly.

"Ella, who is looking into all this for you?" Alex asks.

"Just our lawyer."

"Let me know if you need extra security. I know someone who can help you if this situation becomes more difficult." I understand what he's saying, even though I'd like to pretend I don't. I've heard some of the rumours surrounding the King brothers, who lead security at all of Alex's places of business. It should frighten me, but it doesn't.

"We hope it doesn't come to that," Connor says. "But I'll bear that in mind because I'm sure you'll understand I'll do anything it takes to keep Ella safe."

"Okay. Can we get back to what we were meant to be discussing? And then we can head off, letting you get back to your kids."

Libby smiles warmly and nods in agreement. Alex takes notes.

He's making a to-do list which he'll send me a copy of. He's far too organised for me. I'd always been a spur of the moment person up until recently.

My phone buzzes again. Connor and I both make a grab for it at the same time, but I get to it first. It's my brother. A message and a picture. I read the message first.

I've already called the police. I think you should come home.

My heart sinks at his words and then I open the picture. My gates have been cut open and the camera security system looks as though it's been ripped from the wall. I gasp. Connor takes my phone.

"Fucking hell."

"What's wrong?" asks Alex.

Connor shows him my phone as I stand. "I'm sorry, but we'd better go and see how bad things are."

Libby wraps her arms around me, giving me a hug, "Drop us a message later on so we know you're okay?"

"I will, and thank you."

The two men stand and shake hands. "Remember, if either of you need anything, give me a call and I'll do what I can to help you. And if I can't, we'll get someone who can."

"Thanks. I appreciate it," Connor tells him.

We say our goodbyes and leave the hotel. I'm certain our drive home is going to be a long one.

Chapter 7

AS WE GET CLOSER TO the entrance, I see there are two police cars, both with their blue lights flashing, and a few other cars that look as though they've only stopped to see what's going on. I've always had my personal space when it comes to my home. Only those closest to me know where I stay. It's the one thing I wanted to try and keep private. It was my safe haven, but as I look before me, it dawns on me this isn't a safe haven now as a small crowd gathers.

I close my eyes. If I keep them closed for long enough, maybe, just maybe, I can pretend this is all a dream.

But it's not a dream.

This is my reality. A reality that Donovan has so kindly sent my way. I swear the goings on in my life would make a great movie. In fact, I'm sure it would be a Hollywood blockbuster.

"Ella, are you okay?" Connor asks when he stops my car.

"Yes. Let's get this over with." It's not a lie. I am okay, if a bit frustrated and pissed off at what's going on in my life.

We get out of the car. My dad is with a police officer, but as I glance around, I don't see my brother. My eyes take in the damage that has been caused. Wires hang loosely from the security system that was only put in place days ago, and as for the gates . . . well, the damage is going to cost a tidy sum to repair.

"Sweetheart, there you are." Dad engulfs me the biggest hug, squeezing me tightly as though he doesn't want to let me go.

"I'm fine. Where's Callum?" I take a step back when he lets me go and I feel Connor's hand on the small of my back.

"He's at the house with a couple of officers." He points up the long driveway. I stare ahead and worry fills me. What if someone has been in the house? What if they're still there?

"Dad!"

"Ella, I'm sure everything will be fine. You and Connor can either stay at mine or at your brother's."

"Let's wait and see what's happening here before we think about that." I'd much rather stay here, although I'm sure security will be the deciding factor in that. The police officers are standing together. One is talking into his radio, but I'm not paying attention, even though I should. My mind is racing in different directions. I'm trying to think of this as just a coincidence, but after the note this morning, I know it's not.

Someone is trying to frighten me. And it's working.

It was bad enough when I found out what Donovan did with my house and money, but this is completely different. Someone is prepared to go to great lengths to get back what he owes.

"Miss McGregor, can we go to the house? I will leave officers here at the gate," an officer asks, approaching me. I nod and get back into the car with Connor and my dad.

Connor drives the car up to the house. I stare out the window blankly, not looking at what is usually a beautiful sight. I gasp. Tears fill my eyes as I take in the mess that has been made. All the windows downstairs at the front of the house have been smashed, and I can take a guess that the back of the house is the same.

Callum is standing just inside the front door and he's in deep conversation with two officers. Why? Just why? Donovan might owe people money, but that has nothing to do with me. Why have I been dragged into the disaster that is his life? There's no reason for someone to be frightening me. I won't be bullied into paying a debt that isn't mine.

I get out of the car and stand, surveying all the damage that has been caused. It's a mess. My eyes roam the house and I already know whoever was here has been inside. Callum stops talking, looks in my direction, and I see a deep sadness in his face, which confirms that someone has been inside. Connor takes my hand in his, offering me security, but I'm not feeling safe. Not at all.

My dad is walking towards the garage. My eyes follow him and I gasp when I see my other car. I drop Connor's hand and automatically start walking. What the hell? The windscreen and windows are all smashed and it looks like someone has gone to a lot of trouble painting words on the car.

I read the message out loud:

"He owes me. I want what I'm owed. You'll be hearing from me."

Everything is happening too quickly. Images flash through my head about what might have happened if I'd been at home. My body shakes uncontrollably as I read the message over and over. I stand, dazed, unsure what to do or say. My heart is racing and my legs are weakening. I mentally give myself a pep talk to stay on my feet. There are too many people here for me to go into panic mode. Although, at the moment, I want to jump in my car and race off. Away from here. Far away where no-one can find me.

I close my eyes briefly. This isn't fair. I've not done anything wrong. Fear grips me. Right now, I'm also angry and I want to lash out.

"Ella! Please talk to me?" I open my eyes and Connor is standing before me. "What are you thinking?"

"Right now? That we can't stay here tonight and that I'll need to get the whole property secured."

"Ella, come on. What else is going on in your mind?"

I shake my head. "I honestly don't know. This is getting out of control. I'm not sure what or who I'm up against and it's frightening me. And here I thought Donovan had fucked up before, but this . . . this takes it to a whole new level. I don't know what to do. This isn't a fight against Donovan."

"Ella." Callum calls my name and I turn to see him with my dad. They both share the same look of concern.

"I'm fine, but I just want an end to all this." Connor pulls me into his arms and holds me tightly. Usually, this would have a soothing effect on me, but not tonight.

"What do I need to do before we can leave?" I ask, pulling back from his hold.

"Let's go and ask." He takes my hand in his and we walk back toward the front door. "Officers!"

We stand on the doorstep, speaking to the officers. I don't pay much attention to what is being said. I just want to grab some clothes and leave. Get as far away from here as I can. Dad and Callum talk in hushed voices to the side. I catch them glancing in my direction. Callum keeps running his hand through his hair and his eyes dart around, not settling on anything for too long. My dad's eyebrows are drawn close together as he listens to my brother.

I don't even care enough to find out what they're whispering about.

"Ella, we can go inside and grab some things," Connor says, bringing my attention back to now.

"Okay."

We follow an officer inside and I gasp at the mess and destruction. The lamp and vase on my sideboard are both lying on the floor in the hallway, smashed. Pictures that lined the walls are on the floor as well. Tears fill my eyes when I see a picture of me and my mum smashed. Why?

Why would they do this?

"Miss McGregor, I know this will be hard, but can you look

around and tell us if anything is missing? Don't worry if you don't notice anything tonight. I know this must be a lot for you to take in." I nod at the officer. In the living room, it's the same. Pictures and ornaments smashed up all over the floor. Cushions from the couches scattered around the room, as though someone has been looking for something.

I wander around downstairs, and although lots of items are broken, it doesn't look as though anything is missing. Although, I'm sure I won't know exactly until I start cleaning up the mess that has been made.

That's for another day.

The officer follows Connor and me upstairs. The main bedroom door is open and I glance inside; it's a mess. I close my eyes and silently pray to myself that whoever was here is caught, and quickly. Connor enters his room and packs an overnight bag. I wander along the hall to the end bedroom. All the other rooms have also been turned upside down. The door is still closed, so I open it and step inside. Everything is where it should be. Looks as though whoever was in the house didn't enter this room.

As I pack a bag, the officer stands in the doorway, watching me without saying a word. He must see this sort of thing on a daily basis, whereas, I don't. I don't even think I've played the victim of a criminal offence in any of my movies.

"Are you ready?" I turn, hearing Connor's voice, and watch as his eyes glance around the room. "Well, at least they haven't been in here."

"Yes, I'm ready. Dad and Callum have both offered to have us stay with them."

"I know, but what do you want?"

"Can we go to a hotel tonight, and then tomorrow we can think about everything else? I don't think I'll be good company and I don't want them tip-toeing around me."

"Of course we can," he says, taking my bag from me.

We walk back downstairs and outside, where Dad and Callum are standing still talking to a police officer. "Sweetheart, are you okay?"

"I'm fine, Dad. It's just been a shock. Connor and I are going to stay at a hotel tonight. I hope neither of you mind. I just want some space tonight, and tomorrow we can analyse everything that's happened."

They glance at each other before shrugging their shoulders, as though in defeat. "Yes. You have to do what is right for you," Dad says. I hear the sadness in his voice and I know he wishes I was going to his house. With the small crowd that had gathered at the gates, I don't want to risk their privacy. "Okay, why don't we meet up for lunch. Trevor has already cleared tomorrow for you both."

"Lunch would be nice."

"Officer, is there anything else you need from us?" Connor asks.

"I need to know where you'll be staying, should we need to contact you."

"Of course. And what about the property?"

"There will be someone here all night."

"Thank you."

"Ella, I've already been in touch with the insurance company," Dad says. "I will come over first thing in the morning. The security company and the glazers will both be here at nine a.m."

"Thank you."

I walk over to the car, leaving Connor speaking to them. My head is all over the place. I don't want to speak to anyone. I wait on him and nervously look around. This is meant to be my home. The one place I've always felt safe. But as my eyes travel as far as I can see, I'm now wondering if the intruder is still lurking somewhere, watching me.

This is no longer home.

"Come on. Let's go. Is the Hilton in town okay?" Connor asks. I nod and get into the car.

Chapter 8

"THERE'S SOME BAD GUYS AND they're going to come looking for me. I need your help. Please, don't push me away now, not when I need you the most. You can make all my problems go away."

He always has a story. Why should I believe him this time? "How?"

"Just pay them. Give them what I owe them. I promise, Ella, I'll make it up to you." I stare at him. He looks like a little lost boy. Totally alone and unsure of what to do. But I know exactly what I'm going to do, or rather not do. There's no way I'm paying off his debts. I don't care who he owes money to this time. I won't help him.

"You're full of bullshit. I don't care. You're not getting so much as a penny from me."

"Ella, you have to pay. They know we're together. They'll come after you."

"But we're not together and haven't been for a long time. Go away. I don't care about you anymore."

"Don't say things like that. You know I love you."

I can't help but laugh at his choice of words. "Love? You don't know the meaning of the word."

I stand by the window and he starts walking toward me, crossing his arms, holding onto his shoulders. There's no smile on his face. An ache builds in my chest as I look at his sadness, but I have to remember this isn't my fault. He's brought all this on himself.

The room starts spinning. Everything seems to slow down as he approaches me. "Ella, please. I need your help?"

"I'm sorry," I say quietly, turning away from him and looking out the window in time to see a van stopping and eight men jumping out. They see me. One guy has a huge dirty smirk on his face as they all rush toward the front door.

Bang.

Bang.

Bang.

The front door is forced open and I hear their footsteps coming toward us. "Ella, they will hurt us both," he says, falling to his knees before me.

"Do you have what you owe me?" the guy who enters the room first shouts as he stalks toward us.

Donovan turns and shakes his head. He has tears running down his face. "Well, this pretty little thing will have to pay for you." The guy reaches out, touching my face. He runs his fingers down my cheek before running them along my bottom lip. Bile rises.

"I'm not paying anything for this arsehole!" I yell.

"At least we can both agree on Donovan. But you see, pretty lady, you are his insurance. You were with him when he took out the debt and he promised me you would be good for it." He pulls me into his hold and presses his lips to mine.

"No . . ."

"Ella!" I bolt upright in the bed, pulling the covers up around my body, even though sweat drips from me. My heart is racing and I can't control it. Warm arms wrap around me and I try to push them away. "Ella, it's me. I won't hurt you. It was just a dream."

I turn to him and my breathing starts to slow when I see him. It was just a dream. "There. That's better. Are you okay now?" he asks.

"Yes."

"I don't need to ask who or what it was about."

"No." I snuggle into the warmth of his body.

"Do you want to talk about it?"

"Not really. I just want my life to be normal."

"Your life has never been normal so why change it now?"

"You know what I mean."

"I do, and everything will settle down, hopefully sooner rather than later. I messaged Alex when you fell asleep."

"Oh." As soon as we were here, I lay down and closed my eyes then nodded off to sleep. I had completely forgotten he and Libby had wanted me to let them know how everything was.

"They're both concerned about you, and Alex wants to help. All you have to do is say and he'll arrange someone to look into all this for you."

"But isn't that a job for the police?"

"Yes, but how long will it take before they get any answers? I'm not sure I'm prepared to wait that long. Especially when we don't know who we're dealing with. Donovan is one thing, but this is something else."

"Can I think about it? I don't want to rush into something and then regret it."

"Of course. Now, come on. Let's try and get a few more hours sleep." He pulls me back down in the bed, wrapping his arms around me. I rest my head on his chest and allow myself to drift back to sleep, safe in the knowledge that he won't let anything bad happen to me.

HIS SOOTHING TOUCH helped me to sleep, and now, it's waking me up. My eyelids are no longer heavy as I open my eyes. I'm still in the same position I fell asleep in, resting against him. "Morning," I say, looking up into his gorgeous face.

"Morning. You look better. Tell me you feel better."

"I do. What about you? Did you get back to sleep?"

"Yeah, for a bit. Are you hungry?"

"No."

"Ella . . ."

"Honestly, I'm not, but I'm sure by lunchtime I will be so don't fuss. So what will we do to pass the time?" I ask, running my hand down his firm abs.

"Not what's in your head," he says, grabbing my hand and stopping me from continuing my exploration of his body. "We need to talk."

"Really? You want to talk when I can think of so many more interesting things to do? Fine." I huff. "Can it wait until I've soaked in a bath? Or better still, you could join me in the bath. Help me relax. I feel all the tension here." I sit up and roll my shoulders, moving my neck from side to side.

"You do know you're impossible at times?" I don't turn around but I feel his warm, soft lips pressing lightly against the back of my neck. I close my eyes and moan. "Well, if you want a bath, woman, you had better go and run it and I'll join you in a few minutes."

I angle my head and kiss him before jumping out of bed. He laughs and I can't help but smile. I need this. I need a distraction from all the crazy memories of my dream. It all seemed so real.

Connor is still laughing when I enter the bathroom. I shiver, thoughts about the men Donovan owes money to firmly in my head. Are they coming after me because he's told them I'm good to cover his debt? Are they going to hurt me if they don't get what they want? If I paid them, would that be an end to it, or would someone else come looking to me to pay off more debts?

I open a small bottle of bubble bath and pour it into the running water. I watch as bubbles form, filling the bath. After testing the water, I undress and climb in.

As I lean back, the bathroom door opens and Connor enters. With his eyes on me, he removes his boxers before climbing into the bath. I wriggle forward, allowing him room behind me. The warm water rises around us as he sits down behind me. He wraps his arms around my stomach and pulls me closer to him. "There. Is this what you were after?"

"No, but it'll do. I'm in your arms so I'm happy." I don't have to look at him to know he's smiling. I can feel it.

The warm water splashes around us. This is the perfect antidote for stress. A long and sensual bath for two, to bring us closer together. I wish I had some of my own toiletries with us instead of the hotel ones. We'd make good use of those, especially with a warm massage.

He gently rubs my stomach; slow circular movements. I close my eyes, enjoying the warm feelings spreading through my veins.

"Is that good?"

"Mmm, yes. I love your touch."

"What else do you love?"

My eyes fly open and my chest tightens as I realise what I've said. I've been avoiding asking myself what he means to me because I'm not ready to admit my feelings. When the mess that is my life is sorted out, I will ask myself how I truly feel about him. But at the moment, there's just too much going on.

I take a deep breath to steady my growing nerves. "I love the warmth of the water that surrounds us. It's almost as soothing and comforting as your touch, which is also very distracting, in a good way."

"So, you're in a loving mood. That's good to know."

"I know what I am in the mood for."

"You're always in the mood for that." He removes one hand from my stomach and I feel him adjust himself. I also hear the groan he makes as I push my arse closer to him, allowing me to feel what is making him so uncomfortable.

I stand up slowly and turn around; his deep eyes are watching me intently. I wait for a moment, silent and still. The only noise I can hear is the water splashing against the side of the bath. I take a step toward him and lower my body. His lips curve into a mischievous smile.

"This isn't what I had in mind when I said I'd join you in the bath," he says, moving his arms to rest on the side of the bath.

"It's what I had in my mind." I lower myself onto him. He groans, throwing his head back and closing his eyes.

I don't move. I allow myself to adjust to the feel of him deep inside me. After a few moments, he opens his eyes and grabs hold of my hips. I smile as his expression changes. "Can I tell you what I love right now?"

I close my eyes for a split second, unsure of what he's going to say next. "Tell me."

"You taking control."

I lean forward, wrapping my arms around his neck, and press my lips to his. It seems I'm all about taking control today.

Chapter 9

"ELLA, HOW ARE YOU FEELING today?" my dad asks as we join him at the table in the hotel restaurant.

"Not too bad," I tell him as I sit down. I have Connor to thank for that. He took my mind off everything earlier.

Connor and my dad greet each other, but my eyes scan the restaurant. An eerie feeling rushes over me and I'm not sure why. Goosebumps spread over my skin and the hair on the back of my neck stands. I run my fingers through my hair and shake it loosely in an attempt to calm myself down.

What the hell has got into me?

The last time I felt like this, Donovan had been following me in London.

Is he here now? Lurking somewhere? Watching? Or is it someone else? The person who caused all the damage at my home last night?

"Ella, what's wrong?"

"I don't know. Something doesn't feel right. I feel as though someone is watching me," I say without looking at either of them. My eyes are still scanning the restaurant, but there are so many people here, I don't know where to look.

"Do you want to leave?" my dad asks and I finally look at him.

"No, it's fine. I'm sure it's just my overactive imagination playing tricks on me. So, how are things at the house?" I ask. I try not to look at Connor because I know he's going to be concerned by what I've said, but I can't help it.

His jaw is clenched tight. Lines of concentration deepen along his brows and under his eyes. His whole expression is tight with the strain. This isn't just affecting me; it's having an effect on everyone close to me. I turn back to my dad.

"Well, security is now fixed. Broken windows have been repaired, and Mary is in cleaning at the moment." Mary is Dad's cleaning lady; he'd be lost without her, and so would I at times. Today, I'm grateful it's a job I don't have to do myself.

"So, I can go back then?"

"Yes, but I'd like to talk to you about extra security."

I look at Connor, and he's nodding in agreement.

"Look, I don't want someone shadowing my every movement. I know what you're going to say, but this is something I don't want. Having said that, I'm prepared to let Alex have someone look into this mess for me. It's not something I want to do, but I'm being left with little choice."

"I'll call Alex," Connor says, standing and already dialling his number on the phone. He walks away from our table.

"Ella, I'm not sure about this," Dad says quietly.

"Neither am I, but really, what else can I do? I don't want to live in fear of anyone. And I think you and I both know the King brothers will find out who Donovan owes money to."

"But, sweetheart . . ."

"Dad, don't. I don't want to think about the details. I just want to be safe."

"Okay." He sighs in defeat.

"Done," Connor says, sitting back down and taking my hand. I nod.

Lunch is quiet. My dad really isn't happy with what I've decided. But it wasn't his decision to make, and it's not one I've made lightly. The King brothers have, over the years, been linked with various . . . shall we say . . . incidents, but neither of the brothers has been arrested.

I remember a few years back, there was a story about Libby's friend being kidnapped, and it was the King brothers who found her and supposedly killed the man and his associates who took her. I'm not sure how much of that story is true, but I'm not sure I want to know either. I just know that I don't want to be linked to Donovan forever.

"So, do you want to check out and go home?" Connor asks as we all finish eating.

"Yes. May as well get it over with."

"You know I'm going to worry about you," Dad says.

"Yes, because that's what parents do. But, please, try not to." I reach across the table and take his hand. He's hurt and concerned; it shows in his expression. "Dad, I'll be okay."

"Your words aren't comforting me."

"Well, then, maybe my words will. I promise I'll take care of her," Connor says.

"I don't doubt that, son, but you have to understand, she means to world to me."

"And to me. Always has and always will."

"Okay. I expect at least one of you to check in with me later."

Dad gives Connor all the new codes for the security while I look around, still feeling as though someone is watching me, but I don't see anyone who looks even remotely suspicious.

"ARE YOU READY?" Connor asks as we sit parked outside my house. I stare ahead, my mind racing, searching for answers to all the questions swimming around in my head. "Ella!"

I turn to him. "Sorry, I was a million miles away."

"What are you thinking about?"

"I'm not sure, to be honest. Come on. Let's get inside."

"And settled before the police come over to see you."

I'd forgotten about that. They want me to have a thorough look around the house to see if there's anything missing. We get out of the car and I pause for a moment, glancing around.

"I hope they get here before Julie."

"So, she's still coming over?"

"Yes," I reply as he opens the front door. Julie insisted on us having a quiet night in, with some food and wine. She also asked if Connor and Callum would be joining us, but they have plans for tonight.

We had a slight disagreement in the car on our way back here after my brother called him to find out what he wanted to do about tonight. They're going to some football event they've been invited to with Fletcher. Connor is worried about leaving me alone and I know my brother isn't too happy with the idea of me being in the house unprotected. I tried explaining that I won't be on my own since Julie will be here.

Stepping inside, a fresh smell hits me straight away. Mary and her cleaning products. There's a new vase filled with fresh flowers on the sideboard. As I walk along the hallway, I see all but one of my pictures are back on the wall where they belong, the one of my mum is missing.

Connor is talking but I'm not listening as I enter the living room. Everything looks to be back where it belongs.

But I don't feel at home.

It all feels odd.

There's nothing comforting me as I stop in the middle of the room. Yes, everything here belongs to me and I should be happy, but for some reason, I'm not.

"Ella!" Connor's arms snake around my waist and he rests his chin on my shoulder. Having him with me is what I need, but I already feel as though I'm becoming reliant on him. "Talk to me."

"It feels wrong being here. It's not my home. The incident with Donovan, last night . . . I don't know what else to say."

"I'm not going out tonight. I'll call Callum."

"No, you won't. Julie will be here and I'm looking forward to a girlie night, just the two of us."

"Okay. But I'm going to worry and miss you until I'm back here with you."

"You won't be gone long enough to miss me. I could put money on you being home before I go to bed. And if you're not . . ." I turn in his arms to face him. "I'll be in bed waiting for you."

"Now I have a vision in my head of you lying in bed, naked, waiting for me," he whispers.

"Well, you'll have something to look forward to then." I press my lips to his slowly and thoughtfully. He moves his mouth to cover mine, devouring the soft kiss I started. His lips are warm and sweet. There's a dreamy intimacy to our kiss. A kiss that has me feeling weak at the knees.

"Now I really don't want to go out with your brother," he says, his lips leaving mine and leaving me wanting more.

"As I said, you have something to look forward to at the end of the night. Now, I should see if anything has been taken before the police get here."

"Yes." He presses a kiss on the bridge of my nose. "Let me help you."

We go from room to room downstairs and there doesn't seem to be anything missing. In the office, I start pulling open the drawers in the desk, while Connor looks through the bookshelves. He's been in here as often as me in recent weeks. I'm sure he'll notice if something is missing.

Everything is where it should be.

None of this makes any sense.

I sit in the chair and stare at the computer, wondering what whoever was in the house was looking for. I don't think, I lean forward and power on the computer. I sit impatiently and wait for it to start. Glancing over my shoulder, I notice Connor is still looking through paperwork. When the screen opens, I type in the password and go straight to Donovan's files, but they are all password protected. I wait before typing in my own name and chuckle when his files open before my eyes. The first thing I check is when it was last opened on this computer.

The last time was the day before Donovan left me.

I click on the files to find bank account details for me. Lawyers agreements that have what looks like my signature, all relating to my house. So, this is what he used when he was re-mortgaging my house. There is also a file but it's encrypted so I have no idea what it contains.

"Have you found anything?" Connor asks, leaning on the back of the chair.

"I'm not sure, but I know a man who might," I say, saving the file and sending it in an email to Jonathon. I close the computer down and stand. "There's nothing I can do now, and from what I can see, nothing has been taken. Now, I know it doesn't take you long to get ready for a night out, but you, my sexy man, are going to an event filled with some of the hottest footballers in our country."

"You think footballers are hot?" He takes my face in his hands and tries to hide his amusement.

"Not as hot as my man, but I know some women find them sexy."

"Some women's opinions don't concern me."

"Is that so?"

"Yes, but it's nice hearing that you find me hot."

"Always and forever."

Chapter 10

"CHINESE TAKEAWAY AND WINE. WHAT more could you possibly want?" Julie asks as we sit in front of the TV, tucking into our food, which is absolutely delicious. Chicken chow mein and Peking duck with rice, and prawn crackers. Just what I've thought about all day.

"A new house," I say, without thinking. The jaw-dropping look on Julie's face has me instantly regretting my words.

"Hold on a minute. What the hell am I missing? There's no way you want a new house. You love it here. You love the privacy and the views. What's going on?"

Yes, I fell in love with this house the very first time I walked through the front door, and up until recently, I've always felt the same, but not now. "I did love it. Look, forget I said anything."

"I can't. Tell me what's wrong."

"Donovan, the letters, the fact that someone has been in here looking through all my belongings. When we arrived here today . . . I don't know. I can't explain it. It doesn't feel like home anymore. I think it's time for a change."

"I get it. So, what are you going to do?"

"Go house hunting."

"Connor's already looking for somewhere. Why don't the two of you just look for somewhere together, and you know, make it official between you? A family home, because I can already picture you together with kids."

Kids. Yes, I want kids, but at the moment, all I want is to be happy. "I don't know. He might not want that."

"Please! The man who has been waiting five years for you is going to want you living together. Connor wants the full package. You, kids, a nice house. He loves you. If he could whisk you away to a remote island tomorrow, I know when you come home you'd be Mrs Ella Andrews. He'd marry you in an instant."

I nod, trying to ignore her statement about marriage. I love him too, but I'm not sure I'm ready to discuss our future. What if I do and it scares him off?

"Do you know what we need?"

"No, but I'm sure you're going to tell me."

"A girlie weekend away to a nice hotel. Somewhere we can both relax, enjoy the scenery, and do nothing. Maybe get a few treatments. What do you say?" Julie asks, already sounding excited about the possibility.

"Yeah. Why not?

"Perfect. After we've finished dinner, we'll have a look online and see if we get anywhere."

Julie sticks to her word. No sooner have we finished eating, she has my laptop open and is searching for a relaxing break. It would be nice to get away for a bit just the two of us, have something to look forward to instead of feeling anxious and dreading each day. Because, at the moment, that's how I feel in the morning when I wake up.

A few hotels grab my attention, but they all lack something. My thoughts drift to Stewart House and, for me, that ticks all the right boxes. The hotel, the grounds, and the scenery. "What about Stewart House?" I ask, hoping Julie agrees.

"Oh, I love it there. Why not? And seeing as you are on friendly terms with the owner, we might get it at a reasonable rate."

"That's not why I suggested it."

"I know. Do you want to sort that tomorrow, and hopefully we can get a few days before you start filming?" I nod. "What about the charity work you plan on doing? When does that start?"

"I can start anytime I want."

"How many nights will you be out helping?"

"Only one night at the moment. I'd love to do more, but I'll wait and see how my schedule is."

"You do know I'm proud of you for wanting to make a difference?"

"Yes, I do, and although I'm a bit nervous about it, I'm really keen to help out and see if the work the charity is doing will make a difference."

"I'm certain it will, and with you fronting their campaign, how could it not?"

Since we've decided on me phoning Stewart House tomorrow, Julie opens another bottle of wine and we sit back to watch a movie. Sometimes it's strange watching people I know in a film. It never felt strange before I got into acting. The movie is just at a really good bit when my phone starts ringing.

"Ignore it."

I glance at the screen and see my brother's name. "Hey, Callum. What's wrong?" I can hear sirens in the background. Wherever he is, it's noisy.

"I'm in the back of an ambulance with Connor." Time stops with his words and my heart stops beating. Dark images flash through my head. I'm imagining all sorts of possibilities, but that's not going to tell me what's happened. Only my brother can do that. "Ella, I need you to listen to me."

"Okay," I say softly, looking at Julie, and I'm sure the concern I see in her eyes mirrors my own. "I'm listening. Julie will call a taxi." She nods her head, picks up her phone, and walks toward the window.

"I'm not sure what's happened, but Connor has been beaten up, and badly."

"But, how? You were meant to be with him. How could this happen?"

"Ella, I don't know. He went to the bathroom and when he didn't come back, I went looking for him. Fletcher and I found him unconscious."

I stare ahead, seeing Julie before me, but not really seeing her. Tears fill my eyes. My body shakes uncontrollably.

"Ella. Ella! Please. Are you okay?" I hear his voice and open my mouth to speak but nothing comes out.

Julie is right beside me, taking the phone from my hand. "Callum, our taxi is on the way. What hospital are we going to? . . . Okay. Yes, she'll be okay . . . We'll see you soon."

She takes my hand. "Ella, come on. We don't know how he is. He'll need you to be strong." I nod silently, trying to understand.

Everything is done on auto-pilot; from getting dressed and putting on shoes, to locking up the house and setting the alarm. Julie let the taxi into the grounds when the driver buzzed to let us know he was here.

Why Connor? Why him? Julie tells the driver our destination before taking my hand in hers.

I close my eyes and my tears fall. I don't believe this has been some random attack. Not with everything else going on. No, this has been planned and calculated to hurt me. Or to scare me into paying off Donovan's debts, and right now, that doesn't sound like such a bad idea.

I believe Connor has been hurt because of me.

This is all my fault.

I'm to blame for bringing Connor into my life.

Opening my eyes, I don't turn to Julie. I stare out of the window, watching the darkness outside. Right now, I hate the fact that I live so far out of the town. It's taking so long to get to the hospital.

Julie's talking to me. "Everything will be okay. Connor will be fine," she says, her voice hushed. I nod weakly, unconvinced by her words.

I know she's trying to reassure me, help me stay positive, but it's not helping. I need to see Connor. I need to know what's happened to him, but most importantly, I need him to be okay. Not knowing anything about his injuries, other than he's unconscious, has me imagining the worst possible situation.

"I should call my dad."

"I'm sure Callum has already done that."

"Well, I should call Connor's parents."

"No. Let's wait until we know how he is before you go worrying them."

Maybe she's right. As soon as I know how he is, I'll have to call his mum. She's going to be so upset, and she'll have every right to be.

I should send Alex a text, especially if he has the King brothers looking into who Donovan owes money to. I'm praying this has nothing to do with that, but deep down, I'm certain it does.

I'm on my way to hospital. Connor has been beaten up.

Alex: I've just been told. Cole is already looking into it. He has a few leads on Donovan

How the fuck does he already know this?

Me: This is my fault.

Alex: No it's not. Do you want me to come to the hospital?

Me: No. I'll send you a message as soon as I know how he is, but thanks for the offer.

I'm not sure if I should be concerned or happy that Cole already has leads on Donovan. For now, though, I'm going to put it to the back of my mind and focus all my attention on Connor. He's going to need my support and love.

Chapter 11

SICKNESS REARS ITS UGLY HEAD as Julie and I follow a nurse who is taking us to a private waiting room, where we've been told Callum is waiting for news on Connor. The nurse won't tell me anything. I have to be able to tell his parents something positive when I make the call and tell them he's in hospital.

When we arrived, Julie went straight to the reception desk and gave them Connor's name. I looked around at the waiting room feeling completely numb. Lots of staff rushing about trying to go on with jobs. Some patients sat quietly waiting to be seen, while others were noisy and aggressive toward the staff.

I hate hospitals. I don't think anyone likes hospitals very much. Why would anyone like them? They're full of sick or injured people, but the staff seem lovely here.

The corridor is long and quiet compared to the waiting area of the A&E department. The nurse stops in front of a door. She opens it slowly, and inside the small room, is Callum. He sits leaning forward with his head in his hands. I shiver seeing my brother look so deflated and concerned. He turns his head slowly to the side. He's as white as a ghost, and offers me a small smile as I enter the room.

"Miss McGregor, I will get the doctor to come and speak to you as soon as he's available," the nurse says, and I thank her before she leaves the room.

There's nothing familiar about this waiting room; it's cold and clinical, not warm and inviting. The chairs don't even look comfy. I take a seat beside my brother and take his hand in mine. Julie sits opposite us and I can see the concern on her face as she watches Callum. He looks lost.

"Callum, please. I need you to talk to me. I need you to tell me Connor is okay. Please?" I glance at Julie and she can only shrug her shoulders. Rubbing my thumb along his hand is all I can do to offer him my support.

The room is almost silent. All I can hear is our breathing and the ticking of the clock on the wall. I close my eyes and try to gather my thoughts. I need to stay positive because I know Connor needs me, but it's hard. I have an inability to stay focused as my brother's body shakes beside me. Tears fill my eyes, and I know if I open them, my tears will fall. My body is weak and my mind is numb.

I need Connor to be okay. I need someone to come through those doors and tell me he's awake and wants to see me.

"Ella, I'm so sorry I couldn't help him." I open my eyes and look at my brother. His own eyes are filled with unshed tears.

"It's okay. This isn't your fault," I say as he wraps his arms around me, and I lean my head on his shoulder.

"Callum, how bad is he?" Julie asks.

"I'm not sure. He was unconscious when I found him. There was blood everywhere. So much blood I'm not even sure what injuries he has."

My tears fall at my brother's words. I clasp my hands together and say a silent prayer to God, asking him to keep Connor safe. Callum rubs my shoulder in the same way our mum used to do when we were children when she was trying to soothe and comfort us. It always worked.

"Ella, I called Dad and Trevor. They should be here soon."

"Okay," I whisper through my tears. "This is all my fault. If it wasn't for me, Connor wouldn't it be in hospital."

"Enough!" snaps Julie. "This isn't your fault. I can't sit here and listen to you blaming yourself." I hear her words but it doesn't make any difference. If Connor wasn't in a relationship with me, he wouldn't be here. He wouldn't be lying in a hospital bed after being beaten up.

Callum and Julie talk in hushed voices, although I don't know why because there's no one here to hear their conversation. "Did nobody see anything?" she asks him.

"Fletcher and I saw two men running away from the gents' bathroom. Fletcher chased after them but didn't see who it was. We don't think it was anyone who attended the function tonight."

"Where is Fletcher?" Julie asks, moving in her chair. It looks as though she's as uncomfortable as I am.

"He wanted to come here, but it made more sense for him to go home to Jess. He wants me to phone him as soon as we have news."

I close myself off from their conversation.

Numbness slowly seeps through my body. I can't move and I don't want to think about any of the situations running through my mind, because each one is as bad, if not worse, than the last.

He shouldn't be in here.

I should speak to Trevor, and as soon as it's possible get Connor moved to a private hospital, I know he has private medical insurance that will cover this.

I'm clinging to hope that God will answer my prayers to keep him safe. Time has stood still; the hands on the clock on the wall don't seem to be moving. I turn my head to the door and watch as strangers walk past our room.

I shrug out of my brother's hold and stand, rolling my neck from side to side I stretch the knots out that have formed from sitting against Callum's shoulder. I feel both sets of eyes on me as I start to pace the floor. Every muscle in my body aches and I have no idea why.

Loud footsteps in the corridor start to slow down and the door opens. I lift my head to see my dad and Trevor standing in the doorway. My dad's eyes are filled with sadness as he looks at me. I rush toward him and he engulfs me in his arms.

"He's going to be fine sweetheart," Dad says softly as I sob in his arms. "He's a strong lad and it'll take more than this to keep him down."

I hope he's right.

Trevor clears his throat as he sits down beside Julie. As Connor's agent, I'm hoping he can keep this out of the news for all our sakes. We don't need swarms of reporters descending on the hospital, looking for a story.

"Ella, come on and we'll both sit down." I let my dad lead me back to the chair I was sitting in only moments ago. Callum takes one hand and my dad takes the other. I'm grateful they're here. "Do we know anything yet about his condition?"

"No," Callum says.

"I'll wait five more minutes then I'll go and see what I can find out," Trevor says.

I don't know if I can wait five more minutes. It feels as though I've been waiting for hours. I remove my hand from Callum's and look at my phone and realise we've been here in the hospital for not even thirty minutes.

It's going to be a long night.

There's a television on one of the walls, which Trevor switches on. I suspect he's trying to fill the silent, uncomfortable air with a little noise. I glance at it before returning my gaze to the floor. The others chat amongst themselves. I don't bother listening to the conversation, never mind engaging with them.

My phone buzzes in my hand, and everyone stops talking. I lift my eyes and they're looking with anticipation.

Dread fills me as I look at the name on the screen.

Donovan: I hope Connor is ok. If he's hurt, it's your fault. I've told you before and I'll say it again. He's not the man for you.

Fear grips me. Takes me hostage. I can't speak. I squeeze my dad's hand, gripping onto him as though my life depends on it.

No, not my life. It would seem I'm putting everyone close to me at risk.

"Ella, let me see." It's my dad's concerned voice that filters through my head. I look at him as I hand over my phone. "What is it with him? He's behind this attack on Connor. Why the hell can he not leave you two alone? He was the one that fucked up. If he wanted to stay in your life, he shouldn't have been so selfish and greedy. Now, because you're finally happy and in a better place, he wants to destroy that. Well, I won't let him. He's finished."

Everyone seems to have an opinion on this as they all start talking. "Ella, what are you thinking?" Dad asks.

"Connor wouldn't be hurt if he and I weren't together. Maybe I should walk away now, before it's too late."

"You can't do that," Julie says, grabbing my attention. "He loves you and I know you've fallen for him."

"Julie is right. That wouldn't help either of you. We just need to find a way to keep you safe." My phone buzzes again and my dad reads the message. "It's Alex. He's asking if there's any news yet." I watch as my dad types out a reply saying as soon as we know anything I'll send a message.

I should call Connor's parents. I know I have nothing to tell them, but as other people know, I don't want them to hear it from anyone else. It should come from me or Trevor. "We have to let his parents know."

As I finish speaking, the door opens and I watch the floor as shoes squeak across it and stop. I lift my head to see a doctor taking a seat opposite me.

"I have an update on Mr Andrews." The even tone of his voice has me thinking my prayers have been answered. Anxiety fills this small waiting room as we wait with bated breath to hear what he has to tell us.

He clears his throat and I suck in a deep breath. He smiles and that gives me hope. "Mr Andrews is now conscious." My body sags with relief at his words. "He is asking for you, Miss McGregor." I can't hide my smile and my eyes dart to Julie. She smiles and I realise my prayers have been answered.

"Can I see him?"

"I'll take you through to him in a minute." All I want to do is kiss him and apologise for all the pain I've caused him. "Mr Andrews has taken more than a few knocks to the head. He has bruising and cuts to his face, head, and upper body. We've cleaned him and stitched him up. I would like him to stay in hospital but he's already asking to go home. It's in his interests to stay so we can monitor him."

"I'll have a word with him," I say before looking at Trevor. "I'll call his parents after I see him." Trevor nods in agreement with me.

I stand up. "Ella, can you tell Connor I'm sorry I wasn't there for him?" I look at Callum as my dad moves seats and tries to reassure him that this isn't his fault. My brother might be looking at the floor but I can still see the pain and sorrow on his face.

What a pair we make. Callum is blaming himself and I'm blaming myself.

"Give him a kiss from me," says Julie as I leave the room, following the doctor.

Everything seems quieter as I walk beside the doctor; the waiting room is not as busy. My trainers squeak on the floor and I find myself smirking as I realise we're walking in line with each other.

We've walked through many doors and taken so many turnings, I have no idea how I will find my way back to the waiting room. Although, I'm sure once I see Connor, I won't want to leave him.

We stop outside a door within the A&E department and there's a security guard standing at the side of the door. "I've ensured Mr Andrews has privacy whilst he's being treated within the department."

"Thank you. I appreciate that," I say as he opens the door.

Chapter 12

STRENGTH AND DETERMINATION; IT'S WHAT he needs to see in me. I won't allow myself to be weak, not when he needs me the most.

I square my shoulders back and keep my head high. My heart thumps deep in my chest and my head spins round and round. I'm not sure if that's from the alcohol or from seeing him. I stare ahead and take in the sight before me. He might look battered and bruised, but he's sitting up in bed, smiling as I step toward him. For that, I'm grateful.

"You look . . ."

"Yeah, let's not go there, with how bad I look. You, on the other hand, look as you always do. Pretty amazing."

I move the chair beside his bed, but he tugs gently on my hand, "I need you closer," he says, pulling me toward the bed. I sit down beside him, conscious that I don't want to hurt him. I don't want to cause him any more unnecessary pain.

I sit and stare, not wanting to take my eyes off my man. I take in every bruise and cut on his face. He has stitches above his left eye. Four small stitches; it shouldn't leave a scar. There's a cut under his right eye, but it doesn't look too deep. And then my eyes drop to his lips. There's no cuts or bruises around them and I smile. I'm scared to move closer, but all I want to do is wrap my arms around him and squeeze him tight before kissing him.

I just need him.

He's okay. He's really okay.

"I'm glad you're here," he says, softly nuzzling in and placing the softest of kisses on my neck. This simple act captures my heart yet again.

"Where else would I be?"

"I'm not sure." He shakes his head and winces briefly from the movement, but I notice it. I cradle his face. I reach across the bed to press the alarm, but he pulls my hand back, stopping me. He lowers his gaze from mine and something doesn't feel right.

Does he blame me?

Of course he does. This is my fault.

I can't sit here and watch him struggle with the pain. "I'll go and let you rest," I say, trying to move from the bed, but his grip on me tightens. Our eyes lock and I see all his concern and fear, but I see something else too.

"You'll do no such thing. I need you here. I shouldn't say it, but you belong with me." I take in his last words and my body shivers.

"I do," I say, meaning the words and trying not to think about all the times Donovan has said I belong to him. The way Donovan said it or sent it as a message scared me. But with Connor, I'm not scared.

He's right. We do belong together. It's just taken me longer than him to realise it.

"Talk to me. What happened tonight? Callum said he found you covered in blood. Where did all the blood come from? Did you see who did this to you?" The questions leave me in a rush.

"Slow down. Yes, I saw them and I should be able to give a good description of the two of them. As for the blood. I don't think it was as much as Callum is making out, but . . ." He points to the back of his neck where there is a dressing. I gasp. How did I not see this? "From what I've been told, I have a nasty looking cut. It's not too sore," he says and I notice him wince in pain again.

"I should go and give your parents a call and let Callum come and see you."

"Please don't call them. My mum will only panic."

"I have to. I don't want them hearing it from someone else, or reading about it."

"What do you mean?"

I sigh heavily. I didn't want to tell him this, not yet. "Donovan sent me a message saying that it was my fault you were hurt."

"That fucking bastard. I had a feeling this had something to do with him."

"He is right though. It is my fault."

"There's no way I blame you. We're in this together and we'll get through it together. You and me, we're a team."

I nod.

We can get through this. We just need to keep fighting our corner. Show the world that nothing can break us. Show Donovan that he can't hurt either of us. We are stronger. I'm a stronger person having Connor in my life.

He brushes his fingers across my check. Warmth spreads through me and my emotions get the better of me.

I lean in, doing what I've wanted to do since I walked through the door. I give in to the need to feel his lips against mine and I brush my lips lightly against his. The minute our lips touch, our connection is made, and a soft sigh escapes his mouth. My eyes shut and I'm struggling to think. I pull back a little to ensure he's okay, but his grip on me tightens and he holds me firmly where I belong.

Lips part and tongues mould together as we sink into the depths of our kiss. And as I always do in moments like this, I lose myself to him.

Our lips break and I rest my head against his, our noses touching. Earlier I was worried and upset and now I'm just happy that he's okay.

"I don't want to stay here," he tells me.

"Tough. The doctor wants you to stay. I'd love to take you away from here, but, sorry. I'm with the doctor on this. You should stay to get monitored at least for a while. It would make me happy."

"Would it? I'd rather be alone with you. Other than a few cuts and bruises, there's not much wrong with me. I feel okay."

"You feel okay because of whatever medication you have been given. The doctor only wants to monitor you for a short time. He won't keep you in here for days."

"I hope not," he mumbles. "I'll stay a few hours and that's it."

"Fine, and you'll have me for company until the doctor decides to let you go."

"You don't have to."

"I know, but I want to be here with you. But I do need to call your parents and there's a few other people here wanting to see you." He looks puzzled. "Callum is here, but there's also Julie, my dad, and of course, Trevor."

"Okay, you make the call and please tell my mum I'm fine. She doesn't need to be getting herself stressed over me. And, I'll see everyone else." His phone buzzes beside him. He picks it up and I watch his playful expression of moments ago change to something else. His nostrils flare and there's a tightness around his eyes that wasn't there before. The smile on his face is gone and is replaced with a thin white line. For a minute, I think he's going to throw the phone across the room, but he doesn't. Instead, he slams it down on the bed, keeping it firmly under his hand.

"What's wrong?"

"Nothing. Nothing for you to worry about," he says, without even looking at me.

I leave the room, feeling no better than I did when I entered the hospital. Yes, Connor might be okay, but his reaction to the message he received tells me I should be worried. I'm not sure

I've ever seen him look so angry. He looked almost as angry as he did when he found Donovan at my house.

Was the message from Donovan? What is he hiding?

I walk without thinking about the direction I'm going in and surprise myself when I see I'm outside the private waiting room. Opening the door, I walk in with a smile on my face.

"Well, how is he?" Julie asks, standing as I enter the room, her eyes narrowing as she watches me.

"He's a bit battered and bruised. Apart from that, he wants out of here."

She sighs and sits back down. "Glad to hear it."

"You can all go and see him. I'm going to call his parents."

"Don't you think it's a bit late to be calling them?" Trevor asks.

"Yes, it is, but I don't want them hearing this from someone else or in the news."

"Are you okay?" Dad asks, standing up.

"Yes, I'm fine. A little tired."

"That will be the alcohol from earlier," Julie chimes in.

Callum, Dad, and Trevor all leave the room. "Are you not going?" I ask Julie.

"No," she says, shifting in the chair. "I think my friend needs me more than Connor. So you can tell me what's wrong after you've called his parents."

I nod and make the call.

As I speak with Connor's dad, Julie's gaze stays on me. I'm glad he answered the phone and not his mum. I know she would panic and she has every right to. I tell him that when he's released from hospital, I'll get Connor to give them a call. His dad is grateful that I've phoned and tells me to take care of his son.

I sigh heavily after the call and sit down opposite Julie, who is still watching me intently. "I'm waiting for you to tell me what's wrong."

"I'm not sure. Connor is hiding something from me. He

received a message while I was in the room, and I swear, the look on his face was thunderous as he read the message. But when I asked him about it, he never said anything."

"I'm sure it was nothing."

"I think it was a message from Donovan."

"What does he have to gain from sending Connor a message?"

"I don't know what he hopes to gain. He's still sending me messages when he has no reason to." I put my phone down on the seat beside me, lean my head forward, and rest it in my hands.

"Ella, we know Donovan is playing games, and after tonight, we can presume he's upped his game. From his message to you earlier, it's very clear he knows about Connor's attack. Is that because he was in some way behind it? Or was it those he owes money to? Now, the one thing I know is Donovan is to blame and not you. I've watched you battle with your conscience tonight, blaming yourself. This isn't your fault."

I know deep down she's right, but I can't help but feel responsible.

I've called Connor's parents. Now it's time to drop Alex a message.

I've seen Connor. He's got a few cuts and bruises but he'll be fine.

Straight away there's a reply.

Alex: Glad to hear it. I should have something positive for you in the next few days.

Me: I don't want the details.

Alex: It's okay. I won't be given those either.

Me: Thank you and I'll speak to you soon.

I sit upright in the chair and stare ahead, looking at the wall above Julie. I'm biting the inside of my cheek as I think about Alex's text message.

"Penny for them," Julie says, walking the short distance across the room and sitting down beside me.

"I wish I wasn't thinking about anything. There's so much going on. I'd like normality in my life."

"Hardly," she scoffs. "You wouldn't know what to do with normality. But, all this shit with Donovan, it will eventually disappear. One day, you'll wake up and realise he's not messing with you anymore. He'll get tired of it. Either that, or the guys he owes money to will catch up with him and he'll be the one disappearing."

"Maybe." I shiver at what she's implying and stare straight ahead.

"Look, if you're still worried about Connor keeping something from you, you need to just come right out and ask him. But, be prepared that he might not tell you. Not because he's hiding something from you, but because this is Connor, and he'll do everything in his power to protect you."

I offer her a weak smile. Yes, she's probably right, but what if she's wrong? And he is hiding something from me.

There's a niggling feeling in the back of my mind and I can't shake it away.

Chapter 13

"MUM, I'M FINE, HONESTLY. STOP fussing . . . Yes, I'll see if Ella and I have time to fit in a trip to see you before filming starts . . . I don't need looking after . . . Of course not . . . Look, we're nearly home . . . Yes, I'm still looking for somewhere."

I'm listening to Connor's side of the conversation with his mum as I'm driving us back to the house. I hope he's doing a better job of convincing his mum that he's okay than he has done with me. In my opinion, he's far from okay.

Talking to his mum, he sounds and looks happier. There's no strain in his voice, and considering he's still sore, he seems in good spirits. But he's been different with me. Something is wrong, but he won't tell me what it is when I've questioned him.

My windscreen wipers swish back and forth, trying to clear the rain that's falling heavily. Callum brought my car to the hospital earlier on with my dad. We could've just got a taxi, but right now, I'm thankful I have something to concentrate on, even if it is the rain outside.

Something has Connor on edge with me and I don't know what it is. I can pinpoint when he changed; last night when he received that text message.

"Love you too. We'll see you soon," he says, ending his call. I glance briefly in his direction, but he's already turned and is looking out the window. If I'm truthful with myself, he's hardly spoken to me since I went back into his hospital room after calling his parents. I'm certain he pretended to be sleeping a lot.

He's going to have to speak to me at some point. Give in and tell me what's wrong, because right now, I'm beginning to think *I've* done something wrong.

I have though. I've brought him into my fucked up life.

No, I didn't.

I wasn't looking for anything when I found him, and I'm glad I did. But something deep within tells me the happiness I've had recently is going to be short-lived. A feeling of dread fills me as I stop at the gate and enter the code for them to open.

Driving into the grounds, I look over my shoulder and check the gates are closing behind us. I find myself sighing when they do. Connor is still facing the window. The silence between us is unbearable. I hope it's not like this for the rest of the today because I don't know how I'll stand it.

Stopping the car, I don't even look at him as I get out and walk toward the house. I know he's out when I hear the car door closing. I fumble with the key in the lock. Why the hell can I not do something so straight forward as putting the key in the lock and open the door?

"Here, let me," Connor says, taking the key from me and opening the door. I step inside and switch off the alarm, still without looking at him.

I walk toward the kitchen and there's a part of me that's hoping I hear his footsteps walking up the stairs. That he'll go and rest, fall asleep, and wake up in a better mood, because the one he's in at the moment has my own mood simmering away, just below the boil, ready to explode. But his footsteps follow me. In the kitchen, I switch the kettle on and open the patio doors. It might be raining, but it's humid.

His footsteps stop and I know he's there. "Ella."

I turn to facing him; he's standing by the table. "What is it?"

"Nothing, forget it," he says, staring at the floor.

"Maybe we should forget it. Forget us. It's clear to me you blame me for last night. So maybe you should pack up and move out!" I shout, staring at him, willing him to say something, anything. To argue back with me. At least then I'd know he cared.

But nothing.

He can't even bring himself to look at me. For the first time in five years, Connor looks lost and alone.

I want nothing more than for him to open up, to tell me what is wrong. Put my wandering mind at rest, but as I take in the sight of him, I don't think he will.

After what feels like an eternity, he lifts his head. Goosebumps spread over my skin when I see his dark expression. In this moment, I want to take back the words I've just said because I didn't mean them. They were said out of anger and frustration.

"Connor?" I'm scared now, because I see something in his expression I don't think I've seen before. Regret.

I hope I'm wrong, but the longer I stand here looking at him, my fears are confirmed. There's an unpleasant emotion filling the air around us. And, right now, I wish I had a magic wand to put things right between us.

If only I knew what was wrong.

His phone buzzes from his jeans pocket, and I want to rush toward him and take it, to see who is calling and sending him messages. He shifts uncomfortably and I sense he wants to read the message that has just come through, but he doesn't make a move for the phone.

For God's sake. Just read it and then tell me what's wrong.

Connor draws in a sharp breath and the expression on his bruised face is pained. My heart sinks because I know I've said words I don't mean, but the reality is, this is what he wants.

"Connor, please speak to me. Tell me what I've done."

"You've not done anything." I want to sigh with relief, but I don't because his mood is still flat.

"What's wrong then?"

"Nothing. I'm going upstairs to pack. I can't be here." I freeze. "I'm sorry."

He's sorry. Is that all he's got?

"Why the hell would you do that?" I scream at him.

"I'm going to do what you told me to do," he says, turning his back to me.

"No, you're doing this because something is scaring you. Your mind was already made up before I uttered the words you and I both know I didn't mean. Something has frightened you, or someone has got to you, telling you to stay away from me. So why now? Why? You've waited all this time for what? To walk away from me. Was that the plan all along? To play me? If it is then you're no better than him."

I stand in the middle of the kitchen, deflated at the turn of events. The Connor I know would put up a fight, not run and hide. I hear his footsteps trudge up the stairs.

For whatever reason, he thinks he's doing the right thing, but deep down, his heart is breaking. I can see that.

This has to be a dream. A hallucination.

I'm frozen to the spot as tears fill my eyes. A deep chill settles over me and reality hits me hard. This isn't a dream. This is happening because of Donovan Bell.

At the moment, I have no proof, but in my heart, I know this is connected to him. I almost laugh as I think about the turn of events. This could, in fact, be written in a movie script. *Scripted reality*, the story of my life.

I wouldn't even need a script to play my own part, because I'm the one who has and is still living through the mess that is my life. Maybe when my life is back to what resembles normal, I should put this idea to Trevor.

I look around the kitchen for something to do. Something to keep my mind occupied. I walk the short distance to the work surface and make myself a cup of tea. I glare at the mug as I put spoonful after spoonful of sugar into it.

I don't even take sugar.

With the huge mug in my hand, I sit down and close my eyes. I hear Connor upstairs, but I don't move. I just sit, waiting. Hoping that when he finally walks down the stairs, he comes to his senses and tells me what's going on and doesn't leave me. He knows I need honesty in a relationship.

My stomach twists violently as it hits me. I open my eyes and take a drink to calm me down. He's going to walk away from me, from us, so he doesn't have to lie to me.

Seconds feel like minutes. Minutes feel like hours.

His footsteps coming back down the stairs grab my attention. I stand with my mug still in my hand and walk slowly into the hallway. He's standing there, hand on his suitcase, with his back to me.

I open my mouth to speak, but I can't find any words. I need to figure out what to say to him. He takes a step toward the front door.

He's really going to do this. He's really going to leave me. Connor Andrews, the man who waited patiently for me to be his, is giving up at the first hurdle. The man I thought I could trust with my damaged heart. He's going to walk out that door and take my heart with him.

"So, that's it? What the hell was all that you just told your mum? You lied to her. You hate lying. Connor, talk to me. Tell me, please?" I don't even recognise my own pleading voice.

He releases the suitcase from his hand and turns around to finally face me. "I won't see you broken because of me. I won't be the cause of your tears."

"If you walk away now then you are the reason I'll be broken in two. You will be the cause of my tears." I don't even bother to lift my hand to wipe away my falling tears.

"You're strong, Ella. You'll get through this mess without me. I'll only drag you down when I fall." I take a step toward him. He raises his hand, keeping space between us.

I hate this.

He looks down at the floor briefly before bringing his eyes to mine. Pain, sadness, fear . . . it's all there for me to see. His eyes study me and I know he's struggling to walk away. I want him to offer me words of comfort, and for a split second, a small smile graces his lips, and I think he's realising the mistake he's making.

Instead, I hear the words I've been dreading. "I'm sorry, Ella."

He turns, puts his hand on his suitcase, and opens the front door then walks away without looking back.

The door closes behind him and he's gone.

I stare at the door, willing him to walk back through it. When I hear a car or a taxi's engine, I know he's gone.

"Damn you!" I shout, throwing my mug of tea at the door. It smashes hard and falls to the floor. "Damn you for not taking the risk and telling me!"

I sit down on the bottom step and my tears fall heavily.

Am I really that bad a person? Do I deserve all the crap that is in my life?

Maybe I deserve it all and more.

Maybe I'm not worthy of Connor Andrews.

If only I was strong enough to say those three little words.

Chapter 14

I'M STILL SITTING ON THE first step. My tears have long since stopped when my front door opens. My heart beats fast as I lift my head, but my spirits fall dramatically when I'm met with Julie, her eyes full of the same sadness and regret I saw in Connor's. She studies me for a moment before rushing toward me, her shoes crunching against the broken mug on the floor. She pulls me to my feet and takes me in her arms.

"Oh, Ella, I'm so sorry. I'm sorry. I'll clean up that mess later."

I stare ahead at the front door that he walked out of as Julie holds me protectively in her arms. I will myself not to cry again. I don't even know how long I've sat on the step or what time it is. What I do know is that it's still raining outside. Julie's clothes and hair are wet from dashing the short distance from her car to the front door.

"Have you eaten today?" she asks.

"I had breakfast in the hospital with Connor."

"Bloody hell. You need to eat. I can make dinner." I don't want food. All I want to do is walk upstairs and crawl into the bed we've shared. Fall asleep with his scent surrounding me. "Let's go and sit down."

She guides me through to the sitting room. "What are you doing here?" I ask.

"Callum called me. It was me or your dad and I think he went for the safer option for Connor. He said you would need me. So here I am."

"Callum?" She nods. I stare at her. "Connor's staying with Callum?" My brother the traitor. Why would he do that? I'm going to kill him for taking sides.

"Yes, but only for tonight. I believe he's going to his mum's tomorrow on an early morning train. What the hell happened?"

"I wish I knew."

"Start at the beginning."

"Well, you already know about the message he received last night. He's been strange with me since then. One word answers as though he had nothing to say. He couldn't even look at me when we got home. He says he doesn't blame me, but what's the saying, actions speak louder than words? Well, his actions speak volumes. He blames me, but that's okay, because I blame me too."

"You are not to blame. Do you hear me?" Tears fill Julie's eyes as she watches and listens to me. I nod. She understands. She doesn't agree, but at least she understands.

Five years with Donovan and I never felt this bad about him leaving me. I was angrier about the way he left, but this feeling in the pit of my stomach tells me I might not recover from Connor leaving me.

Donovan used to tell me all the time that he loved me, and it felt nice. I thought we were building a future. I would tell him I loved him on an almost daily basis. But now, I realise I said it out of habit and not because I loved him.

As I sit with my best friend offering me comfort, I know what I felt toward Donovan wasn't love, because the day he left me, my heart didn't shatter in two.

Love is waking up with a smile on your face because the first thought of the day is about that special someone who makes your heart all warm and fuzzy. Love is closing your eyes at night, smiling as you drift off to sleep with the same thoughts that you started the day with.

Love is the undeniable ache in your chest when you aren't around your someone special. Love is so hard to describe, but when you have it in your life, you find yourself grinning from ear to ear. It's all the silly things you take for granted, like his hand in yours, or his arms wrapped tightly around you as you lie securely, snuggling into his arms. Seeing his face with that perfect white smile when you open your eyes in the morning light. The strength he gives you when he's around.

You don't have a choice in who you fall in love with. It happens when you least expect it. Well, that's what happened in my case.

I wasn't looking for love

Love found me.

"I love him," I say softly, and the smile that comes to my lips is easy as I think about my feelings for him.

"Oh, Ella, I know you do." My heart is racing. "You will be okay. I know you will."

My phone ringing in the distance startles us both. "I should go and answer that," I say when it stops ringing and then starts straight away.

I make my way into the kitchen. Trevor's name flashes across the screen. I take a deep breath and answer. "Hi, Trevor. What's up?" I ask, trying to even out my voice.

"I'm glad I've finally managed to get you. I know this is really short notice, although it wouldn't have been as short if you had answered my earlier calls."

I have no idea what he's talking about. "Just tell me."

"I need you on set at eight a.m. tomorrow."

"Really?"

"Yes. Filming is ahead of schedule. I'll come around and pick you up just after seven and I'll hang around tomorrow in case you need me."

"Okay. I'll be ready."

"See you in the morning," he says, and ends our call.

"Well?" Julie asks as I switch the kettle on.

"I'm on set tomorrow."

"Brilliant! Or is it? I thought it was still a few weeks before you started filming. Have you even read the script?"

"Yes, and yes, of course this is good, but I'm not sure I'm going to be in the right frame of mind."

"You'll smash it on set and it will help you. This is the distraction you'll need because I can already see how torn up you are. Now, I was going to suggest opening a bottle of wine and ordering a curry, but we better leave the wine tonight. We need you fresh tomorrow."

She has a good point.

THE CAR HORN sounds louder than it should. I nervously walk toward the front door with Julie behind me. She stayed last night to keep me company, saying something about not being on my own. I'm glad she did, because it meant I didn't spend the whole night in tears. And, this morning, I'm relieved that I actually look not so bad.

"You've got this," she tells me as we walk outside after setting the alarm. Trevor's car is parked beside Julie's and he's anxiously waiting. I don't know what he's worrying about; there's no way we'll be late.

"Thank you for staying with me."

"I'm here for you always. Now, go on and break a leg and enjoy today. Just think, you get to ogle a couple of sexy men all day."

"Julie!"

"Okay, not the best choice of words under the circumstances but there are a few hunks on the show." The car horn blares, making us jump. "Go before he gets impatient. I'll be here tonight."

"You don't have to."

"I know that, but someone needs to look after you."

I watch as she gets in her car and waves before driving off.

"Ella McGregor, get a move on instead of standing there dreaming," Trevor says.

"Sorry," I say, getting into his car.

"It's fine. I have a few things to discuss with you," he says, starting the engine and driving away from the house.

"I'm all ears."

"Well, Michelle from the charity has been in touch, wondering when we can film the TV commercial, and I've told her this weekend or next because you're on set every day this week. She'll get back to me with all the details, but be prepared to be filming Saturday and Sunday." Exciting. This makes me happy. This will give me purpose. "She also asked if you still want to help."

"Yes," I say without hesitation.

"Okay, well how about tomorrow after shooting? She'd like you to meet the family she's working closely with."

"Yes. Just tell me where I need to be and when."

"I'll find out later. Are you looking forward to today?"

"Yes, even though I'm a bit nervous."

"You, my dear girl, have nothing to be nervous about."

I sit back in the seat and stare out the window, watching the early morning of a new week whizz by. But my thoughts drift to Connor.

Has he already left my brother's to travel up north to his parents? I thought Callum would've at least been in touch with me. I rummage around my bag. I take my phone and type out a message because I'm not sure I'd be able to hide my anger with him in an actual conversation.

> *You're my brother and I never thought you'd take his side over mine. But I wanted to let you know just in case you're interested, I'm on set from today. I'll be home tonight should you decide you*

want to talk to me.

Callum: I love you and I haven't taken his side over yours. And if he wasn't already sporting a black eye, he would get one from me for leaving you. Who's with you?

Me: Trevor and he's staying with me today.

Callum: If it's okay can I come over and see you tonight?"

Me: Do you usually need to ask?

Callum: I'll see you tonight.

I check my messages and emails and I don't know why I'm surprised there's nothing from Connor. I sigh heavily, dropping my phone back into my bag. "Everything okay?" Trevor asks. I nod in response and go back to watching the world go by.

I hope today goes well, because Julie's right. I do need a distraction. I don't want to think about Connor, but I'm sure he won't be far from my mind.

Chapter 15

"OH. MY. GOD. I'VE HAD so much fun today," I say, sliding into Trevor's car, relieved that the day has gone so well and that the cast made me feel welcome.

"Yes, I see that. I wish your dad had been on the set today to watch you. To see that sparkle in your eyes we all feared was lost as far as your career is concerned. I've loved seeing the smile on your face. Especially when you looked so miserable when I picked you up this morning. I won't ask what's wrong, but I'll say this, Connor sounded as miserable as you looked when I talked to him."

He's spoken to him. My heart skips a beat just hearing his name. All day I've tried hard to put him in the back of mind. He's never been far from my thoughts, especially when we finished filming and talk turned to the storyline Connor will feature in.

"Ella, can I tell you something?"

"Yes."

"Connor will always, and has always, done what he can to protect you. You need to remember that. He hasn't given me any details, but I know he wouldn't want to hurt you."

"But he has," I say with a sigh. "How am I going to able to work with him?"

"Ella, you are always professional. Look at how you've handled

Donovan. I'm sure this will be no different."

"This is very different." I love Connor, and in the show, he's meant to play my love interest. The producers were excited about working with us, knowing we were a couple. They said the chemistry between us would make for some very intimate and believable scenes. Nothing between us would be an act. I know we would each pour our heart and soul into a kiss because we do that with every kiss we share. This is what the producers had seen when we were together and I know this is what they want to see in scenes we are together.

I'm not sure that's what they'll get from either of us now.

I think about his words as we start the drive back home. They spin around and around in my mind, making me dizzy. For whatever reason, Connor left to protect me. But why? What threat has been made? If he doesn't communicate, how am I supposed to understand his reasons for leaving? Will it make any difference knowing the reason? No. At the moment it won't. All I know is he's left me and taken a part of me with him.

I've not thought about the time, but as Trevor drives me home, I notice it's getting darker. It's almost eight p.m. I was so immersed in work that I hadn't realised the time. There were only a few scenes I was in that needed to be re-shot, and not because of me, which I was pleased with. I was worried I wouldn't fit in. The other actors have all been with the show for a number of years. I'm the newbie. The man who plays my gangster dad is an absolute sweetheart. He reminds me of my own dad; tough on the outside but a real heart of gold. Most of my scenes today involved him.

Tomorrow, I've to be on set at the same time, and I'm excited and looking forward to it. I just hope I get a decent sleep. Although, it's my first night on my own in weeks, so I'm not sure I will.

My phone buzzes.

Callum: I thought you'd be home.

Me: I'm on my way. I'll be there in less than 5 mins

Callum: Okay are you hungry?

Me: No.

I wonder if my brother will be able to shed any light on Connor. Maybe he will, maybe he won't. I'm not sure I'm ready to hear excuses.

There are no messages on my phone from Julie, and after speaking to her earlier in the day, I didn't expect there to be. She had messaged around lunchtime, asking how everything was going. I called her when we stopped for something to eat. She was only checking on me to see if I wanted her to come over tonight. I told her Callum was coming over, but I left out the part that he wasn't staying. She seemed content with my answer and I'm sure my happy mood gave her the reassurance she needed.

The car slows down and Trevor enters the code for the gates and drives through. I used to smile about coming home. Not anymore. It fills me with dread, and not just because I'll be on my own tonight. The car stops beside my brother's in the driveway.

"Thank you for today," I say, turning to face Trevor.

His smile is warm and sincere. "You don't need to thank me for doing my job. What do you want me to say to your dad about Connor?"

"Nothing. Not yet. Well, that's if Callum hasn't already told him. If he hasn't, then tell him he's visiting his parents."

"Okay. Well, that part isn't a lie. If you want to talk to someone, Betty is always happy to talk through issues." I nod with a smile. Betty is a good listener and does offer good advice when she thinks it's necessary. "Go on in and see your brother and I'll pick you up in the morning."

"Trevor, picking me up isn't part of the job. I can make my

own way there."

"Yes, I know that, but . . ."

"Fine." I huff before leaning across and kissing his cheek. I know they want someone to be with me at all times. I'm hoping Trevor hasn't tried to talk my brother into staying with me tonight. There's a part of me that really wants to be on my own. The longer I'm surrounded with my family, the harder it will be when I finally am on my own.

I don't hear Trevor's car drive off until I've closed the front door behind me.

"Well, how did it go?" Callum asks as I enter the kitchen. He's sitting at the island, a mug of tea in his hand, and my mail is sitting in front of him.

"It went great. Better than I expected."

"Brilliant."

"Now . . ." The single word hangs in the air around us as I grab a bottle of water from the fridge. I might not be hungry, but all the talking I've done today has certainly made me thirsty.

"Ella, I'm sorry. I didn't know what to do when he showed up yesterday. He looked fucking lost."

"It's fine," I say, trying to shrug it off. Maybe if I tell myself often enough that I don't care, I won't.

"It's not fine. You look far from fine."

"No, I'm not. I thought everything was going well between us. I thought he truly loved me, but, obviously, I was wrong."

"He does love you."

"Well, he has a funny way of showing it. Yes, I know it's my fault he was beaten up and I don't think I'll ever be able to forget that. And neither will he."

Callum stands, pushing his chair so it scrapes along the floor. He steps toward me. "Ella, that's bullshit. He doesn't blame you. That was the one thing he insisted I tell you."

"What else has he told you? What was his reason after

everything that's happened? Why has he turned his back on me? Why now?" My eyes fill with tears, but I don't want them to fall.

"I wish I had answers for you, but I don't. He hasn't told me anything. What I do know is that his decision to leave hasn't been made lightly. He's heartbroken."

"I don't want to hear it. He's gone and I'm on my own after letting him in. After trusting him. After falling . . ."

Callum wraps his arms around me and I struggle in his hold. "Ssh. I know you love him."

"Yeah, well loving someone sucks. Big time. I don't ever want to fall in love again because this fucking hurts," I say, and my tears fall.

I'm not sure how long I stand with my brother's arms around me, holding me, protecting me. I can barely see with the tears that are streaming down my face. My vision is blurry.

"Come on. You need to pull yourself together. This isn't going to help you," he says as he guides me from the kitchen to the sitting room.

"He's left me," I say, sobbing as I sit down on the sofa.

Callum sucks in a deep breath. "I know and he's a fucking fool for doing so." His words only make me cry again. This time harder than before.

Callum sits down and tries to wrap his arms back around me, but I push him away. "Go home."

"No. I'm here with you for the night."

"I don't want you here. I want to be on my own." I raise my voice.

"Ella, it's not . . ."

"I don't want to hear it. Whatever you're going to say, I really don't care. I just want to be on my own." I don't need to listen to my brother trying to tell me everything will be okay. At the moment, it's not okay, and I want to be left alone to cry and feel sorry for myself, before I have to pull up my big girl pants and carry on with my life. "Callum, I'm going to lock up behind you, set the alarm and go to bed. I'll have my phone right beside me. If I need you, I'll call," I say with conviction as my tears stop.

"I don't know. Dad won't be happy if he finds out you're on your own."

"And who is going to tell him? Not me. Go on. Go home. You have work tomorrow."

"And so do you. If I stay here, there's the added bonus that I'm here if you need me."

"Callum, I'd rather be on my own. With my own thoughts."

"I'm not going to convince you to let me stay, am I?"

"No." He stands and so do I. I follow him out into the hallway. He pauses at the front door with his hand on the handle. "Honestly, I'll be fine."

He gives me a kiss, his eyes filled with sadness before opening the door. I stand and watch him as he gets in his car. I give him a wave before closing the door and locking it. I set the alarm and slowly climb the stairs.

I pause outside the bedroom Connor and I have shared and glance along the hallway. It's not a difficult choice to make, where I'm spending the night. I strip as I enter the room, taking my phone from my pocket. I turn it off and put it down on the cabinet then climb into bed, pulling the bed sheets around me. The smell of Connor still lingers on them.

Tears fill my eyes as I close them. I already know I'm going to have a troubled night's sleep.

Chapter 16

AS I LOOK IN THE mirror, I really wish I had got a decent sleep and hadn't spent most of the night crying. My eyes are bloodshot and the dark circles underneath them show exactly how little sleep I've had.

Not how I should look for my second morning on set.

I almost look as bad as I did all those weeks ago. The morning my dad and brother came home from their holiday. The day I finally told them everything that was going on in my life. And here I find myself withholding the truth about Connor and me from my dad.

This isn't me. I won't go back to that dark place I was in. I don't want to be there again.

When I see my dad, I'll be honest with him and tell him that Connor has done the one thing he promised my dad he would never do to me. Hurt me.

Fear pulled me from sleep on more than one occasion throughout the night. Strange dreams of Connor and Donovan left me frightened and angry. I woke up crying at one point, sweat dripping from my body. I wasn't sure what had scared me so much. I only know that I woke up alone and scared.

After all the weeks of sharing a bed with Connor, I didn't like being alone. I missed his arms around me.

If I don't shake these thoughts, I'm going to look worse than I already do.

I'm dressed, hair is okay, and as for my face, well, I'm sure make-up will sort that before I start shooting today's scenes. I slip my feet into my shoes, grab my phone, and leave the bedroom.

Walking downstairs, I switch the phone back on. It takes a few minutes to power on. I stop at the bottom step when it starts buzzing. I look at all the text messages. Callum, Julie, Jess, and the one that surprises me most, Alex Mathews.

I know I need to speak to him, but I'm worried about what I'll end up caught up in. I don't want those looking for their money back from Donovan to come after me for it, but I also don't want to be responsible for others getting hurt.

Alex's message is from this morning. I wonder if it's too early to call him. I decide it's not and call him before I change my mind.

"Good morning, Ella. How are you?"

"I've been better."

"Can I do anything to help?"

"No, but thanks for offering. Now, you have news for me?"

"Yes. The men from America that Donovan owes money to . . . you won't get any more trouble from them."

"Alex!"

"Ella, everything is okay. There's nothing for you to worry about. Cole only had to do a little digging to find out who Donovan owed money to, and the funny, or not so funny thing is, it was someone known to me. So, there's nothing for you to worry about. A friendly word was all it took. However, Donovan and Miss Hunter have a lot to be worried about."

"I don't know what to say. Thank you."

"You don't need to say anything, especially not thanks. Friends help each other out. Now, Libby has asked for you to get in touch. She wants to run something past you."

"That sounds intriguing. Is tomorrow okay? I'm on set today, and tonight I'm going out with Michelle from the charity to meet a family."

"Of course it is. Just don't forget to call her."

"I won't. Thank you again."

"Bye, Ella."

I sigh deeply, ending the call with Alex. Feelings of relief sweep through me. My life can go back to normal. I don't have to watch over my shoulder and Connor should be able to come back because I'm certain this was his reason for leaving. We have nothing to worry about. I'm not going to be hounded or bullied into paying money for that low-life of an ex.

I need to call him.

The tooting of a car horn makes me jump. I open the front door and Trevor is waiting for me. I grab my bag, lock up, and leave the house.

"Well, you look awful," he says as I get in the car.

"Thanks."

"I'm only telling you the truth. From the state of you, I presume you've not slept?" *Sleep. What's that again?* My poor mind was in overdrive, and all the tears . . . I can't remember ever crying as much as I did last night.

"Not really. Have you heard from Connor?" I ask the question I'm not sure I want to hear the answer to. I tried to call him, but I presume his phone is off, and even if it was on, I'm not sure he'd take my call anyway. Twice through the night I dialled his mum's number, but I couldn't call her.

I just want to ask him one question. Why?

"No, I've not spoken to him. I do need to speak to him today to find out if he'll be on set when he's expected. Am I taking you straight from the set to meet with Michelle at the charity office later?"

"Yes." I notice his quick change of subject.

The engine roars to life and I sit back, trying to relax, with thoughts about today's filming firmly in my head. I push everything else to the back of my mind. I'm sure tonight, when I'm home alone, Connor will be who I think of. He'll be the one I cry myself to sleep over.

My phone beeps and I look at the name on my screen.

I don't need this, not today. Not any day. Why the hell does he keep popping back into my life when I don't want him?

> *Donovan: I told you he wasn't the one for you. Now you know why. You and I should talk.*

I frown and re-read his message, but I don't understand. What the hell is he on about now? Has he not interfered in my life enough lately? And how does he know Connor and I aren't together? A deep shiver runs through me. He's still keeping tabs on me, watching me, following me. Donovan knows something about Connor that I don't. A secret. Is this why he's gone?

"Trevor, while I'm on set today, could you look into something for me?"

"Of course I can."

I need to know what is forcing Connor away. It must be a pretty big secret that he doesn't want out. But what?

"I DON'T HAVE anything to tell you yet," Trevor says, stopping the car outside the charity office. I was beginning to wonder on our drive here if he had forgotten what I had asked. "When you're finished with Michelle, you've to get a taxi straight home."

"I know. Don't go anywhere, and no talking to strange men," I say with a giggle. The way I look now, no strange men would want to talk to me. I look as though I've been dragged through a hedge backward.

"Go on, get out, and behave yourself."

"I always behave," I tell him as I get out of the car and blow him a kiss. I don't look back before entering the charity office.

"I'm here to see Michelle," I say to the lady behind the reception desk.

"Miss McGregor. I'll let her know you're here."

I take a seat and my eyes flit slowly around the area. It's warm and welcoming, with posters on the wall and lots of different information leaflets on the table.

There's a poster that catches my eye; a success story about a young lad. He found himself living on the streets after getting in with a bad crowd. One thing led to another; drugs, theft. His mother put him out after he was caught stealing from her for the eighth time. My heart aches for not only the lad, but his family.

After being on the streets for a little over a year, he sought help, turning to the charity. His story is a happy-ever-after. He's clean, has a relationship with his family, a house of his own, and a job.

I find myself smiling.

"Ella, great to see you," Michelle says, putting her jacket on.

"And you."

"Are you ready to meet the family?"

"Yes."

Michelle and I leave the office together. We're travelling to the east-side of Glasgow in her car. I know the area we're going to is rough with lots of social problems. Michelle has told me drugs and alcohol abuse play a huge part in the local community. She has prepared me for the worst, I think.

"How is filming going?" she asks as we drive.

"Not too bad. I'm just glad to be working again."

"When will your first scenes air?"

"I think in four weeks' time, if I remember correctly."

"It sounds very exciting. Are you sure you'll have time for the charity?"

"I'll make time. I've realised lately that I have to make time for the things that matter to me, and this matters to me. I don't want to be someone who takes everything for granted. I want to help."

Michelle smiles warmly at my answer. For me, this is more important than my career. I want to make a broader difference. I'm not interested in the politics behind the scenes. When I think about my mum and all the amazing things she did for charity, I can't hide my smile. She gave her time freely to help others, and if I can help even a fraction of those she helped, I'll be happy.

Chapter 17

MICHELLE'S CAR COMES TO A stop outside a block of rundown flats. I cringe thinking about a young mum on her own with kids staying somewhere like this.

It's awful. The picture is the same as I get out of the car and look up and down the street. I turn, looking out to wasteland. Not a pretty sight to look at from the windows of the flats on this side of the street. "Who owns these?" I ask.

"The local authority."

"And they think this an acceptable standard of housing? Bloody hell. This is no place for a young family. Is there even a park for a mum to take her kids to?"

"I'll show you that after we've visited. Stacey knows I'm bringing someone with me today but she doesn't know who. She has two young girls. Kelsey is four and Kali is almost two. She had a good life before her husband died. Nice house in a good area."

"What happened?" I ask as we walk to the entrance of the building.

"They had no insurance and she couldn't keep up with the repayments on the mortgage. Found herself in a lot of debt very quickly and didn't know what to do. Not only did she lose her husband, she lost everything."

God, I've not even met Stacey and my heart is breaking for her.

The main door is hanging from the hinges. It's not even secure. Michelle climbs the steps and I follow, taking in all the rubbish lying around. It stinks.

We arrive at the third floor and there's a buggy outside one of the front doors. Michelle knocks, and after a few moments, the door opens. There stands Stacey, who can't be much younger than me, with Kali in her arms, who is crying.

"Hi, Michelle," she says quietly, at the same time trying to reassure her crying daughter.

"Stacey, are you okay?" Stacey's eyes widen as she looks over Michelle's shoulder at me. "Remember I told you I was bringing someone with me?"

"Yes, but I expected someone from your office or the council. Not a famous actress. I feel so underdressed and disorganised."

"Stacey," I say. "I'm Ella. If you'd rather I wasn't here, that's fine." I don't want her to feel uneasy. That is not my intention.

"No. You're just not who I thought it would be." Michelle waits quietly for Stacey. "Where are my manners? Please, both of you. Come in."

The flat is clean and tidy. In the living room, Kelsey is sitting up on the couch, watching some cartoon on the TV. She doesn't even turn when we enter.

"Please, take a seat. Oh, baby girl, come on. Ssh."

Michelle sits down and takes out her folder from her bag. I can't sit down. I take a step toward Stacey. "Here, let me take her and you sit down."

She hesitates, but only for a minute, before handing me her crying daughter. Stacey flops down on the sofa beside Kelsey, giving her a kiss on her head. Her daughter turns around and flashes her mum the biggest, cutest smile I've seen. That look melts my heart. I stand with Kali in my arms and she stops crying and stares at me. I smile at her and she finally smiles back.

"How did you manage that?" Stacey asks, looking at me. "All

day she's cried with me. A few minutes with you and look at her. I'm so bloody useless today." She sighs and rubs her tired eyes. She looks physically and mentally exhausted.

"Stacey, you're not useless. You're a great mum to these gorgeous girls and they both love you. Tell me, have you been out today?" Michelle asks, moving closer beside her and taking her hand.

"No. I've been too tired to do anything. The young lads in the bottom flat must've been having another of their parties. The music went on all night. I was up with the two of them crying most of the night."

"So, you've had another sleepless night? This isn't fair on you or the girls." Michelle releases Stacey's hand and starts writing down some notes and muttering under her breath.

I take a seat with Kali still in my arms and stare at her. She has beautiful big brown eyes and a perfect smile. She looks very much like her mum and sister. Sadness fills me.

"Stacey, Ella has very kindly agreed to help with the charity's promotional work. She will be fronting an ad campaign that we hope will raise more awareness of the challenges that affect people like yourself and those living on the streets."

"Maybe we'd be better on the streets. We'd all get some sleep there."

"Enough of that. None of you deserve that. I'm here to help you," Michelle tells her. "Why don't you tell Ella your story?"

She nods slowly. "We had a good life before. I didn't need to work once I had Kelsey, and if I'm honest, I wanted to be a stay-at-home mum. Graham, my husband, had a good job and we were comfortable. Kali was only two months old when he collapsed after complaining of a sore head. He died two days later."

Bloody hell.

"We had no life insurance. It was always one of those things we kept saying we'd get around to. We had insurance for the house, but I can't remember what the problem with that was. Something to do with a shortfall. I couldn't keep up the payments with no money. I did get a part-time job, a few hours a day, but that wasn't even enough to feed us. So, here we are after losing everything."

"I'm sorry."

"Don't be sorry. You probably don't understand. How could you with the life you lead?"

Her last statement hurts.

"Stacey!"

"I'm being truthful, Michelle. How can she possibly understand?"

"Ella might understand a bit more than you think. Everyone in this life has their own story to tell. Ella."

I can't say anything. Stacey has a point. To the outside world, I have it all, but when you strip back the layers, I'm no different to anyone else.

I sit with Kali and tell Stacey about the whole Donovan situation. I tell her everything, including the threatening messages from those he owes money to. Talking about this isn't as hard as I thought it would be. Yes, I've done an interview with my brother but his questions seemed very selective. But this is me pouring my heart out. The good, the bad, and the downright ugly.

"Wow! I'm the one who's sorry now," Stacey says. "I had no idea. You'll understand I don't get to watch much TV at the moment with these two. I'm sorry that you were put in that position by someone you loved and trusted."

"Me too, but enough about me." I look at Michelle. "What will it take to have them moved to somewhere that is better suited to a family?"

"Ella, I'm working on it. Believe me, I am. These flats along with the others in the street are earmarked for demolition. Stacey is lucky she has a roof over her head, but we can all agree that a young family shouldn't be living in conditions like this. Yes, Stacey has made it look comfortable and nice for the girls, but she's living on charity handouts. Hopefully, when the local authority re-house her, it will be somewhere better."

"Never in a million years did I think this would be my life."

"Don't you have family who can help?" I ask, thinking about my dad and Callum.

"No. My parents died a few years ago. And as for Graham's family, they probably could help, but don't. His mum hasn't bothered with the girls since he died. I think she blames me."

How can his family turn their backs on this gorgeous family? Christ, Stacey isn't anything to me and I don't want to leave her and the girls here when I have to go home. How can someone who is family turn their back on these two beautiful girls? Some things that happen in life don't make sense, and this is one of those.

"What about friends?"

"My friends don't really keep in touch since we moved in here. They don't want to come and visit. The area doesn't have a good reputation."

No family, no friends because they don't want to come to a rough area. Well, in my opinion, they were never true friends. Because true friends would be around no matter the situation. Hearing Stacey's story only confirms how lucky I am, but that's not going to help her.

I look at Kali in my arms and she's fallen asleep. She's a perfect wee girl without a care in the world at the moment, like her sister. But how will it affect them if their situation doesn't improve?

I already know the answer to that because Michelle has said that it's a vicious cycle for those living in poverty.

"Stacey, with Kali sleeping, why don't you take them both to bed and get some rest yourself? We'll go and I'll call you in the morning. Remember, I can help you anytime, day or night."

"Thank you. I appreciate all you're doing for me and my girls. And Ella, thank you for helping the charity."

"Hopefully it will make a difference," I say, handing Stacey her sleeping daughter.

"We'll let ourselves out. Just remember to lock the door." Stacey nods and we leave.

We walk down the three flights of stairs in silence. There's a small group of teenagers standing around the entrance, smoking and drinking. I keep my head down and follow Michelle out to the car. In the car, I take a deep breath and look back at the building we've just left.

"What are you thinking?" Michelle asks.

"That they can't stay there. The cycle needs to be broken or else those two beautiful girls are going to end up hanging around flats, drinking and smoking. Our society is failing those who need it the most."

"Ella, you have to understand, some people are more than happy living like this. They don't want anything else out of life, but others . . . well, you've seen for yourself."

She starts the car and we drive away. Michelle stops at a park, which is only five minutes away from Stacey's flat. It's run down and there's a large group of teenagers hanging around. I'm trying not to be judgemental about them but it's hard when I see some passing around a bottle and each person taking a mouthful.

I want to help Stacey and the girls, break the cycle before it's too late. I'm saddened at how lonely her life is. Yes, she has her daughters, but she's young and should have friends.

Real friends.

Chapter 18

FIVE DAYS HE'S BEEN GONE. No contact. Nothing.

I've been really busy during the day on the set and in meetings, but at night, I've been alone. Being alone makes you think, and I'm tired of thinking. I've given myself a constant headache with all the crap buzzing around in my head.

Whatever happened to normality? When Alex told me that I didn't have to worry about the people Donovan owed money to, I stupidly thought my life would be normal again. I was so wrong.

I sigh, turning over in bed. The same bed Connor and I shared for weeks. I can still smell him if I take a deep breath. I want him here with me. I want him to tell me face-to-face what the hell he has to hide. There's not been a single night this week that I've managed to sleep soundly.

My nightmares are back, creeping around, trying to drag me into the darkness. It's been easy to stay positive when I've been working. Put on a brave face. Act; after all, that's what I'm good at. But alone, it's not so easy. I find myself on a downward spiral and I'm not sure where it will end.

I want the pounding headache to disappear, but I know it won't. Not with all the jumbled thoughts in my head.

Callum and Julie have both been phoning constantly, but I'm doing what I did when Donovan left me. I'm shutting myself away from them. And why? I'm not entirely sure. Julie left me a voicemail last night, saying, 'If I don't hear from you, I'll be over tomorrow and I'm not listening to any of your excuses.'

I don't have to pretend with Julie. She'll allow me to be myself. To have a crying session if that's what I want. But she'll also be the one to give me a kick up the arse and tell me to pull myself together. That's what I need to do, because this moping around and feeling sorry for myself isn't doing me any favours.

I put on an act the other night when I called Libby. She asked how I was and I told her that everything is okay. I'm sure she knows it isn't, but she didn't press. She was so full of energy, asking lots of questions about the charity. I told her all about my meeting with Stacey and her two little girls. She sounded genuinely concerned when I mentioned their living conditions.

We spoke at great length, especially after she told me about her proposal. She would like to host a charity dinner at Stewart House. She wants to involve Jess and me. Both the charities we represent would benefit. She claims it's the least she can do considering what we're doing. I tried to reassure her she doesn't need to do anything, but she wasn't listening to a single word I said. We have arranged to meet here on Wednesday night, and Jess will be here too. Libby is hoping the event can be organised quickly.

I'm sure she'll manage it. After all, she did organise a wedding from start to finish in only five weeks. I'm looking forward to seeing them both.

I should force myself to get out of bed. If only so that when Julie gets here, she doesn't need to drag me from it. And I have no doubts that if I'm still in here when she arrives, that's exactly what she'll do.

This room is a mess.

My eyes scan the entire room as I stand. Nothing is where it's meant to be. I should clean it, but I can't be bothered. The minute I do clean, it will be as though Connor was never here and I'm not ready to let that go. If I wash the bedding, his scent will no longer linger. And while I can still feel and smell him, there's hope in my heart.

Hope that he'll come home to me.

I pass the tall, free-standing mirror and catch a glimpse of myself. It's not a pretty sight. The dark circles under my eyes are a constant reminder of my lack of sleep. My skin is pale, almost grey. *Casper the friendly ghost I am not.*

This is ridiculous. I'm not bloody sick.

But I am heartbroken. I should never have allowed myself to get close to Connor because as soon as I realised I was falling for him, I knew if it didn't work out, it would break me. And I've lost my friend. The one thing I was scared would happen has happened and there's nothing I can do about it.

I wander into the bathroom. Time for a shower and to try and pull myself together.

THE SHOWER WAS warm but did nothing to soothe my mood. And I don't think the way I'm feeling is just to do with Connor. I'm shivering from head to toe, even though I've pulled a hooded sweater over my T-shirt. I hope I'm not coming back down with the cold; that's the last thing I need.

I enter the kitchen and switch on the kettle. I need a warm cup of tea before I do anything else. The noise of the front door opening startles me and I walk into the hallway. "Do you not know how to answer a fucking phone?" Julie is mad as she marches towards me. "I've been trying to phone you and I'm sure everyone else has been doing the same thing."

"I switched my phone off last night and haven't turned it back on. What time is it?" I ask her.

"Eight a.m."

"You're kidding me? God, give me strength. Whatever you're

going to shout at me about, I need tea first. I feel like crap."

"Yeah, you look like it too."

Cheeky bitch. I turn my back to her and walk back into the kitchen, taking another mug from the cupboard and making two cups of tea. I don't have to turn around to know she's watching me; I feel her eyes boring into my back. She has something on her mind and I know she's about to tell me what it is.

"Well?" I ask, placing a mug on the island before her. I sit down, taking a drink of my tea.

"Do you have any idea how I felt not being able to get you on the phone? No, I don't suppose you do. You're lucky I'm here first, but, just so you're aware your dad, Callum, and Trevor are all on their way here, because . . ." She's pacing my kitchen floor, looking everywhere but at me.

Dread fills me and my first thought is *what the hell has Donovan done now?* Whenever something bad happens, his name is usually floating around. She finally stops and sits beside me, not opposite as she would usually do, and takes my hand. I look at her and all I see is sadness and my thoughts turn from Donovan to Connor.

Something is wrong.

"Ella, there's a story. It's everywhere. The papers, TV channels. They're all running with it."

"What story?"

"It's about Connor."

My heart sinks, and as I look at her, something tells me this is the reason he left. I'm not sure I'm ready to hear what she's about to tell me, but I don't have a choice. "Go on," I say reluctantly.

"Well, Mr Andrews has plenty of skeletons in his cupboard after all. Christ, they must've been waiting for someone to open the door. And, boy, have they all come tumbling out."

"For fuck's sake, just tell me."

"Do you know he starred in a porno?"

No, this can't be right. "No. He wouldn't."

"Well, I'm saying starred in, but it doesn't look as though he wanted to."

"What do you mean?"

"Well, I haven't watched it, but Trevor has. There's also pictures online of him in compromising positions with various women."

I stare at her, lost for words. It can't be Connor. His image is very clean cut. "I'm sure it can't be him."

"Ella, it is, but there's something you should know. When I said it doesn't look as though he wanted to star in a porno, I should've said Trevor thinks it wasn't consensual."

Not consensual. He was forced to do this? When and by who? My head is spinning and I'm having a hard time trying to understand what she means. Anger. Fear. Confusion. They are all fighting for a position inside me, and I feel as though my head is going to explode.

I need to breathe. Just breathe.

"Julie, please. You're confusing me. Just tell me what you mean."

"Okay. The video that has been uploaded is a very young Connor, can't be more than fifteen. The women are all older and so is the other man."

Tears fill my eyes. Her words strike me like a blow in my stomach. Nausea sweeps through me. I push from my chair quickly with my hand over my mouth and dash to the sink. Julie's hand rubs lightly on my back as I'm bent over, being sick in my kitchen sink. She turns on the tap, running cold water.

When I finally stand upright, she pours me a drink of water and pushes it into my hands. I take a drink, swallowing the entire contents and then pouring another. The water will do for now until I go back upstairs and freshen up.

"Ella, come and sit back down." Julie gently guides me back to the seat and I sit. "Are you okay now?"

I can't answer her because I'm far from okay.

"You say no more than fifteen?" She nods, her eyes filled with a deep sadness. "He's kept this to himself for all these years that he . . ." I can't bring myself to say the words but I'm sure she knows what I'm trying to say.

I need to speak to him.

He must be hurting. All this time, he's had a horrible secret bottled up inside. I need to see him. I want to help him through this.

"Yes, he has," she says, her voice full of sorrow.

"I need to call him." I grab my phone from where I left it last night and power it on. Julie wasn't kidding when she said everyone was trying to get in touch with me. I don't take notice of any of the missed calls or messages except one; Connor's dad has called a few times and sent a message. I open it.

Ella, can you ask Connor to call us. His mother is worried sick.

"He's not at home!" Where is he? And why did he tell Callum he was going to his parents?

"What do you mean?"

"His dad wants him to get in touch with them. I need to call them."

I call his dad who answers almost instantly. I tell him I've not seen Connor since he walked out on me. This is all news to him. I try my best to explain everything but I fear I'm making the situation worse. As we speak, I can hear Connor's mum crying in the background. My heart breaks for her. Before we end the call, he tells me that he and his wife are going to travel down to Glasgow today. I offer to have them stay here, but he said he'd wait and see how things are when they get here.

I hear the front door open and close as I flick through the rest of my missed calls and messages. I don't even lift my head when I hear them enter the kitchen. "Ella, how are you?" Callum asks.

"Callum, where is he?"

"At his parents' house."

"He's not! I've just spoken with his dad and his parents will be here later today. His poor mum is distraught. Don't lie to me."

"Ella, honestly, I don't know. He told me he was going to theirs."

"Sweetheart, everything will be okay," my dad says, coming into my view with Trevor behind him.

"How can it be? All sorts of things are running through my head."

"Ella." Something about the way Trevor says my name has me pausing. "I know where he is." I get the feeling he's trying to work out what to say to me next.

"You what? How long have you known where he was and about this?"

Trevor walks toward me, but I stand and make my way to the patio doors and stare out into the garden and the green hills beyond. I wrap my arms around my body as sadness and anger roll from me in waves. I hear the mumbled voices of my dad and Trevor, but it's Trevor who stands beside me.

"I'm sorry. It wasn't my place to say where he is."

"Where is he?" I ask calmly.

"In Glasgow at a hotel." These last five days when I've come so close to losing it because he's not been here with me, he's only been a few miles away.

I hesitate, but eventually turn to face him. "How bad is the story on Connor?"

"Here's the thing. The story isn't that bad. Most of it is speculation about how a young and innocent boy ended up in the clutches of some unsavoury actors. Actors who would never have made a name for themselves without doing what they did. The story so far seems sympathetic to Connor."

"Is it true?"

"Yes." His one lonely word has my tears falling. Falling for what the man I love went through as a young boy. Callum is quickly beside me and engulfs me in his arms. I bury my head against his chest and cry.

"I need to see him."

Chapter 19

WE ALL HAVE GHOSTS IN our past, and anyone who tells you any different is lying. I've never questioned Connor's past because I had no reason to. To me, he has always been Connor Andrews, with a clean-cut reputation.

This doesn't change that. Not in my eyes.

He's kept this awful secret hidden for almost fifteen years.

His poor mum. *What must she be going through*?

Why has this now cropped up? Who would want to cause him pain?

His name is spinning around my head. A nightmare waiting to be unleashed. As I sit in the car with Trevor driving, I quickly scroll through my messages and calls. I can't be angry with Trevor, even though it would be so easy to. After all, he lied to me. But I get that he was only looking out for Connor.

There it is. Donovan.

> *You need to call me. You don't need to be associated with someone who has a past like that.*

As opposed to what Donovan has done in his past. He's tried to call me a few times. Even if my phone had been switched on, there's no way in hell I'd answer a call from him.

The car stops. I lift my head and see we're outside the main entrance to the Hilton.

"Ella, do you want me to cancel tonight?"

I had completely forgotten about tonight. I'm out with the charity later, offering help to some of our city's homeless. "No. I'll be there."

"Are you sure?" I nod. I gave Michelle my word and intend on keeping it. "Okay. Ella, I am sorry that I kept his whereabouts from you, but he thought he was doing the right thing to protect you and his family."

"I understand. I'll call you later." He nods and I exit the car. A few people stare as I enter the hotel lobby, but I'm not interested. I walk straight toward the elevators and press the up button. I step inside alone, and when the doors open, I press for the twentieth floor.

I stand outside his hotel room door, staring at it, wondering if he'll even see me.

Enough with the stalling.

I draw in a deep breath, knock on the door, and wait.

A moment later, I hear his voice for the first time in five days. "Go away. I didn't order anything." I knock again, this time more firmly. "Hold on."

I hear the lock turning and I hold my breath as he opens the door.

And there he is. Standing before me, shocked and looking as though he's had as much sleep as me these past few days. My eyes meet his and I offer him a smile.

"Ella."

"Can I come in?"

He takes a step back and opens the door wider. I enter, not stopping until I'm standing in the middle of the room. The door closes and I hear his footsteps crossing the floor.

I turn around to face him. His body is tense and his eyes are dark. I can't make up my mind if he's happy to see me or angry that I'm in his hotel room. My heart is breaking and all I want to do is melt into his arms. But I can't. If that's what he wants, he has to lead.

"Why are you here?"

"Because the man I love is hurting, and all I want to do is take away your pain. Where else would I be?" My smile wavers and suddenly I feel as though I'm about to shed more tears as he looks deep into my eyes.

The corners of his mouth curve and life returns to his darkened eyes. His smile is real as he wraps his arms around me, holding me close. I soak up everything I've missed about him. I breathe his scent and I listen to the strong beat of his heart.

"You have no idea what hearing those words means to me," he whispers against my neck, kissing me just below my ear.

"You're not mad I'm here?"

"I could never be mad at you," he says, his voice full of emotion. "I'm nothing without you in my life."

"Well, you, Connor Andrews, should never have walked away from me. From us."

"I thought it was for the best. I didn't want to bring you or my family shame. I thought if I walked away, the story and the videos would stay hidden. How wrong was I? I should've known after everything he's put you through lately, he wouldn't stick to his word."

"Donovan."

"Yes."

"Let's sit down and you can tell me everything."

He sits down on the bed and pulls my body to his so I'm sitting between his legs, my back to his stomach.

I stare ahead, silently waiting for him to tell me the story I'm sure haunts him.

"Donovan has always known what happened years ago. He was the one that actually made the story disappear at the time."

I shiver, not because I'm cold, but because my thoughts have turned to what he's been through. No one should be forced into a situation like he was. He was only a boy. A young lad.

I sit with his arms around me and listen to him take several deep breaths. He shouldn't be nervous with me. I'm not going to judge him.

When he doesn't say anything, I turn around to face him. "Connor, take your time. I love you and I'm not going anywhere."

Slowly, Connor closes his eyes and I know he's thinking about what I've just said.

"So, Donovan made this story disappear the first time?"

He stares ahead, gathering his thoughts. I know this must be hard for him after all these years and I don't want to make it any harder than it already is. But I do need to know and understand.

"Connor?"

His voice is low and steady as he starts to speak. "I was only fifteen. It was my first time away from the farm and my parents. Everything was meant to be incredible. I was on this huge adventure. I was going to be a star in Hollywood. My agent had taken me under his wing. He was meant to looking after me. He gave my parents his assurance I would be safe. But he didn't keep me safe. Instead, he used me. He threatened me, saying if I didn't do what he wanted, my parents would lose everything. I won't go into the details and I'm hoping and praying you haven't seen some of the footage I know has been leaked."

Tears run slowly down his face. I shake my head, hoping he understands that I've not seen it, nor do I want to.

"I met Donovan a few months after arriving in Hollywood. We were both at the same event. He was there with his family and I was there with my agent, who would hardly let me move from his side. That night, I just wanted to forget about everything I was doing. The women . . . I had no interest in any of them. God, they were all so much older than me and they were proper porn stars."

I nod, offering him the encouragement to carry on.

"I hated that man and still do. That night, I got so drunk and I eventually told Donovan what was going on. He told his dad, who got me away from my agent, and I stayed with them. That is how Donovan and I became friends."

That's the Donovan I remember. Someone who put others first and tried to help.

"When I was twenty and my first major film was about to be released, the agent appeared, trying to blackmail me into giving him money or he would leak the footage. Donovan and his dad dealt with him, tying up all loose ends. I thought it was gone from my life until now. Donovan sent me a message last week saying that if I wanted that footage to stay under lock and key, I had to leave you."

"So, he's gone from protecting you and being your friend to blackmailing you."

"I should've realised he would play this card eventually. Especially when I've never hidden my feelings about you. I couldn't hide them even if I wanted to. Everyone knew how I felt about you, including him. I've always felt a connection between us and I know he hated it."

"I don't know what to say."

"I'm not expecting you to say anything. All these years I've kept this hidden because I was ashamed of what I let happen to me."

"This isn't your fault. You were only fifteen. You were only a boy."

"Yes, I was. But as I've got older, I've realised that I was abused and used for someone else's gain. Fuck. I never wanted my mum to know what I went through, and now, with today's stories, I'll have to tell her and watch her crumble."

"Yes, and soon. She and your dad are on their way here to Glasgow."

"Shit! I'm not ready to face them yet."

"They're your parents and their love for you, like mine, is unconditional. Your mum is distraught. She needs to see her son and wants to protect him as a mother should."

"That's three times you've said that word," he says with a smile.

"And I'll say it until I'm blue in the face. I love you."

His eyes meet mine. "I should've told you about Donovan."

"Yes. But I know now, and together we are strong and we'll get through this. *Together*."

For a moment, I see a brief sadness in his eyes and then he smiles. "How long do we have together until I need to see my parents?"

"I would say a couple of hours before they arrive at my house. Or I'll call them and tell them to come straight here. It's your call."

"We'll call them and ask them to come here." I smile at his answer and press a soft kiss to his lips. "Ella, I'm sorry for what I've put you through. But I want you to know how much you mean to me."

"I know and you don't have to be sorry. I understand your reasons."

"I would do anything in my power to protect you. I love you." He leans in, pressing his forehead to mine. "I love you and I want to show you how much."

Chapter 20

I FEEL HIS FINGERS AT the hem of my t-shirt before his lifts it, pulling it off over my head. His breath is like magic on my bare skin as he trails kisses around my neck and over the swell of my breasts. Already, my body is tight with desire for the man I've fallen head over heels for. I need to feel him.

I pull away, stand at the side of the bed, and quickly remove my shoes, jeans and then my underwear, leaving me completely naked. His eyes wash over me, taking in every last detail. "Your turn," I say.

He almost leaps from the bed and removes his jogging trousers and boxers, and pulls his t-shirt off. I watch, enjoying the show. He might look tired but he's still perfection and still very much mine. His discarded clothes lie crumpled up next to mine on the floor, but neither of us cares. He is as desperate to reconnect as I am; I can see the desire in his hooded eyes.

"I want you," I whisper as I lower myself to the bed, licking my lips. Connor's soft chuckle has me smiling.

"What is it my lady wants?" he asks, a teasing tone to his voice.

"Only you. To touch and to taste."

"I want the same and more. To touch. To taste. To have and to hold. I want you forever." I gasp at his words. "When the time is right, you will be mine *forever*. But right now, I'll settle for being buried deep inside you."

Doesn't he realise I'm already his? I've been his since the day he walked through those doors at the airport.

He lowers himself to the bed, kneeling before me, and pulls me up into a sitting position. He takes a deep breath in. "I have every inch of your body memorised in my head. The way you smell, the way you taste. It's all been here with me." He places his hand on his heart. "I've never been without you these days we've been apart. You need to know that. It was all I could do."

"I've slept in our bed so I could be close to you," I admit. "Connor." I wrap my arms around his neck and lie down, pulling his body with me. "Just me and you."

"Together we can get through anything." He's finally realising it. "You're all I need and want in my life."

He brushes his lips lightly over mine. My hands roam his back before settling on the curve of his arse. I spread my legs further apart, bending my knees. His body is where I want it to be. Skin against skin. My breasts tingling against the firmness of his chest.

The need to have him deep inside me is far greater than I thought possible. I rock my body against him, his erection pressing hard against me. He moves slowly, thrusting against me. But that's not what I want.

"Please, Connor," I beg.

He thrusts hard and pushes deep inside me, filling me. I gasp in sweet agony. My body arches up against his with sheer pleasure. "I need you more."

The rhythm he sets is magical, and I rise to meet each thrust. The connection between us is undeniable. We both feel it. He smiles, his eyes burning brightly.

With each thrust, my body draws him in, my muscles tightening around him as my orgasm builds within. His eyes look as heavy as mine feel, but neither of us closes them. I'm scared to close mine in case he disappears again. Maybe he feels the same.

With every careful thrust, fire spreads through me, taking with it all my thoughts and fears. Taking me on a journey to a height of passion I've never felt before. My body begins to vibrate at the same time I notice all the muscles in his shoulders tense. We both freefall together.

And together is where we belong.

Forever.

I TURN AROUND to face him. He looks much better now than when I first entered the room. He's relaxed and fresh from our shower. "I should go and let you speak to your parents on your own."

"I'm not sure I can do this on my own." I can hear the vulnerability in his voice.

"You can. I have every faith in you, and anyway, I'm out tonight with Michelle from the charity."

His face falls, but I believe the three of them need each other. I'll be here when he needs me, but for now, his parents will need some time and space to come to terms with what Connor has been through.

"Can I ask you a question?" He nods. "The agent that put you in that horrible situation. What happened to him?"

"He died a few years ago. I'm not sure how and I don't care." My mind wanders to who it could be. I know I could find out, probably quite easily too, if I did some digging. But knowing his name isn't going to help matters. It won't change the past.

"I wanted to help you with the charity," he says.

"I know, and you still can. There's going to plenty of opportunities. I have so many things to tell you. I was with Michelle and a young family during the week and I'm hoping Michelle will take me with her the next time she goes to visit them."

"Oh. Where are you helping tonight?"

"On the streets of the city centre."

"Once I've spoken with my parents, can I call you and we can go home together?" I smile at his words, even though my house is no longer home.

"Yes."

There's a knock at the door and I know this is his parents. They called when they arrived and he told them the room number. "I'll get it," I say, kissing him. I leave him standing by the window. "Come in," I say to his parents as I open the door. His mum's eyes are red from crying and there's no sign of her warm, loving smile.

"Ella, I can't thank you enough," she says, hugging me tightly before releasing me. Her eyes dart to where her son stands and I know he's trying to gather his own strength to tell his parents.

We spoke briefly after our shower and his concern about his parents is that he doesn't want to disappoint them. I tried my best to reassure him that he couldn't disappoint them, but I don't think he listened. Hopefully, his parents will have more luck than me.

"You have nothing to thank me for. I'm going to leave you so you can talk. Please be gentle with him."

"Of course we will," his mum says, her eyes brimming with more tears.

"Ella, if you're leaving, you might want to arrange with the hotel to leave through a back entrance."

Connor walks toward us. "Why? What's wrong?"

"There's a lot of press gathered outside," his dad tells us. "It seems someone alerted them when Ella arrived earlier."

"Ella, just stay. Call Michelle and cancel. She'll understand."

"She will, I don't doubt that. But your mum needs you. I think you all need some space as a family. I love you so much and it hurts to walk away from you right now, but I'm leaving because it's the right thing to do. You need time with your parents and I'll be here as soon as you need me."

"I know you're right, but . . . I'll see you later?"

"Of course you will."

"I love you."

"I love you too," I say before leaving the room. Leaving him to be comforted by his parents.

Pausing in the hallway, I hope I've done the right thing. It felt like the right decision. His mum is a very proud and private woman, and her love for her son is unconditional. She will want time to process what he tells her and I know she'll do everything in her power to support him through this.

I take a deep breath. Now, I have a decision to make; do I scurry away through the back entrance, or do I hold my head up tall and walk out the main doors and hopefully not into the lion's den.

My phone beeps in my hand. It's Trevor: *I'm at the hotel.*

> *I'm on my way down. I'll see you in a few minutes at the main entrance.* I type out my reply.

Trevor: That's our girl

I exit the elevator and Trevor is standing inside the hotel's reception. "Why are you here?" I ask.

"Because I had a feeling you'd be leaving soon, although I'm not sure if you're going home or to Michelle. I'd been tipped off that there were journalists here waiting. Someone contacted them after seeing you arrive earlier."

"I'm glad you're here. What should I say?"

"Well, today's story isn't for you to confirm or deny. When and if Connor wants to give his side of the story, that will be up to him. How is he now?"

"You saw him this morning, didn't you?"

"Of course. He's my client and I always look out for my clients, but more importantly, he's the love of your life, and like everyone else who loves you, I'd do anything for you."

"You know you're getting mushy in your old age?"

"Betty will tell you I've always been mushy. Especially when it comes to those close to me. Now, I trust you to say the right thing. If it starts to get out of hand, I'll step in."

"Okay. Let's do this," I say as the doorman holds the door open for us.

Cameras flash in every direction, but I don't let it faze me.

"Ella, you look well considering today's breaking story."

"I am well."

Trevor stays close as we stop because it's clear I'm not getting through this crowd without answering a few questions.

"Miss McGregor, have you watched the footage?"

"No."

"It clearly shows Mr Andrews."

"Is there a question in that sentence?" I ask the reporter who is standing in front of me, blocking the path to Trevor's car.

"No, there wasn't." The woman's face falls with what I think is sadness, and it's clear to me that she's seen some of the footage at least.

"Will Mr Andrews be making a statement on today's story?" a man from the back of the crowd calls out. "Is it true he was abused?"

"I'm sorry. I have no comment to make."

Trevor puts his hand on the small of my back and pushes his way through the crowd. He opens the passenger door and I get in quickly as photographers still take picture after picture.

"You done good girl. Are you sure you still want to go ahead with your plans?"

"Yes," I say without hesitation.

If I can keep myself busy, I won't be wondering how Connor and his parents are.

I shouldn't worry about them. They love him unconditionally.

And the sooner he realises that, the better.

Chapter 21

"I HONESTLY DIDN'T THINK I'D see you tonight," Michelle says as I enter the shelter. "Are you okay?"

"I'm fine. I'd given you my word I'd be here tonight, and my word isn't something I tend to go back on."

"I'm realising that. As long as you're sure. If at any point tonight or today's events get too much, just tell me." I nod with a smile. "Okay, I'm about to give all the volunteers a briefing on what to look out for."

I follow her into another room which is huge and filled with makeshift beds and lots of volunteers. Michelle told me this isn't the only venue used at night to help the homeless in the city; there's another four throughout the city centre. Even with four venues with all these makeshift beds, there are still people sleeping on the streets. It suddenly hits me that our homeless problem is much bigger than I initially thought.

I stand at the back as Michelle makes her way to the front of the room. Any hope of blending in with the crowd is long gone when Michelle announces that I'm here to help. Everyone turns and looks at me. She proceeds to split everyone into groups of two or three and gives each group instructions on which area of the city they will be working in and what to look out for; checking on anyone showing signs of sickness.

Every group has to check in several times. I suppose that's one way of ensuring the safety of all the volunteers. Michelle hopes to get as many homeless people as she possibly can off the streets tonight and sleeping in one of the shelters.

I stand back and watch as each group gathers some boxes. "What are they doing?" I ask.

"Not everyone will take our offer of a bed for the night. Sometimes, we have to earn their trust. They may be scared that we'll go to other authorities. We'll give those who don't accept a bed for the night some basic toiletries such as, face wipes, hand sanitiser, a toothbrush, and toothpaste. It doesn't seem like much, but most people are so grateful. We also provide them with a hot drink and a roll."

"How do you get hot food to them?"

"Well, we can tell them where to go, but most won't, so I have a team of guys who are prepared to take hot food to them. I just call in the destination."

"It sounds like you are very well organised."

"We need to be. There's a lot of ground to be covered in a night."

We take a few boxes of supplies out to Michelle's car. There's a guy coming out with us; Tom. He's young and seems really friendly, but I can't help thinking I recognise him. "Considering you're an A-list star, it should be me staring," he says with a cheeky smile.

"Sorry, it's just you look familiar."

"I'm sure you'll have seen pictures of me at the main office."

"So, you were homeless?" I ask as we put the last of the boxes in the car.

"Yes. I owe my life to the charity and that's why I'm here at the weekend instead of drinking in the pub. And what you're doing is amazing. You will lift the profile of the charity."

"I hope I can help."

"I have no doubts you will, Miss McGregor."

"Please, only Ella."

"Okay, Ella. If I can get some pictures of you helping, is that okay? I'm not sure if Michelle has asked or not but we'd love to have a piece in one of the papers."

"Yes and yes. I'm here to help the charity in any way. You can do what you want." Tom smirks. "Within reason," I add.

"So I can't steal a kiss then?"

"Tom!" Michelle shouts. "Ella is here to help, not to have you come on to her. Ella, you'll need to forgive Tom. He's just a typical young lad."

"He's already forgiven. Look at the smile. I'm sure no one can stay angry with him for long." Michelle gets in the car and Tom winks at me. I get in the car, laughing, because this feels so normal after today and the week I've had.

My thoughts drift to Connor and I type out a message on my phone.

I love you and hope the three of you are okay. X

He replies almost instantly. *I love you and you were right. We did need space.*

I smile at his response.

Our drive isn't long, and before I know it, we're walking along what is, during the day, one of the busiest high streets in Glasgow. But, tonight, the scene is different. Groups of people going from one pub to another ignore everything else.

We've each put some supplies in backpacks. Talk is cheery as we walk. Tom has a knack of making Michelle and me laugh. Someone like him is great company on nights like this because he keeps spirits high.

"Slow down, guys," Michelle says as we approach a large shop with a double doorway. There are at least two people there.

"Hello, Mack. How are you tonight?" Tom asks the man

sitting up in a sleeping bag. I try not to stare, but it's hard not to.

I can't even begin to estimate what age he is. His dirty, ripped clothes hang loosely on his undernourished frame. His matted hair is long and greasy. The shirt on his back is spattered with blood and covered in mould and saliva from his hard nights on the street.

This is so wrong.

I want to say our country is fucked, letting this go on. But this isn't just our city, our country's problem. This is a worldwide problem. That needs to be addressed.

"I'm not too bad," Mack says, adjusting his sleeping bag. "I see you've brought a new friend, but I'm hoping she's not from social services." Michelle's words about trust ring loudly through my ears.

"No, she's not from social services. This is Ella McGregor."

"She could be a movie star," Mack says, and Tom laughs. "What's so funny, young man?"

"She is a movie star. One of the best," Tom replies. As Mack studies me, movement at the other sleeping bag catches my eye. I can't hide the gasp that escapes my mouth as I take in the sight before me. Tears fill my eyes.

A young boy, maybe twelve or thirteen, sits up and stares at me. I can hear Mack and Tom talking; he's asking why I'd want to be on the streets helping the likes of him when I could be sitting in my warm house.

I tune out their conversation and concentrate on the small boy. He's not as dirty as Mack so I presume he's not been on the streets long. The lad's deep blue eyes stare at me and he blinks rapidly as though he recognises me. "You're Ella McGregor."

I bend down to his level. "Yes, I am. How do you know me?"

"I saw your last movie with my mu . . ." He doesn't finish his sentence and sadness creeps across his expression. A moment ago, his face was full of light, and now, all I see is darkness. He slumps back against the door, fidgeting with something around his neck. There's a gold cross between his fingers.

Michelle is on her phone, calling in for hot food and drinks. "So, our young scrapper is with you again," Tom says to Mack.

Again?

"Yes. He's a good lad. I gave you my word I'd look out for him. It seems I'm stuck with him."

"I can leave you at any time, old man," the boy says, his voiced laced with humour. Michelle and Tom laugh, but I can't. My eyes are filling with tears and there's nothing I can do to stop them.

What has happened to our society? A young boy who should be at home with his family, going to school, playing football with his friends. Why is he not at home?

"Miss Ella!" It's Mack's voice that brings me away from my thoughts. "Is this your first night out?"

"Yes, and it won't be my last."

"Mack, can't we offer you both beds in the shelter tonight?" Michelle asks.

"Not tonight. The boy won't go and I won't leave him on his own." And with Mack's words, my tears fall. Tom hands me a tissue. I want to give Mack a kiss for what he's doing for the boy, and as for him, I want to take him in my arms and tell him everything will be okay. That there's someone to look out for him and protect him.

But most of all, love him.

"Miss Ella, don't cry. He's fine with me. No harm will come to him."

"Ella, do you need a minute?" Michelle asks.

"No. Can I sit down with you?" Michelle and Tom look at each other. Tom smiles and Michelle shrugs her shoulders.

"It's been a few years since a nice young thing sat next to me. It's a bit dirty down here," Mack says.

"I don't mind." I sit down beside them. Tom snaps a few

pictures. "Tom, I don't mind pictures of me, but I want the privacy of Mack and the boy kept exactly that. Private."

"Understood," Tom says, and Michelle smiles.

"Mack, can I ask you a few questions?"

"Of course. I'm an open book."

"How old are you? And how did you end up here?"

"I'm forty-nine, and this was the last place I expected to find myself. I had a great life, a good job, a nice house, a wife and a daughter. But my daughter was killed in a car crash. I was driving when the other car hit us. I survived and she didn't." He takes a deep breath to steady his wavering voice. "Things went from bad to worse. I started drinking, couldn't stop, or rather, didn't want to. It hid my grief. While I was drinking myself into oblivion, my wife was submerged in grief and I couldn't see it. We should've been helping each other. Instead, I couldn't even help myself. In the end, I lost my world."

"Mack, I'm so sorry for your loss."

"Thank you. I've accepted my fate. But . . ." He turns and looks at the boy who is now drinking and eating. I never even noticed the food was here. "He shouldn't be out here."

"I agree."

"Ella, we have others to see," Michelle says.

"Yes, I know. Mack, it was nice to see you." My eyes turn to the boy. "And . . ."

"My name is Jack."

"Jack. That's a nice name."

"Thanks."

"Miss Ella, I can see the worry in your eyes. I promise I'll look after Jack until he decides he can trust again."

"Thank you." I lean forward and give him a kiss.

"And where was your camera when a hot young thing was giving me a kiss?" Mack says to Tom, laughing.

"Maybe next time."

"Oh, I hope so. Miss Ella can come and see me anytime."

We leave Mack and Jack and walk further along the street. Tom tells me that's the first time Jack has told anyone his name. He tells me that Jack must feel a connection to me. I might even be someone who he could trust.

Crazy, but I already know that my thoughts for the rest of the night and the next few days and weeks are going to be of a boy lost without family and friends, living on the streets.

This is wrong. So wrong. Where did our system fail him and why?

Chapter 22

"YOU DID GREAT TONIGHT," MICHELLE says as we stand at the doors to the shelter. I'm glad she thinks so. I got off to a wobbly start after meeting Jack. I hoped I wouldn't cry tonight. I told myself I would hold it together no matter what I saw, but seeing Jack . . . that was all it took. My eyes drift to the road. Connor is in the taxi that's waiting for me.

"Thanks, but . . ."

"I know you're worried about Jack. I am too. He's been with Mack for the last week. I'm keeping an eye on him, but at the same time, trying to gain his trust. As I said at the start of the night, trust is a big issue for anyone living on the streets, regardless of their age."

"He's so young. What about social services?"

"Yes, I should contact them, but the thing about kids like Jack is that, if I do report him and they put him in temporary care, he'll run away again. He would then move on to a new area and we wouldn't be able to keep an eye on him, and the cycle would continue. He would run every time social services got involved."

"There must be something that can be done. My heart is breaking at the thought of him sleeping in that doorway."

"Ella, go home. There's nothing more you can do. He could do worse than Mack. He's a good man. I'll catch up with you during the week."

"I'll go home, but you'll see me tomorrow night. Same time and place?"

She smiles and nods her head as if knowing what I was going to say. I walk slowly to the waiting taxi and get inside, the weight of the world on my mind.

"Hey, you," Connor says as I slide into the seat beside him. "What's wrong?"

"Nothing. How did it go with your parents? Is your mum okay? And how are you?" I ask, changing the subject because I'm not sure now is the right time to answer his question. I need to hear how he is.

"I know what you're doing, but I'll let you get away with it for the time being. It went okay with them. Better than I expected. It was easier to talk about than I had imagined. Yes, there were lots of tears. I'm relieved that it's out in the open, although my mum is blaming herself."

"It's not her fault."

"I know that and you know that, but she says she shouldn't have let me leave. Now, are you going to tell me what's wrong?"

Now who's the one changing the subject?

"Do you mind if I wait until we're home?"

"No, of course not." He wraps his arm around me and I snuggle in. I know my thoughts should be about Connor and us and everything he's been through, but I can't stop thinking about Jack. The same thoughts and questions are whizzing around my head like a racing car on a race track.

What's driven that young boy to flee from his home and live on the streets? Seeing him has put my life into perspective. Yes, there's been a few crap things happening lately, but it pales into insignificance. If my helping out with the charity and raising awareness helps children like him then it will all be worthwhile.

"OKAY, WE NEED to talk," Connor says as we walk up the stairs. "You need to tell me about tonight. Or maybe it's me?"

"It's not you, honestly. But I do have loads of questions."

"And when you ask, I promise to answer you truthfully."

We enter the bedroom and I strip down to my underwear. Connor takes a t-shirt from the drawer and hands it to me. I put it on and inhale, smelling him.

I cast my eyes around the room. He's already been here tonight. His case is unpacked. I smile.

He pulls the bed covers down and I climb in and watch him undress, leaving his boxers on. His eyes are a little red and puffy. It's been an emotional day with his parents. God, it's been a hugely emotional day for me and I'm still struggling to adjust to all the facts about Connor, and now also, Jack.

Connor climbs into bed beside me and I snuggle into the warmth of his body, needing the closeness. The closeness I've missed this week when he wasn't in bed with me. "I've missed this," he says.

"Me too. Tonight was eye-opening. I thought I would be ready for whatever I saw. God, I was so wrong. I'm so disappointed in our society. The system is failing miserably and even children are falling through it and living on the streets. It's not right." There's a long pause and tears roll down my face.

"Ella, you can and will make a difference. I'm certain of it. When are you next going back out?"

"Tomorrow. I need to see if he's okay."

"If who is okay?"

"Tonight I met a man called Mack. He's forty-nine and lost everything after turning to drink when his daughter died. He's been on the streets for a few years, but there was a young boy with him. I'd say about twelve or thirteen."

"Shit! Really?"

"Yes, his name is Jack and I can't stop thinking about him

sleeping in a shop doorway. It's not right. He's only a boy. He should be at home and safe. Mack is looking out for him. Some of the things Mack said truly touched me. He's a man who cares deeply, especially about Jack."

"Oh, Ella. I'm not surprised you were quiet coming home. It's been a tough day for you." His arms tighten around me, and I hear a sigh of what I hope is contentment as I snuggle into him. I can only hope that he's taking comfort having me in his arms. I've longed to be in his arms like this.

"You've had a tough day. You've had a tough week," I say, my thoughts filled with Connor alone in that hotel room all week. Hiding from me and his parents, trying to protect us. I wish someone was there to protect Connor all those years ago, and then he wouldn't have gone through that abuse.

"Ella, I'm sorry I've caused you unnecessary pain. You have to understand I thought what I was doing was the best for you and my family. I never wanted that footage and story to get out. It's from a part of my life I'd much rather forget."

"Connor, you don't have to apologise. I get why you thought leaving me was the right thing to do to protect everyone you love. But don't you see that those who love you will always be there for you? We all want to help you and support you. I'm angry that you had to go through the unthinkable. I wish someone had been there for you to step in and help you. To protect you."

I turn in his arms, so that I can see him. A lonely tear runs down his face. I lift my hand and wipe it away. "You are incredibly brave. I'll be here for you any time you want to talk."

"I know this is news to you and my parents but I'm hoping you can all put it behind you like I have. I've fought hard with my demons over the years. Some things, as you know, are better staying in the past."

And it's someone in my past that has caused Connor so much pain. What did Donovan hope to gain from putting this story and the footage into the world? I'm sure it was just another attempt to drive a wedge between us.

"I'm not sure the media will see it that way. Your story is already in their hands, minus the facts. You and I both know they have a way of twisting a story to suit themselves, unless . . ."

"They are presented with the facts." He frowns knowing as well as I do what the media is like. I nod. "I know what I should do, but I don't want to hurt you or my mum."

"I'm sure your mum has told you the same as I'm going to tell you. I will stand by you no matter what you decide."

"Me and you, will we be okay? Regardless of what I decide?" he asks.

There's no hesitation on my part. "Yes. We *will* be okay."

"Glad to hear it. Now, I'm hoping having you back in my arms means I'll get a decent sleep."

I yawn and wipe away the last of my own tears. "Me too." He pulls me closer to him and I close my eyes.

FEAR PULLS ME from my sleep. I awaken to an empty bed. Not what I had hoped for after our first night together. My breath comes in a deep rush as I try to think what's troubling me. I can't forget this nightmare; it's not my usual. This time it's about a little boy, lost and searching for someone to love him. The face kept changing in my dream. One minute it was Jack staring at me, the next it was Connor.

I'm alone, and something about my nightmare is scaring me. I reach across to Connor's side and it's cold. He's been out of the bed for a while. I roll over, pushing the covers off, and throw my legs off the bed.

I had a great sleep when I was wrapped in Connor's arms, but since he's not in the bed with me, I guess he didn't sleep so well.

I hope he's listened to me about sharing some of the facts

of his story. The media, if handled the right way, can be a good thing. He might even save someone; another young actor who is being pushed into the same position he was in. I don't understand some people in our industry. They use and abuse others for their own gain. It's wrong.

After going to the bathroom, I go in search of him. Downstairs is silent and dark, although there is light coming from the kitchen. I wander into the kitchen and the patio doors are open. A light wind blows inside. I step out onto the deck. "What are you doing?" I ask.

"I was restless. Tossing and turning," he says, without turning to face me. "I didn't want to disturb you. What brings you out here?"

"You. I woke up and you were gone. I missed having your arms around me." I decide not to tell him about my nightmare. He has enough on his mind without me adding to his worries.

"Come here." He holds out his hand as I walk toward him, already feeling that familiar pull between us. When I'm in front of him, he pulls me down onto his lap, his hand resting on my stomach. "You do know how much you mean to me?" he asks, a thick sadness to his voice.

"I have a pretty good idea."

"I'm worried about the fallout from this story. I don't want my past tainting our future together. And I certainly don't want it to affect you and your career in any way." There's a shake, an edge in his voice.

"This isn't going to affect either of us. Our future together and our careers. I think you need to tell your story. To be truthful and not leave any part of it out. From what Julie said about the press, the story that was printed today was very sympathetic. I don't think you have anything to worry about."

"I'm not sure."

"I understand your reservations. I wasn't sure about going

public about Donovan, but I'm glad I did. It might not seem like a good idea, and if you do go public, you have to tell your parents, so they know to expect the story in the papers."

"They'd like to have lunch with us today before they go home. And I meant to say last night, Mum said thanks for the offer to stay here but she thought we'd need the space."

"Lunch would be nice, and they are more than welcome here anytime. But I'm glad it's just the two of us."

I close my eyes and inhale. The sweet aroma of the mug of coffee on the table takes over my senses. The bitter, yet inviting smell fills the atmosphere, making my taste buds ache for a taste of the creamy, smooth coffee.

"I can hear you deep in thought. What are you thinking about?"

"I'm thinking your coffee smells delicious."

He laughs lightly. "Have some if you want."

"No. I know what I would like, though," I whisper, as a vision of us making love out here as the sun comes up has me smiling.

"I'm sure that can be arranged," he says, kissing the back of my neck.

Chapter 23

"YOU CAME BACK. WE DIDN'T expect to see you again so soon," Mack says as I stop and sit down beside him and Jack, handing them each a hot cup of tea and the bags with the hot filled rolls. Michelle and Tom smile warmly.

"I just thought I'd keep an eye on you, make sure you're behaving yourself."

Mack laughs and Jack sits up, rubbing his eyes. "Me? I'm always behaving. Not sure about the young lad though. He's always up to mischief."

"Is that so?" I ask, turning my attention back to Jack. His eyes are red and heavy and his face looks a bit puffy. "What's wrong, Jack?"

"Nothing. I'm fine," he snaps. He's anything but fine. I frown, looking at Michelle. I can see she's concerned about him too.

"He's got the start of a cold," Mack says.

"How about I take you both for something to eat and drink inside a café?"

"Miss Ella, you have a lot to learn," Mack says. "If we leave our spot, someone else will take it and we'll have to move on. I like this spot. I've been here for a while."

"Okay, I understand," I say, not really understanding, but I can see it's important to Mack.

"I think I should go and get you both extra blankets and medicine for Jack, unless you want to come into the shelter and see a doctor?" Michelle says. Tom nods in agreement.

"He won't go," Mack says. "Medicine, blankets, and some water will be fine."

"Got it," Michelle says before walking away.

"Mack, what do you both do during the day?" Tom asks as he sits down beside us.

"Well, since the lad is with me, my days aren't quite so lonely. For the first time in years, I feel as though I have a purpose. We might be living on the streets but that doesn't mean I've no principles. I ensure he and I go and wash up in the morning in the public toilets. One of the attendants is really nice. He opens them ten minutes early for us. And with the toiletries and toothpaste that are given to us, we at least look clean at the start of every day. Although, depending on the weather conditions, we might look like our normal scruffy selves by lunchtime."

"What about food?"

"Well, we get hot food and drink from the charity at night. I usually beg, and on a good day, by mid-afternoon I can have enough money to buy us both a roll and maybe some sweets as a treat. On a bad day, I try to give the boy food, but he's a stubborn wee lad and always halves whatever I give him."

I can't help but smile at his words. Jack might only be a boy, but he's thoughtful and caring. My eyes drift to him and he's shivering. Tom sees it as well and he takes off his jacket and wraps it around his shoulders. I inch closer to Jack and wrap my arms around him. I expect him to push me away or at least argue with me, but nothing.

I rub my hands on his arm, offering him a little comfort. "Mack, when did he start feeling unwell?"

"Late this afternoon. He's had a few cups of hot tea but

wouldn't take anything to eat."

I feel Jack's head and I think he's got a bit of a temperature.

"What are you thinking?" Tom asks with concern.

"I don't know. I think it might be flu, but I'm hoping just a virus." Tom and Mack sit talking but I don't pay much attention. My attention is on the boy who has now snuggled into the warmth of my body, still shivering.

My phone buzzes and I take it from my pocket and read the message.

Connor: What time do you want me to pick you up?

He had wanted to come with me tonight, but I didn't want Mack or Jack to feel overwhelmed and Connor agreed with me. I know I need to gain their trust, and bringing someone else with me so soon most probably wouldn't sit well with either of them.

Connor isn't going to like my reply. I know it, but given the circumstances, I hope he understands.

Me: You won't need to pick me up. The boy I told you about is unwell. I'm staying with him.

Connor: What hospital are you at? I'll come to you.

Me: No he's not at the hospital.

Connor: Do you mean you're staying on the streets with him?

Me: Yes.

I frown as my phone starts ringing. "Everything okay?" Tom asks.

"I'm about to find out. Hi, Connor."

"Ella, you can't stay on the streets with him. If he's sick, he should be in hospital." I'm certain Tom and Mack can hear Connor, but I don't care, as long as Jack doesn't, and at the moment, he's sleeping in my arms.

"You're right about the hospital, but he wouldn't go. And if he did, there's every chance he would run away. I'm not prepared to take that chance, so if me being here with him all night means he gets the right medicine and is looked after, then I'm prepared to do that." Tom smiles but then I see his worry. He doesn't have to stay.

"Ella, fucking hell. I'm not letting you stay there on your own."

"I'm not on my own. Tom is here at the moment and Michelle is away getting medicine and blankets. And when or if they leave, I have Mack for company."

"Do you realise this is dangerous?" Connor shouts.

"Yes, but it's my choice to make."

There's a long silence. "Tell me where you are. I'm coming to you."

I look at Tom and Mack. Mack nods his head and tells me it's okay.

"Fine," I say with a sigh and tell Connor where I am.

"He sounds like a good man. He's only worried about his woman," Mack says.

I feel bad because I've added to his worries. He has enough going on in his own life without me causing more problems. "He is. He wanted to come with me tonight but I didn't think you'd appreciate a new face."

"As long as he's not a social worker, he'll be okay. And anyway, he can't be that bad if he's a friend of yours."

"He's a good soul. An actor as well."

"We'll end up needing security for you two," Tom says, and I can't make up my mind if he's joking or not.

"No one will even know we're here except Mack and Jack. Mack, do you know anything about Jack's background?"

"He doesn't talk much about family, except his mum, but she died a few months back. From what he says, they were really close. It was always just the two of them. From what I read between the lines there were no aunts, uncles, or grandparents."

"What about his dad?"

"I think that's why he's here, because of him. I didn't want to push him on this. I want him to tell me when he's comfortable and when I've gained his trust."

And there's that word again.

The three of us sit talking. I turn off from the conversation when it switches to football. Although, I do hear Mack say he's a huge fan of one half of the old firm. The team Fletcher plays for.

"Sorry it took so long," Michelle says, re-joining us. "I have some paracetamol and I got a prescription for an antibiotic. You should have seen me trying to lie to the doctor. Not something I want to do again."

"Thank you," Mack says, and I know it's because she hasn't returned with the doctor or a member of social services.

"Don't thank me yet. If this doesn't help him, I'll be left with no choice," she says softly.

"I understand."

"Okay, Tom, which of us is going to stay with the boy all night?" she asks.

I hope she's not offended that I'm staying. "I've already said I'm staying."

"Ella!"

"Don't say a word. I couldn't go home knowing Jack is sick. Connor is coming here." She frowns. "Don't ask."

"I won't. I'm not sure about leaving you, but I do have others Tom and I should go and check on."

"I know that. Go. I'll be fine."

Connor arrives, and if he's shocked, he hides it well. Michelle agrees to leave reluctantly with Tom after telling me about the medication for Jack. She also informs me that she'll check back on us in a few hours.

I'm introducing Connor to Mack when Jack stirs in my arms, waking up. Perfect, it means he can take the medication now.

"Hey, I know you," Jack says, rubbing his tired eyes.

"Jack, this is Connor," I tell him.

"I know that. I'm not stupid. Why is he here?"

"Because with you sick, I wouldn't go home, so he's come here to keep an eye on me. Make sure I don't get into any trouble. Now, I have some medicine for you to take." I give him the correct dosage of medicine and he laughs at me. "What's so funny?"

"I bet you get into loads of trouble, Ella," he says.

"She does," Connor says.

The night goes quickly. Jack drifts in and out of sleep for most of it and Mack does too. I get the feeling he wanted to make sure Jack was okay, but he was exhausted. Michelle and Tom come back a few times to check on us. Connor and I talk most of the night because there isn't much else to do. It's funny; I'm still not tired.

We talked about the lunch we went to with his parents. It had been good to see them yesterday afternoon looking so much better than the day before. His mum looked as though a huge burden had been lifted.

Connor has also decided to go public and tell his story. I know he'll find it tough because he's dredging up the past. A past he doesn't want to think about. I've told him he's not alone when he does this. I'll be right by his side.

It's five forty-five a.m. and the sun is rising. "This is very different to how we spent this time yesterday morning," Connor says, bringing a smile to my face.

"It is. I'm sorry."

"What are you sorry for?"

"For refusing to come home last night."

"Don't. I understand completely, especially after seeing how Jack has been through the night. He needed you. And your caring quality is one of the reasons I love you." He leans over and kisses me.

"Oh, no. I can't be doing with mushy stuff first thing in the morning," Mack says, stretching. "How has he been?"

"Restless," I say. "But his temperature is coming down."

"Thank God for that. I was worried about him."

"He'll be fine. Hopefully when he wakes up, he'll feel hungry. We can get you both some breakfast."

"Miss Ella, you should think about going home. Get some sleep yourself."

"Mack has a point, Ella."

I know he does, but I want to make sure Jack is okay before I leave them. Jack stirs in my arms, sitting up and rubbing his eyes.

"I wasn't dreaming then," he says, looking straight at Connor. "You're really here. I can't believe I've spent the night with not one, but two celebs."

"You look and sound better," Connor says, and I have to agree. I watch as Connor opens his mouth as though he's going to speak, but he stops himself.

"I feel better thanks to Ella."

"You have nothing to thank me for. Anyone would've done the same."

"No, they wouldn't. My own dad and his girlfriend wouldn't and couldn't." I look at Mack and his eyes fill with unshed tears at this small piece of information.

"I'm sure that's not true," I say, trying to sound hopeful, even though I want to keep my arms around him and never let him go. I hear the hurt in his voice.

"It is, but don't worry about me. I'm better off without those drug addicts in my life, even on the streets."

Now I think I get it. Why this boy has fallen through the system; it's because no one has bothered to report him as a missing child. I can't imagine a father not caring enough about his own child. How could he not even notice his son was missing?

"Miss Ella," Mack draws my attention to him. "I don't want to be rude, but you really should get going because if you're still here when the city gets busy with people, someone is bound to recognise you and that will bring attention to us."

"I understand." I tell Mack about the medication that Jack should continue to take today and I tell them I will see them both tonight.

Connor hands Mack money and tells him to make sure they both eat well today. Mack isn't happy with the amount Connor has given him and argues with him that it's too much. Connor then takes my hand as we walk away, leaving two people who have found a way into my heart in a very short period of time.

Chapter 24

"YOU'RE AWFULLY QUIET," MY DAD says as we sit in my front room. He's right, I am. There's so many things going through my head, it's hard to keep up; Connor, Mack and Jack, but also Donovan. It's been a bit too quiet lately from him. I'm not sure if I should be worried or not. Dad and Trevor came over an hour ago to talk through the fact that Connor is joining me on the set this week. I'm excited about that; we both are. Trevor has also talked to Connor in great length about the interview he'll be giving this week too. He's really nervous about putting his story out there, but as was pointed out to him, it is out there, he just needs to give the facts.

"Sorry. I have a few things on my mind."

"Care to tell us?" Dad asks.

I look at Connor and he nods, already knowing part of what's on my mind. "I can't stop thinking about a young lad who is living on the streets."

My dad gasps and his eyes dart between me and Connor.

I start at the beginning and tell my dad and Trevor everything about my nights on the street helping the charity, including staying there the whole night to make sure Jack was okay. I give them every last detail because I need them to understand. That our society is fucked up. That this happens. It shouldn't be going on in this day and age. We're not living in the dark ages, but to see the problems on our streets, you'd think we were.

"Sweetheart, you get more like your dear mother with each passing day. But do you know how dangerous that was?"

"Yes, but Connor was there with me. He said the same as you when I told him I wouldn't be home, but then he came and stayed with me, Jack, and Mack."

"Okay, so what do you plan to do? I know you and you'll want to do more than you're already doing, so tell me."

"I don't know. That's why I'm feeling so troubled."

"What does your heart say?"

My eyes drift around the room. I'm deep in thought. There's so much I want to do. The voluntary work with the charity is just a starting point for me. "My heart wants to protect him, to help him. Not just Jack, but also Mack. Jack deserves a home, a family, someone to love him. He can't spend his life on the streets. His mum loved him, but she's gone, and from what he said, his dad isn't interested in him."

"You really do sound like your mother when you're passionate about something, and you might not know it, but I think your mind is already made up on what you want to do."

"I want to help."

Connor squeezes my hand.

"When are you going back out with the charity?" Dad asks.

"Tonight." I can see the raised eyebrows of both my dad and Trevor, but neither of them says anything, even though I sense my dad is itching to speak.

We don't talk any further about my volunteer work, although we do talk about what Libby wants to do for the charities. I tell them I'll be seeing Jess and Libby this week to discuss this. Everyone seems genuinely interested in the event.

Things have changed for me. I said at the beginning I would only volunteer two nights a week, but with the way I'm feeling about it, I'll need to look at my schedule. I won't be out on Wednesday night because that's when Libby and Jess will be here. But I do intend helping out on as many nights as I can.

"ARE YOU OKAY?" Connor asks as we sit outside in the garden, having some lunch. "You're deep in thought again."

"Sorry. Yes, I'm okay, I suppose. There is just so much going on in my mind. I should be concentrating on you, but I just can't get Jack out of my head. And I know Jack isn't the only kid on the streets, but it's breaking my heart knowing he and others are out there alone with no one caring for them."

"Don't worry about me. I already feel as though a huge burden has been lifted from my shoulders. Just being able to be open and honest with you and my parents has helped me in more ways than you could realise. And as for Jack, you care and I'm sure you will make a difference to the lives of many homeless people up and down the country when the campaign launches."

"I don't know if that's going to be enough for me."

"What do you mean?"

"We all know that my main reason for going into this was because of what Donovan did, but now that I've seen the problems for myself, a lot more is needed than just an ad campaign and some volunteer work."

"Such as?"

"I don't know. I'm no politician. But I think the government and local authorities need to be doing more. Money has to be made available to help. The conditions Stacey is staying in with two little girls is not acceptable. Local authority housing and private lets should be an acceptable standard. And don't get me started on how it's been possible for Jack to fall through the system. If his dad is a drug addict, shouldn't they all be on the radar for social services?"

"You sound as though you should be an MP," he says with a smirk.

I laugh. "I've no time for that at the moment, but you never know what the future might hold."

"I can tell you our future holds great things. That I'm certain of."

I ENTER THE sitting room and look around. Everything is as it should be, but again, there's an odd feeling running through my body. This really isn't home anymore. Maybe I should do what Julie suggested and bring up the idea of Connor and me looking for a home together to him.

He's sitting on the sofa, newspaper in his hand, studying the front page. I happen to know that story is about him, although it's not too bad, it just isn't factual.

I walk across the room and lift the newspaper from his hands before putting myself in his lap, wrapping my arms around his neck. His dark eyes are shining, full of contentment. He pushes his forehead to mine, sighs, and wraps his arms around my waist. "This is nice," he breathes softly against me.

"It is."

"Ella, you have something on your mind. Tell me what it is."

"Okay. I know you're still considering looking for a flat."

"Yes, but so much has happened lately."

"Ssh!" I press a light kiss to his lips. "Let me finish. Instead of looking for a flat, how would you feel about looking for a home? For both of us."

His face lights up. "What about here?"

"This isn't home, and if I'm honest, it hasn't been for a long time. I don't want to be here any longer. I'm not sure what I'll do with it yet. Sell it, keep it. We'll see."

"I'd love nothing more than for us to be living together in

our own home. So, it'll be a yes from me. I think we should start looking online now."

"Really?"

"Yes. I'm not giving you a chance to change your mind. You go and grab the laptop and I'm going to call the estate agent and tell them there is a change to my plans and see if they have any family homes suitable."

He kisses me quickly before I jump from his lap. Excitement fills me. We're going to do this. I pause in the doorway and turn back to him. He said *family home*. Not a home for the two of us, but family.

I watch him for a moment as he talks to the estate agent on the phone. He's clear about what he's looking for. I smile, listening to his end of the conversation. "Five bedrooms at least, good sized family room on top of living room and, most importantly, a large garden."

He looks at me and all I can do is smile. Everything is clear to me.

Our future.

Our life.

Together.

Forever.

Chapter 25

"YOU HAVE BEEN ONE HARD lady to get a hold of the past few days," Libby says as I greet her at the front door. She hugs me tightly before casting her eyes over me.

"Sorry. It's been a busy few days. Who am I kidding? The past week has been non-stop. Come on through. Jess is already here, and my friend Julie."

"I hope you have lots of great things to tell us," she says. "I've been worried about you."

"You don't need to worry about me. I'm fine." She walks beside me and greets the others when we enter my sitting room.

Julie has already opened a bottle of wine, and four glasses stand tall on my coffee table. Libby takes a seat and opens the briefcase she's brought with her, taking out piles of paperwork. "This is my kind of business meeting," she says as Julie hands her a glass of wine.

"Cheers. To friendship."

"To friendship."

"Now, Ella. Please tell me . . . you and Connor, you're okay?" asks Libby.

"Yes, we're fine. Hoping to get our lives back on track and forget about all the other stuff we've had to deal with. We're going to look for a house together, somewhere that feels like a family home."

Julie lets out a squeal. "Why didn't you tell me?"

"I'm telling you now."

"Oh, I know the perfect place. Only seven houses. Nice neighbours and one house happens to be going on the market this weekend," Jess tells us.

"Where?"

"In the estate we stay. It's gated and very private." Sounds like somewhere we'd both consider. I'll mention it to Connor later. I think I'd like to be around people. Have nice neighbours.

"Ladies, before we get down to the important work, can we just take a few minutes so my so-called best friend can fill us in on what the hell is going on?" Julie sits back in the chair, folding her arms across her body. She stares, waiting for me to start talking.

Libby and Jess both agree and they all grab their wine glasses, sit back, and wait for me to tell them a story. I tell them everything from Connor leaving because he thought it was the best, to him opening up and telling me what happened. Connor won't mind me telling them now because he is doing an interview. I tell them that this house isn't home. Julie already knows this.

And then I tell them about Stacey and her two gorgeous girls, and also about Mack and Jack, before I sit back and take a much needed gulp from my own glass of wine.

Libby and Julie both seem stunned. I've not had a lot of time, and when Julie and I have spoken, I've only given her brief details. I'm the one who's stunned when I turn to Jess; tears are rolling down her face. I put my glass down and move to her. "Hey, it's okay."

"But it isn't okay. Hearing stories like these leave me feeling upset and angry. No child should be living on the streets, just like no woman should live in fear of violence against them. When is our society going to realise that just because they live behind rose-coloured glasses, doesn't mean everyone else does? Sorry. I blame the hormones. They're still all over the place."

"Don't apologise to us because you're passionate about the cause. Our passion is what has brought us all together."

Jess smiles. It's true a meeting of chance between us and our passion has brought us together, and I'm sure a solid friendship will be formed between the four of us.

"Okay, let's discuss my plans and then we can go over the big event at the end of the football season" Libby says confidently.

Football event!

I glance at Jess and she shrugs her shoulders.

Libby either doesn't notice our questioning glances or chooses to ignore them and carries on talking. "Four weeks this coming Saturday night, we will host a fundraising event at the hotel. This will be an invitation, ticket only event. We can accommodate two hundred and fifty people. My chefs will put out an incredible four or five course meal, we'll have dancing, and you two will both give a speech about the charities the event is for."

Jess and I look at each other.

"Don't you dare tell me no. The main event of the evening will be a charity auction to raise funds. I've already got my dad on this for marketing and I know that between all of us, and partners and family, we have the right connections to have all tickets gone within

a week."

"You really don't mess around, do you?" Julie says.

"No, I don't. I've spoken to Alex and I want to do this to help. I've heard how passionate you are and that's inspiring. You both lead busy lives, yet you're still finding the time to help others. You've put me to shame."

"Me too," Julie pipes up.

"Libby, you have the hotel to run and three kids. And Julie, the hours you work, you're lucky if you have time to do anything else."

"Stop! Don't make excuses for us," Julie says.

"I'm not."

"Ella, you don't understand. If it wasn't for you and Jess, would I be sitting here now? The answer is no. And you'll want to know why I want to help. The reason is quite simple, and I'm sure Julie will agree with me; the passion you have rubs off on others. You make everything look so easy."

"It's anything but," I reply.

"Yes, I get that. After sitting in the hotel and hearing your story and watching you live your life in the public eye. And now, tonight hearing about Jack, I totally understand. I'm on board with you to help where I can, and Ella, you have Alex's backing one hundred and ten percent. Now, with that being said, Jess, I know you've helped organise end of season charity events at the club. Alex has already spoken to Peter about this year's football match being a little, shall we say, different."

The three of us stare at Libby, wondering what the hell she's on about. Well, I have an idea. Alex mentioned the football event when we all met.

"Here's the thing. Fletcher already has his football team and the club have already said that money raised on the day is for the charity." This isn't news to any of us. So where is she going with this story. "So, how can we make more money for the charities? Simple. We get the match televised, not just in Scotland."

"And why?" I ask, trying hard to follow where she's going with this.

"Because people would pay money to watch sexy footballers play against equally sexy A-list celebs. I'm talking the cream of Hollywood."

Jess and I look at each other, I'm sure with the same puzzled expression, before we both slowly smile.

"That is amazing," Julie says with enthusiasm.

"I can't take the credit for this one. Alex has already done most of the ground work. And with my dad's connections and Trevor's in the business side of things, I'm certain you will pull this off."

I'm not quite sure what to say.

"Ella, say something."

"Tell me what I need to do."

The smile on Libby's face is contagious. "Your first job, along with Jess, will be to hold a press conference, telling the world the plans, and then you're in charge of getting a team together. My dad, Alex, and I'm sure Trevor, can all handle the PR side of things. Peter has ensured me the club will handle ticket sales and everything else to do with a football match."

"You really are organised," Jess says.

"Well, Alex is."

We sit, laughing and drinking. Talk changes from the events and charities to everyday stuff; men, sex, or lack of it as Julie pointed out. Jess said she knows more than a few single men, all of them footballers. Julie's eyes lit up when Jess suggested she would set her up on a date.

"What about Callum?" I blurt out after having a few too many glasses of wine. It's a good job I'm not on set until lunchtime tomorrow.

"Been there, tried that. We're better off as friends."

I stare at my friend. "When?"

"A few years ago. We went out on a few dates. But it was strange. He's your brother and one of my closest friends, and we decided we'd be better staying as friends."

I'm not sure Callum feels the same. I've seen the look on his face when they're together.

The front door opens and closes. Connor is home. He went out with Michelle and the charity tonight. I felt guilty because I couldn't go.

I lift my eyes and he's standing in the doorway, looking mighty fine. I sigh.

"Evening, ladies. Looks like you've all had fun."

I hear a low rumbling laugh. I turn my head and Julie is covering her mouth with her hand. "What?" I ask.

"Just you, and that dreamy noise you make every time you see him. It's funny. But I don't get it. He's okay to look at, but that's it," she says smirking.

Cheeky bitch. If she wasn't my best friend and I didn't think she was teasing, I'd probably be throwing her out of my house.

"She'll get it eventually when she finds the one. Every time you lay eyes on them, your heart skips a beat," Libby says with a smile full of warmth, and I know she's thinking of Alex.

"Just being near your other half makes you feel calm and content," Jess adds.

"Oh, please. You three must be drunker than me," Julie says, standing up. "Taxi for Mathews and Adams before they say anymore mushy stuff and make me sick."

Connor strolls into the room and sits beside me. I throw my arms around his neck. "Miss me?" he asks. Julie makes a horrible boaking sound and I could happily throttle my friend right now.

"Yes, I did, but how's Jack?"

He feigns a look of being wounded, but I know he's teasing. "Jack is okay. He was worried about you not being there. He thought you were ill, then thought he'd upset you in some way. I told him you were busy working on a few things for the charity and that you'd see him tomorrow."

I turn away from him and my body quivers. I take a deep, pained breath and close my eyes. Images of a disappointed Jack filter through my mind.

"See that look right there," says Libby, and I open my eyes. "That is a look of someone so committed to what they're doing. That helpless, guilty feeling spreading through you . . . lose it now. You are doing far more than you know."

"Maybe, but it's still not enough."

"When will it be enough?"

"When I have Jack off the streets and where he belongs. With someone who'll love him and care for him." Connor squeezes my hand now I'm no longer clinging to him.

"You mean with you?" Jess states, and as she says it, I realise that's what I want. Stupid, I know. What do I really know about him? Not a lot. But I do know he doesn't deserve the hand he's been dealt in life.

I know absolutely nothing about bringing up a child, let alone a young teenager.

"Watch this space," says Jess, standing. She sways lightly on her feet. "Julie, have you called a taxi?"

"Yes, and we can leave these two alone to do whatever."

"Whatever?" I question Connor. He smirks and nods. Whatever works for me.

Libby gathers up the papers from the table, putting them back in her briefcase. Connor and I walk them out when the taxi arrives.

"Ella, thanks for having us," Jess says, kissing me on the cheek. "I know you and I have a lot to do. I'll give you a call late tomorrow night after you've been out."

"Tonight has been fun, and yes, phone and we can make a start on things."

Jess steps to the side and Libby hugs me as though her life depends on it. "You are a remarkable woman. Don't ever change for anyone. And with regards to Jack, you have to go with your heart. Speak to you soon."

"Well, you, my friend, are full of surprises. I love you and everything you stand for. I'll do whatever I can to help, you know that don't you?" Julie's grip on me is fierce.

"Yes, I know that. Now, go on and get home. I'll speak to you tomorrow. I love you." Connor wraps his arms around my waist, his head resting on my shoulder, and we watch them all get into the waiting taxi.

"I think you and me need to talk," he says as we go inside, closing the door behind us.

"Can talking wait until tomorrow? I liked the sound of whatever."

"I like the sound of whatever too." He sweeps me up in his arms, throwing me over his shoulders in a fireman's lift.

"The lights!" I squeal as he takes to the stairs.

"I'll get them after I've taken care of my woman."

Chapter 26

I STAND IN THE MIDDLE of our bedroom, where he so delicately put me down. He's standing before me, watching, eyes popping, and smiling. I'm bad. I've not even asked him how the rest of his day on set went. He had a few more scenes than me to shoot today, which meant I was away from the set long before him. And as far as I'm aware, he went straight to the shelter.

"Do you know how much I want you?" he asks, placing his hands on my hips. My nipples harden and I'm sure he sees them through my top. His gaze shifts from my face and, slowly, he casts his eyes over my body.

"Yes," I say breathlessly. "Because I want you just as bad."

"Hmm, I can see that." He runs his tongue along his bottom lip. I close my eyes momentarily before loosening my top, taking it off and allowing it to fall weightlessly to the floor. Next, I reach around my back, unfastening the clasp on my bra. I keep my eyes on his as I remove the bra.

From the mischievous look in his eyes, and the wicked smile on his face, I can presume he's happy with what he sees.

I unfasten the button on my trousers, shimmy them down to my hips, and they fall to the floor. I'm standing in only my lace underwear. I place my hands on the waistband. "Leave them," he says, dropping to his knees.

A delightful shiver of want runs through my body as the intensity of his gaze upon me grows.

He reaches out and pauses for a long, drawn out moment, before pulling the waistband down and sliding my knickers down my legs. I step out of them and take a step closer to him. He slides his hands up the inside of my legs, spreading them a little further apart. Then he's right there, parting me with his fingers. "You're wet," he murmurs. I close my eyes, unable to watch my man kneeling, still fully clothed, on the floor in front of me.

He slides one finger carefully inside me, pulling out before thrusting two back in to me. I cry out. My back arches and I swallow hard as he thrusts into me harder. I grip his shoulders tightly.

I'm moaning and panting, my hips moving shamelessly as he continues to thrust his fingers into me. I'm completely naked and should feel an ounce of embarrassment, but I don't. I've never been so turned on.

My breathing comes in a fast rush when his tongue connects, teasing me. In this moment, he owns me completely. I throw my head back as he licks and sucks. My legs weaken at the knees, and if he keeps this up, it's only a matter of time before they give way and I fall to a heap on the floor.

With my body quaking, I come hard, every tender muscle tightening around his thrusting fingers. I cry out, gasping his name.

He removes his fingers and takes hold of my hips, holding me steady. He kisses my stomach before rising to his feet. I open my eyes and he looks pretty pleased with himself.

"Happy?" I nod because I'm incapable of words. "Good, but I'm nowhere near done with you. You are mine, all night long, or as long as you can keep your eyes open."

The last part might be where we have a problem, but I smile and kiss his lips. "I'm yours," I whisper.

I look over my shoulder, my eyes going to the bed we've made ours. I take a step back and then another. For each step I take, Connor takes a step toward me. The back of my legs touch the bed and I gently ease myself down. I slide up to the centre of the bed. "You're still dressed," I say, watching him.

He undresses quickly and I've barely got my breath back when he's crawling up the middle of the bed, spreading my legs until he's hovering above me, hands either side of my shoulders. The scent of sex fills the air around us. "You're so perfect, Ella."

He dips his head, his lips meeting mine, kissing me deeply, sliding his tongue into my mouth, teasing and coaxing. Everything about Connor lights up my world, from the look in his eyes when he thinks I don't see him watching me, to the way he makes me feel in moments like this.

I run my hands through his hair, tugging lightly. His hand slides down and up my body as his lips move, and he nibbles and licks just below my earlobe.

I gasp when he thrusts deep inside me. The connection we share is way more intense in moments like this. It's like a drug, completely and utterly addictive, and it's one I'm more than happy to be addicted to.

I clench around him, gripping tightly, loving the feeling of him inside me. His hips grate against mine and my back arches, rising to meet each thrust. He grips my shoulders hard. I don't care if he's marked me.

Light smoulders in his dark brown eyes, almost glowing as they focus on me. The muscles in his arms and chest harden and strain with each thrust, pulling almost out before slamming back into me harder and deeper.

I cry out and hear a low, rumbling sound.

He tightens his hold on my shoulders, thrusting harder. I grab the bed sheets as my core tightens and fire spreads through my veins.

My heart is hammering. His broad shoulders tense. He's

close, and I'm closer to the point of drowning in him. So lost in him. Everything around me darkens and I only see his eyes, the intensity burning brightly.

Our bodies move in an exquisite harmony with each other. We belong together.

My building orgasm takes over in a rush and has me sobbing his name. His hips thrust harder against me as he loses control, his body shuddering and his head thrown back. My entire body is tingling and pulsing, filled with uncontrollable joy.

My world is filled with only Connor Andrews.

He is my everything.

He lets go of my shoulders and rolls off me onto his side, pulling me with him. He kisses the top of my head and I snuggle in, our legs intertwined. I close my heavy eyes.

Tiredness has overcome me.

His deep breathing evens out and the slow rising and fall of his chest is comforting. I can't describe the love for my man as he holds me protectively, but I always have the perfect night's sleep in his arms.

Everything always feels so much better when we're together.

"Ella, are you going to sleep? I have something I need to ask you." His voice is low but there's something alarming about it.

"What's wrong?"

"Has Donovan been in touch today?" My body tenses and I try to prise myself from his hold, but he refuses to release me. Just hearing that name has me on edge. My breathing has already quickened.

"No. Why?"

"He messaged me today."

I stare blankly at the ceiling, trying to anticipate his next words. "His message just said, promise me you'll take care of her."

I close my eyes. "And?"

"That was it. I thought he'd been in touch with you. I don't think you'll get any more trouble from him."

I'm not so sure. Trouble and Donovan go together.

"It's strange." I inch closer to him again, settling my head on his chest, getting into my favourite sleeping position. "These last few days I've been so busy with everything going on in my life, I'd like to say I haven't given him a thought. But, I've been thinking it's been too quiet. I don't think it's the last I've heard from him, but on the off chance it is, then I'm relieved. I won't be angry and I don't want to hold a grudge."

"Ella, you don't need to be understanding."

"No, I don't. But I also know that I don't wish him any harm, even though that's what he's wished on me with his antics."

"You are a better person than me," he says firmly. "I'm not so sure I can be so forgiving. I won't make a promise to him, but I will make promises to you. I promise to care for you and to protect you. And I promise to love you forever."

I lift my head and his gaze is steady. "I'll always love you." My voice is barely a whisper against his skin.

I snuggle back into my favourite position, his fingers running through my hair. There's a smile on my face as I close my eyes.

Tonight, there are no demons from my past. No skeletons in Connor's closet.

It's only us.

A future to look forward to together.

Chapter 27

"I HAVE SO MUCH TO tell you," Michelle says, excitement lacing her voice.

"Go on then," I say as we exit her car, and I already know where our first stop of the evening is from where she's parked her car. Mack and Jack. And I'm glad, because I missed them last night.

"Well, thanks to your dad's very generous donation, we're in the middle of purchasing an old derelict building. All going well, we should hold the title deeds in about six weeks."

"That's incredible."

"It is, and it's all thanks to you."

"Nonsense. It's all to do with hard work."

"And friends in the right places."

"What will this building be used for?"

"This will be a home for thirty to forty homeless people. They will all have their own bedroom. I'm so excited about this project. We'll have a games room, and a meeting place. There'll be a lounge and a kitchen. We'll be able to employ permanent staff, including a cook and housekeeper. There will be a member of our organisation there twenty-four-seven to provide advice. This is a huge breakthrough. This will be used as a stepping stone for homeless people. It's our way to bring them off the streets and help prepare them for moving on to a home of their own.

We will provide them with the support we can in making the transition back into normal society."

"I'm so pleased, and I'd love to help wherever I can. I also have news of my own. I missed last night . . ."

"Ella, we don't expect you here every night. God, I'm not even out here every night."

"I know that, but I want to. Anyway, last night I had a meeting with Libby Mathews and Jess Adams." I stop as we round the corner. "Alex, Libby's husband, is amazing and, so far, has organised a football game at the end of the session. All profits will be split between your charity and the women's aid charity Jess does so much work for. Libby is also organising and hosting a charity event at Stewart House. As soon as I have the details, I'll let you know, because I think someone from the charity should be there."

"I don't know what to say except thank you."

"No thanks needed. Now, can I go and see my boy? I've missed him." A strange look crosses Michelle's face and we carry on walking. It's only when we get near Mack and Jack I realise what I've said.

"Ella!" Jack calls out my name as I approach them. He stands and rushes towards me, wrapping his small arms around me. "I was worried about you," he says.

"Hey, you don't need to worry about me. Do I not look okay to you?"

"You look better than okay, Miss Ella," Mack says. "Lad, if you don't let her go, she won't be able to breathe."

"Sorry."

"I'm fine. Let's sit down."

"He's been looking forward to seeing you all day," Mack says, and I smile. "So have I. These visits of yours, Michelle's, and the other volunteers are the highlight of my day."

"I'm glad they are, even though I think you deserve more than a visit from us."

Mack shakes his head as though not wanting to listen to me any longer.

Michelle and I have a busy night ahead. We left the office early so I could spend a bit more time with Mack and Jack. Some of the others we see aren't as pleased to see us when we take supplies and food to them.

"Ella, Connor told us last night that he started filming with you yesterday," says Jack, his voice full of warmth and excitement.

"Yes, he did. Did you ever watch the show?" I ask him.

"Yes, with my mum. She loved it." I love hearing the happiness in his voice as he speaks about his mum.

"Hopefully you can get to watch it again. It wouldn't be the same as watching it with your mum, but maybe Michelle could organise something at one of the shelters." Michelle nods and smiles.

"That would be great, but I'll see." And there it is. The trust issue. I hope and pray that I gain his trust eventually.

We spend twenty minutes with Mack and Jack before we leave them.

"Ella, talk to me. What's wrong?" Michelle asks, her voice full of concern.

"I hate walking away from Jack each night."

"We all do. The streets are no place for a boy like him. He's a good kid. It's a pity his dad isn't interested in him, because that boy has so much love inside him. Just waiting to give it to right person."

"Hypothetical question. If someone was to offer him a home, what would the correct procedure be?"

"Ella, you're getting too involved."

She's right and I know it. "Maybe I am, but seriously, how can I not? Please, I'm asking a question."

"Okay. Well, social services would have to be involved. They would then have to seek out his dad and or any other family members to establish why he isn't staying with them. Reports would have to done and submitted on his wellbeing. He would then be placed in temporary foster care or a residential children's home. If he was unhappy about foster care or a home, a request could be made to the panel asking for special permission for him to stay with the person that wants to look after him. This is all hypothetical, and there's lots of red tape involved, especially as he's living on the streets. He might not even want to go and stay with you."

I sigh heavily. "I just want to get him off the streets. It doesn't have to be with me, but it has to be with a family who will support him and love him, but most of all a family who will let him enjoy his childhood."

"Ella, the minute social workers are involved, there would be a chance you or I would never see him again. He might run, or he could end up staying somewhere far away."

"I understand."

"I hope you do. It's a huge risk on your part. He's twelve. Are you ready to be a mother to a moody pre-teen?"

Michelle really has got me sussed. "Is anyone ever ready to be a mum?"

"I don't suppose they are."

We carry on with the rest of the night, seeing and helping a few others. I've noticed that a few of the regular men aren't in their usual spots and I question Michelle about it. She tells me she's managed to find permanent spaces in a few of the hostels spread across the city.

I ask about Mack and she tells me he was offered a space but he refused saying he, 'wouldn't leave the young lad.'

Mack's had a hard life and suffered greatly, losing everything that was important to him. But I see a man with great qualities and sheer determination. To me, this is his way to make amends, to help out. Most importantly, Jack has given him a purpose in life. A life that, after talking to him, I believe he had all but given up on.

Mack cares a lot more than he lets on about the boy he's taken under his wing. They might both be living on the streets, but he's looking out for him the only way he knows how.

They're like family.

Family.

They both deserve to be part of a loving family.

As we make our way back to Michelle's car, she stops dead in the street. "I knew there was something else I was meant to tell you. The council have refused to rehome Stacey and the girls. The reason behind it is because she's not on the streets. Can you believe that?"

"No, quite frankly, I can't. I think I need the name of whoever you deal with in the council. What gives some arse in a suit the right to make decisions that affect a young family? I'm sure he or she is sitting in a nice house, not giving a second thought."

"Yes, you've got a point. But remember when you first met Stacey, she made judgement on you because of your career, so some could say the same about you."

"They could try. I'm trying to make a difference, not sitting at home every night pretending that there aren't others who aren't as fortunate as me."

"You are making a difference. Every single day."

I hope so.

If I only change one person's life, I'd like it to be Jack's. But I hope I can change the lives of many. Use my status to influence the powers that be and make a difference.

Chapter 28

"WHY ARE WE HERE?" CONNOR asks as I park the car in the driveway of Jess' house. Her car and Fletcher's are both in the drive. This isn't really a social call. Jess has the keys to the property that's up for sale on the right hand side of this small, yet prestige estate.

Their front door opens and Jess walks out carrying Emily in her arms, with Fletcher following. I get out of the car quickly, only to pause and look around. It's a beautiful estate, and Jess was right. With the gated entrance, there's plenty of privacy but the added bonus of neighbours. Or in our case, friends.

A family home. I hope.

"Glad you could make it. Does he know yet?' Jess whispers as I greet her.

"No. Jess, Emily is gorgeous." I look at her daughter and I can't help but smile. I know Jess's story, and seeing her surrounded with her happily-ever-after fills me with so much hope.

Connor and Fletcher are standing at the side, talking, and I'm sure it's about tomorrow's game.

"You want to hold her?" Jess asks.

"Yes." I don't hesitate, and when Jess places Emily in my arms, my heart melts. Jess reaches into the back pocket of her jeans and holds the key in her hands.

"Fletch, Connor, come on." My man looks dazed and unsure.

"Where are we going?" he asks Fletcher.

"To see a house. That's all I know. But I'll tell you something for nothing, that look in Ella's eyes when Jess handed her Emily: priceless."

I switch off. I don't want to hear either of them talking about me being broody, although looking at this one, it's hard not to be.

Jess opens the door to the house. I step inside first and gasp. It's beautiful. The hallway alone has stolen my breath. It's light and airy, but has a feeling of warmth, and there's a grand oak staircase before me. It's stunningly beautiful and I'm already in love. Very neutral, and whoever stayed here before has taken care of it. Emily stirs in my arms and I rock her gently and walk further into the hallway.

Only one set of footsteps follow me and I know they're Connor's. I look over my shoulder to see him staring. "I can't describe how I feel seeing you with a baby in your arms. It's too much for my emotions to take in. The look on your face right now, I can already see you in this house with our baby in your arms," he whispers against my skin.

"One step at a time," I say, and I can hear a soft laugh coming from the front door.

"Ella, I'll take Emily and you two can go and have a look around." I reluctantly hand Emily back to her mum. "When you've had a look around, come back into ours and you can have cuddles and tea and I can give you all the details. This house has just come onto my books, and as yet, I haven't put it on the open market."

"Okay, we'll see you in a bit." Fletcher and Jess leave us on our own and I honestly don't know where to start. This is all overwhelming.

Connor takes my hand and pulls me toward the first door on the right. It's enormous. It reminds me of my sitting room at the moment with large bay windows overlooking the front of the property. The colours are light and neutral meaning we can put our own stamp on this home. Connor keeps my hand in his and we walk silently around the room, pausing at the windows and looking out.

The next room is at the back of the house, and I presume it could be a dining room, but it could be used for anything. It has patio doors out onto a large decked area, and the garden is definitely big enough for a family to play together or have a big party. Beyond the garden, the landscape is all green. I think there may be a farm, but I'm not sure; I'll ask Jess.

Next up for me is the heart of any home, and as I enter, I pull my hand from Connor's and walk in. I love the size of it and the layout; everything is so practical. This is a homely kitchen. It reminds me of my dad's kitchen, the one my mum could always be found in. There's a stunning archway that leads to either a dining area or a comfortable family area. Then there's a conservatory off of that. There's just so much space.

I sense Connor hasn't entered. I look over my shoulder and he's leaning against the doorway. "What?"

"I don't need to see any more of the house. Your reaction has sold it for me. If you decide this is the house you want, then it's ours."

I step toward him. "This was meant to be a joint decision."

"It is. If you're happy, I'm happy. This is a family house. A home that will fill as our family grows in numbers." He wraps his arms around my waist, smiling, pulling my body tight against his, leaving no space between us. He presses his lips to mine in the gentlest of sweet kisses.

"We should go and see the rest of the house," I whisper breathlessly against his lips.

He grabs my hand and we wander through the rest of the house. Downstairs, there's another room at the front, which could be used as an office, and a utility room with a toilet.

Upstairs on the first floor, there are four bedrooms, two of which are en-suite, and a family bathroom. On the second floor, we both stop and gasp. The whole floor is one big bedroom, with windows overlooking both the back and front of the property.

"This is home. This is us," I say, turning to face Connor.

"It is. But are you sure about these new neighbours of ours?"

"Hey, you. Our new neighbours are our friends. And you, Connor Andrews, will need to learn to play nice."

"I'm sure I can manage that. Let's go and speak to Jess and get the details for this and find out when we can move in."

"Really?" The excitement in my voice is undeniable.

"Yes. You're right. It feels like home. Our home."

With his words ringing loudly in my head, we leave our home for the time being and make our way back to Jess and Fletcher's. Jess meets us in the hallway. "Well, I'm dying to hear what you think."

I look at Connor and wait for him to speak. "I think you need to give me all the details, including a moving in date."

"Really? You both love it? I'm so happy." Jess squeezes my arms before pulling me toward her kitchen. Connor is laughing as he follows us.

Fletcher is walking around the kitchen with his daughter in his arms. My thoughts drift to my conversation with Michelle about being a parent. I have a vision in my head of Connor with a baby in his arms, with Jack alongside him, smiling and laughing.

I need to give myself a shake because this is only something I would do with Connor's backing, and although we've spoken, we haven't come to any decisions. *Yet.*

"Fletch, can you make tea while I go over a few details with Connor?"

"Jess, I'm a bit busy."

I walk toward Fletcher. "I can take Emily, or you can show

me where everything is and I'll make tea."

"I already like having you as neighbours," he jokes, handing me his precious daughter. "Jess, we will have babysitters on tap." I shake my head, but I'd be more than happy to look after her any time. With Emily in my arms, I sit down beside Connor and listen as Jess tells him every detail she can think of regarding the house. Jess tells us that a moving in date would be up to us and how quickly we want to take things. Connor tells her that once his lawyer puts in an offer, which he'll instruct him to do straight away, there will be nothing to hold us up.

"There might be a hold up," I say. "My house. I haven't decided what to do with it yet."

"Ella, what you decide to do with the house will have no bearing on us buying this home." I hear the steadiness in Connor's tone. Jess's eyes dart between me and Connor and she's smiling. She knows this house is already off the market.

As Fletcher brings over cups of tea and joins us, talk turns to the event Libby is organising at the hotel. They are both as excited about it as I am. Libby and Alex have done brilliantly with this. I'm sure it will be a great night.

Talk turns to the charity football game at the end of the season. I've spoken to Connor briefly about it, but as I listen to the two men, I can hear the excitement in their voices. They sound like two small boys. It dawns on me that this football match is going to be much bigger than I anticipated

Connor slips his arm around the back of the chair, his fingers circling lightly against my bare arm. "You know," he whispers, "you're going to have to hand her back. I have all these visions in my head and each one I love more than the last."

"Visions?"

"Okay. I was wrong," Fletcher says, his voice teasing, turning his attention to Connor. "It's not Ella that's broody, it's you. And I don't blame you. When I saw Jess with my sister's baby in her arms for the first time, it knocked me for six. The emotions were so overwhelming. Then when Emily was born, seeing Jess holding her the first time, my world was complete."

I blush, because I feel as though I'm on display. "Enough," Jess scolds her husband. "Ella has more than enough going on in her life at the moment, and I believe she's as old fashioned as you."

"What do you mean?"

"Well, you believed in marriage first before anything or anyone else came along." As Jess says it, the circular motions that were comforting stop. I daren't look at him because I'm scared of what I'll see.

"I might have been a bit of a rogue, but, yes, I had and still have old fashioned values. So, God help any boyfriends of Emily's in the very distant future. They won't stand a chance with me."

We all laugh and my mood lifts. Our laughing startles Emily, who cries in my arms. "Time to hand her back." I stand and walk around the table, and it's Fletcher who reaches out for his daughter.

I watch him with her and he seems like such a doting, hands-on dad.

Dad.

My mind has turned to Jack again. I'll need to talk to Connor, because I need to know if there's a possibility of us helping him. Of him being part of our future. I know Michelle said that this is something I need to think about, but I don't want to just think. If I waste too much time, it might all be too late.

"Ella, are you okay?" Jess asks, as I stand staring into space.

"Yes. Sorry. I was just thinking about Jack."

"Who is Jack? You not satisfied with one man, you have to have two?" says Fletcher, his voice laced with humour.

"Jack is a young boy living on the streets. I thought I told you the other night when I got home?"

"Jess, you were a bit drunk. If you did mention it, I wouldn't

have understood because all you were doing was rambling on."
I want to laugh but I don't. "Ella, tell me about Jack."

I fill Fletcher in. Connor takes my hand, squeezing it softly as I talk about Jack's dad and his drug problems. I'm stating the facts as I know them. Fletcher's face falls and I see sadness and confusion in his eyes.

"Bloody hell! And I thought some of the women's stories were bad at the refuge. This is awful. What can be done to help him?"

I tell him everything Michelle has told me and he sits quietly, taking it all in.

After I've finished, I change the subject back to the house, because I don't want everyone feeling sad about Jack's situation.

"It's time we make a move," I say, when I realise we've been here for over four hours between viewing the house and just talking. "Let you both get on."

Fletcher and Jess walk us to the front door. Connor tells Jess he'll pop into her office tomorrow after he finishes filming for the day. She tells him to give her a call and she will keep the office open in case he's running late.

"Ella, if there's anything I can do to help with Jack, please let me know," Fletcher says as I say goodbye. "I didn't have an easy childhood with my mum and I ran away a few times, but I always ended up back with her after maybe spending a few nights at a friend's house. I can't imagine what that lad must be going through. I mean it, Ella. Anything at all."

"Thank you."

"Promise me?" Fletcher asks, kissing my cheek. I nod slowly before getting into the car. I know Fletcher had a tough life; his mum was an alcoholic. It's been well documented in the press over the years. But I couldn't miss that his voice was shakier than normal, as though he was living through my revelation about Jack. Maybe he was.

"Are you sure you want to do this?" I ask, reversing my car out of the driveway and stopping to look at the house.

"Yes, of course I do, but I think we have a lot to talk about."

"Yes, we do."

"That's fine. We'll talk, but the house will be ours regardless of the conversation we're going to have. And just so you know, you can talk to me about it when you're ready."

I smile and drive away.

He knows what I want to talk about, and yet he's giving me time.

Time for me to get this right in my own head. But this is a conversation for now.

I think I've fallen for him all over again.

Chapter 29

I DON'T LIKE COMING HOME alone anymore. It doesn't make any difference if it's during the day or late at night. After seeing the house in Jess's estate, my mind is made up, and my heart is happy to move on.

Let go of the past.

I park the car in my drive and stare ahead. I'll always have good memories from my time here.

Getting out of the car, I grab the bag of shopping from the back. Today, when Connor finishes on set, he has a meeting with Trevor. I thought I'd make a start on dinner. I'm not going out with Michelle tonight. I'm going to miss it, but I think Connor and I need some time together before tomorrow, when he gives his interview.

I have to give Connor my support. God knows he's always been there when I've needed him. He's nervous about doing this and has already spoken to his parents and told them about the interview. It will be tough, but he'll get through it with my love and support.

Something catches my eye, making me pause as I walk toward the front door. I'm immediately on guard when I feel the hairs on the back of my neck spike. The wind is picking up and it's probably just something blowing around. I put my bag down and walk toward the garage. I look out to the back garden and there's nothing to see except the trees swaying in the wind. No papers blowing about.

I know I saw something. I'm just not sure what it was.

As I look out past the garden, I know without a shadow of a doubt that I'll miss this view. Although, if we move into the house we saw yesterday, that view is pretty spectacular too.

I draw in a deep breath, expecting the fresh air to hit my senses, but I'm taken by surprise when an all too familiar scent fills the air. My legs are pulled away and my body falls to the ground. I put my hands down to break my fall, but I land heavily and awkwardly on my hand.

I bite down on my lip, trying to mask the cry that's fighting to escape.

Pain shoots through my wrist and I'm scared to move it in case I've broken it. My eyes dart along the ground and I see his feet.

I don't need to lift my eyes to know who is standing there, but I do anyway. I tilt my head upward until I meet the gaze of the man who has caused so much pain and suffering, not just to me, but to the man I love.

Donovan.

He's hovering above me with a metal pole in his hand. My eyes dart around, looking for something, anything I can use against him.

"It took you long enough to come home. You left the set over an hour ago. Where have you been?" he shouts at me.

He's been following me.

Stay calm, Ella. You need to stay calm.

I drag myself back to my feet and stand, facing him. "I had a few things to get at the shops."

I want to scream at him, tell him to go away and leave me alone, but I don't. Instead, I try to hide my growing fears that he's going to hurt me.

My stomach churns as various possibilities run through my mind as he stands there tapping the metal pole against the side of his leg. I'm scared, really fucking scared right now. I can't even try and get help. My phone is in the bag with the shopping.

"Aren't you pleased to see me?" he asks.

I want to grab that pole from his hands and hit him with it until all I see is red. I'm sure that's what he plans to do to me, or why else would he have it in his hand?

What or who will stop him?

No one, because it will be a few hours before Connor is home. I'm on my own with this mad man and I think he knows it.

There's no one here to protect me.

"No. I was hoping I had heard the last from you. Wishful thinking on my part."

"Now, Ella. That's not what I expected. You should be welcoming me with open arms, not standing there wondering how you can hurt me. We have unfinished business to sort out."

"I don't think we have."

"Oh, I don't know. You're moving house so we should discuss this place."

I laugh at him. *Who the hell does he think he is?* "Why would we need to discuss *my* house?" He's not just been following me today. The only way he could possibly know about me moving is if he was following me yesterday. My heart beats rapidly in my chest and sweat drips down my back.

With his free hand, he reaches out, touching the wrist I landed on. I flinch and pull back, crying out as the pain shoots through it and up to my elbow.

"Because this is the home we shared. If you sell it, we should split the money."

I shake my head wildly because I don't actually believe what I'm hearing. He expects me to give him money. "You won't get a penny from me. This is my house. It was never yours. You never paid anything toward it, so you won't be getting anything. Not now. Not ever."

"But we lived together, shared a life together."

"Yes we did," I say, nursing my hand. "But you seem to be forgetting it was you that walked out on me. You that stole from me, and I was left to pick up the pieces."

"You haven't done too badly. Sleeping with my best friend. Got yourself a new job. And I know you're, once again, the talk of Hollywood. All because of me. You can thank me later."

He's delusional. Yes, I might be the talk of Hollywood, but only because I refused to keep quiet about what he did.

"You are on every director's radar. 'Ella McGregor, the bonnie lass from Scotland.' The girl everyone wants to star in their movies."

"That's good to know," I say smugly. I'm terrified right now, but he doesn't know that. I won't let him see my fears. "We have nothing to talk about." I'm inches from his face. I can feel his breath. I can also see the puzzled look on his face. His eyes widen.

"Ella, we have lots to talk about, so why don't we start with Connor? You need to end things with him. Stop leading him on. He has loved you for all these years and you're going to break his heart. His heart is delicate, as you now know."

I take a step away from him. "I'm not listening to this crap."

He grabs my wrist, squeezing it tightly. Tears sting my eyes and I cry out. "If you want me to stop hurting you, I think you'll listen to me and do as I say."

I nod, not knowing what else to do.

His eyes run up and down the length of my body, and when he looks into mine, a new, deeper sense of fear sets alarm bells ringing in my head. The look on his face haunts me. I close my eyes when I feel the metal pole against the side of my body.

"You were always beautiful, Ella. And even now, when you're trying to hide your fears, the beauty still shines from you." The way he says my name has me looking around for a way to escape his clutches. My entire body shakes, and any hope I had of being strong and standing up to him all but vanishes.

He knows I'm weak.

He leans in closer, his forehead against mine. His lips are almost touching mine as his grip on my wrist tightens. I don't move or make a sound. "I think now is a good time for you and I to sort out our unfinished business inside. Although . . . we could do that out here. I know you're happy to have sex outside. Maybe we should wait until sunset."

Heat rushes through my body as I hear his words. Anger fills my veins and I take a step back, raising my uninjured hand, and slap him hard across the face. He's been here, in hiding, watching my every move.

He strikes my hand with the pole and then laughs. Tears flow freely down my cheeks as I cry out in pain. "If you'd behave, I wouldn't have to hurt you. Do you think I like our situation? I don't, but I have to make you understand that you belong to me, not him."

My heart races as I think of what to say to him. We stand for what seems like forever, with me not talking and him watching and waiting. His back is to the front of the house and we're not far from my car.

I see something. Movement.

"We'll talk, but here," I say, suddenly aware that someone is here.

"I want to do more than talk, but talking is a start," he says, and I feel the bile rising in my throat.

"Why can't you just accept that we're over?" I ask, looking over his shoulder and seeing a man coming slowly toward us. I think it's Cole, Alex's security. He puts his hand up and mouths, 'everything will be okay.'

I'm too scared to believe him. I'm face-to-face with a mad man, and another man I don't really know is creeping up behind him.

"We'll never be over. You and I are good together."

"I don't think we are," I say as Cole comes into focus and lunges at Donovan. I take a step backward and watch on helplessly as Cole takes him to the ground. Donovan fights against him.

I lose all focus.

I'm dizzy.

I'm scared.

And so bloody confused.

Darkness surrounds me and my body crashes to the ground.

Chapter 30

"ELLA, PLEASE WAKE UP."

Connor? My head is foggy but I hear his pained voice and feel his hands on my arm. My body feels heavy. "Ella!"

I'm surrounded by darkness, and it's safe. Hearing Connor's pain, I open my eyes, tears already filling them. Connor is the first thing I see and I focus on him. His eyes meet mine, deep lines of concern around them. He offers a forced smile; not the one I'm used to seeing on his handsome face.

"Ella, you're okay. You're okay," he tells me over and over, rubbing the top of my arm and giving me a kiss on the tip of my nose.

I close my eyes and everything hits me all at once. Donovan, at my house, lying in wait for me. Following me for weeks. Cole . . . he saved me. Opening my eyes, I try to sit up, putting weight on my hands. I cry out with the pain.

Connor sits on the bed beside me and holds me close. "It's finished now. He can't hurt you again," he says softly.

We sit like this for a few moments and I try to calm myself. My heart is beating so fast, and I can't control it.

"Deep breaths."

I pull back from his hold and he fixes the pillows at my back. I get as comfortable as I can. My eyes glance around the room.

I'm in hospital.

"There's my girl," he says, pressing another kiss to my nose before smoothing down my hair and tucking it behind my ears.

"Where is he?"

"The last I saw he was handcuffed and being pushed into the back of a police car."

"You saw?" When did Connor get home?

"Yes. I arrived shortly after you fell to the ground. He was struggling against Cole until the police arrived."

I shake my head. "How long have we been here?"

"Not long. I promise I'll fill in all the missing blanks once the doctor has checked you over."

"Okay." I take a deep breath as Connor moves and a doctor comes into view. I grab Connor's hand, wanting him to be with me. He smiles, and this time it's not forced or fake.

"Miss McGregor, my name is Doctor Hardy. Can you tell me where you have pain?"

"My wrist," I say, holding it out. "And my head, at the back."

"Okay. I'd like to check you over and make sure there are no other injuries and then I'll get you sent for a scan. I think your wrist is broken, but an x-ray will confirm this. And I've been told you banged your head when you fell."

"Will she be okay?" Connor asks.

"Yes. The scan is just a precaution and we'll wait and see what the x-ray says about her wrist. Hopefully it won't need any surgery. Now, I'll go and organise this and I'll have a nurse come in and check your blood pressure. Miss McGregor, if you have any concerns, all you need to do is ask."

"Thank you," I say.

"What about security?" Connor asks.

"No one knows Miss McGregor has been admitted, but your own security is outside the door."

"Thank you," Connor replies as the doctor leaves.

"Security?"

"Cole. He's here." I don't know what's going on. Why is Cole here? Why was Cole at the house to start with? Not that I'm complaining, because he saved me. Was I always in danger? Has he been following me as well?

"Why?"

An older nurse comes into the room, smiling.

"I told you. I'll tell you everything when you've been thoroughly checked over."

I huff. "Miss McGregor, this young man of yours is right. Plenty of time for talking later. Now, blood pressure first. Then I have a few family members who would like to see you and there are two police officers who would like to speak to you."

"MISS MCGREGOR, YOU'RE really not a patient person," the nurse says to me with a warm smile. Connor stands by the window, nodding his head. Traitor. All I want to do is get out of here, and all everyone else wants to do is keep me here. It's been a long night. "I'll be back in about an hour to check you over, but if you need anything, press the buzzer."

"Thank you," I say, trying to sound cheerier than I feel as she leaves the room. My wrist is in a cast, a clean break the doctor said, so I don't need surgery.

With a smile on his face, Connor sits down on the bed beside me. "She's right about you; you're not very patient."

"I don't suppose I am. You should tell my dad and Callum to come back in and then I think you should tell me everything. I've waited long enough. I feel as though when I was telling the police officers what happened I was lying to them."

"Fine," he says, typing out a message on his phone. It buzzes instantly. "Your dad and Callum are on their way back from the canteen. But you didn't lie, you told the officers the facts as you knew them."

Connor wraps one arm around me and I lean back into the warmth of his body. I take a moment to think about how today has turned out and how much worse it could've been. But I'm not going to dwell on what might have happened. I'm going to stay positive.

Tonight was meant to be about me being there for Connor. About us spending some time together. Well, we're still spending time with each other. It's just not how I imagined it.

Connor's fingers run up and down my arm and I know if I were to close my eyes, I might just fall into a restful sleep.

The door opens, pulling me from my thoughts. "You look fed up," Callum says as he comes into view.

"I am."

"Sweetheart, there's no point in being fed up. The doctor will let you go home soon enough," Dad says, before giving me a kiss on the cheek and taking the empty seat by the bed.

"I know. Now that you're all here, would anyone care to tell me what the hell happened today and why Cole was at the house?" I look at each of them, waiting for one of them to start talking. "Well?"

Connor clears his throat. "Cole was there because, as much as I wanted to believe that Donovan was going to leave us both alone, you still had doubts, and when I spoke to Cole about it, he agreed with you. He said someone that has gone to all the trouble of following you and frightening you wouldn't just give up and vanish, even though I hoped and prayed he did."

"But Donovan has been watching me for weeks at the house." I keep my eyes on Connor and hope he understands what I'm about to say. "He said he saw me early morning outside."

"Ella, if I had known he was following you, I would have taken you far away. I'm sorry."

His eyes leave my face. I reach up with my good hand, tilting his chin so he sees that I don't blame him for any of this. "You have nothing to be sorry about," I whisper, pressing a kiss to his lips.

"Sweetheart, we all hoped we had seen and heard the last from Donovan. Now, hopefully we have," Dad says. "I'm just thankful that Cole was still investigating."

"Me too. Is he still here?" I ask, thinking I should thank him.

"No," says Connor.

"Oh!"

"He's going to come and speak to you tomorrow. Something about tying up loose ends."

"Okay. What about Julie? Does she know I'm here? And Trevor? I'll need him to speak to the producer and director for me."

"I've not called Julie yet. You can do that when we leave, and as for Trevor, he's already let them know. We both have a few days off and we can relax." Connor is right. I'll call Julie. She's going to panic regardless of when she finds out.

We all sit talking, and I try to convince my dad and brother to go home, but they want to stay. Something about wanting to hear what the doctor has to say when he comes back to see me, and hopefully discharge me.

"Miss McGregor." Doctor Hardy enters the room, carrying my notes. "I'm happy to let you go home, but please take it easy for the next few days. You will have follow up appointments to attend and I have a prescription here for you. If you have any concerns, please come back in."

"I will," I say. "And thank you."

The doctor leaves the room. "Sweetheart, we'll drive you both home, if that's where you're going?"

Connor glances at me. He's leaving this decision up to me. "Yes, we'll go home." Dad and Callum leave the room, giving me a moment alone with Connor.

"It will only be home for a short time," Connor says. "All being well, we'll be in our new home in six to eight weeks."

"Something to look forward to in our world of madness," I reply, standing up.

Connor wraps his arms around my waist. "We have lots to look forward to, and our mad crazy world will go back to what we class as normal."

"I'm sorry our plans for tonight changed," I say.

"Don't you dare apologise. This isn't your fault, but the plus side is, I get you to myself for a few days. I'll still do the interview tomorrow and then we can lock ourselves away from everyone until we go back on set."

"That sounds like a very good idea."

He nods, pressing a kiss on the tip of my nose before taking my hand.

Chapter 31

FILMING FIVE DAYS A WEEK and being out with the charity most nights, and trying to help Michelle when I can with the new shelter over the past six weeks is starting to take its toll on me. I'm tired; really tired. I've not seen Julie properly in weeks. Not since the day after Donovan. A two-minute telephone conversation every few days isn't nearly enough. Especially with everything going on in my life. I need a night out or a night in with my friend. But I feel guilty for even thinking about having a night out when I think about Jack. I know I shouldn't, but I can't help it.

Tomorrow is the grand opening of the new shelter which will provide a permanent home for a number of our city's homeless people, including Mack and Jack. Social services have agreed to Jack staying there for the time being. Michelle didn't think they would, but they did agree with her that she thought he would run if he was put into care, or if they tried to reunite him with his dad.

Jack doesn't know it yet, but Connor and I have already approached social services about him coming to stay with us. Initial background checks have been completed and references have been given. I have no idea if it will work out, but I'm hopeful, and I've also been saying a prayer every night.

Jack has wormed his way into my heart, and if this doesn't work out, I know I'm going to be more than a little upset. We do have a backup plan in the name of my dad, if our plan to have Jack live with us doesn't happen. Dad has also approached social services. So we'll have to wait and see what happens with Jack's dad.

There is a plan C, should A and B both fail, and that is he would stay at the new shelter permanently. Whatever happens, Jack will still be in our lives. He'll be loved and cared for, and he'll attend school, where I hope he makes many friends. Because he deserves some happiness. Over the last few weeks, I've seen a different side to him. He's been confident and happy, and for a lad so young, having been through so much, it's brilliant to see.

Tonight, I have no plans. I'm under strict instructions to do nothing except relax from both Connor and Michelle. Her words were, 'If I see you tonight, we'll fall out.' Connor had to work later than me, so he promised he'd bring a pizza home. He called about ten minutes ago, saying he's on his way, and I can't wait to see him. Sounds crazy, I know, but today on set we had no scenes together, so I've kind of missed him.

The speed at which time flies past is too quick. There are parts of my life I wish I could slow down. Like my time with family and friends. I've grown to really appreciate what I have more than I ever thought I would.

Family and friends I'll never take for granted.

The TV is on, but only for background noise. I used to love the silence, but not so much anymore. I'm excited about moving house next week. I still can't believe Connor and I have bought a home together. Our new life starts then. A whole new chapter. We can say goodbye to the old, to the past, and look forward.

With a sigh, my thoughts drift back to Donovan. Who would've known that him leaving me, doing what he did, would change my life completely? Maybe one day I'll get the chance to thank him for what he did, because now I see he's done me a huge favour. I received a letter from him, hand delivered and already opened by Trevor. I'm sure Trevor was worried about what was inside it.

Donovan's letter was brief and straight to the point, apologising for all the pain he caused before he left me and for all his actions after. He pleaded guilty to a number of charges. I didn't attend court. I didn't see the point. He's currently in prison. And, as for Katherine Hunter, I believe she's back in the States.

The sound of my car in the driveway grabs my attention. I know it's Connor and I smile. The car door slams closed and I silently curse him. He needs to get his own car now. The front door opens and bangs closed. I swear he's just kicked it shut with his foot. I can only presume his arms are full.

"Hey, honey. I'm home!" he calls out.

"Don't *honey* me. Slamming my poor car door closed."

"Sorry, babe," he says, entering the front room with not one but two large pizza boxes and a bottle of Cola. Who does he think he's feeding? And since when did we start drinking Cola? I stare at him, puzzled. His grin is huge. "I've brought someone to see you."

I frown and then quickly try to hide my disappointment that I'm not getting a quiet, relaxing night.

My frown and disappointment are short-lived when Jack walks into the room. I jump from my seat and rush toward him, drop to me knees, and wrap my arms around him. "How, and where is Mack?" I ask Connor.

"When I spoke to Michelle, she agreed to Jack coming here as long as he was happy to stay, and as for Mack, he's staying at the shelter tonight."

Jack is staying here tonight. Not on the streets. Tonight, he can stay in comfort, and hopefully it will be the first of many nights with us.

"Thank you." Tears fill my eyes and I hold Jack at arm's length to look at the boy who has changed so much in the short time

I've known him.

"You have a lovely home, Ella," Jack says when I finally put him down. I try not to think too much about his words. I don't want him to feel intimidated or scared here. Being here might be too much for him. I hope not though. Connor puts the boxes and Cola down on the coffee table and leaves the room. Jack joins me on the couch and I watch as he nervously looks around the room. His knees bounce rapidly and he rubs his hands together over and over.

I can't believe he's here.

I rub the back of my neck as I watch him. I think I'm more nervous than him.

"Glasses for the Cola," Connor says, breaking the silence. "What's wrong?"

Jack and I both answer at the same time. "Nothing." Jack looks at me and a slow smile spreads across his face. "Sorry," he says.

"You have nothing to be sorry for. We have tonight and we can do whatever you want."

"Do you have Scrabble? Mum and I used to play it."

"I'm sure I have it somewhere," I say. "After we've eaten, you can help me look for it."

"Deal."

Connor smiles, handing me a slice of pizza. Jack is already tucking in. I eat in silence, watching and listening to Jack and Connor. They're talking about Fletcher's football match this coming weekend. Fletcher has organised with Michelle for some kids to attend. Jack is going and he's so excited about it. He's not met Fletcher yet, but will meet him and the rest of the players at the game.

Jack now looks a bit more relaxed than when he arrived. I suppose my reaction would've made him nervous too. But now I'm trying to keep my thoughts calm and positive. I can't think of the worst case scenario. We have to all have a happy ending. Jack has to have a happy ending. I'd sacrifice my own happily-ever-after to ensure he gets his.

Connor hands Jack the TV remote and he sits back, enjoying his pizza and flicking through the channels.

I sigh when he stops. "Really? Football news?" I say with amusement.

"I can turn it over," Jack says.

"You will do no such thing," I reply with a smile and sit back. This is how I'm picturing nights in the new house. Fun and laughter. Peace and happiness. But more than that, I see stability in Jack's future.

We watch the football news. Connor clears away the boxes. Jack and I go for a quick tour of the house and we find Scrabble. I let him pick which room he wants to sleep in. He picks the small back room. The same room I sought comfort in all those months ago, when I thought my world was crumbling.

Downstairs, we play a few games of Scrabble. Jack is really quite good at it. He's very intelligent. I'm glad he'll be going to school in the next few weeks, as soon as Michelle and social services sort through the paperwork. Or maybe I'll be the one getting to pick out his school, if it's decided in our favour for him to live with us.

"Can we watch a movie?" he asks. "It's been a while since I watched one."

"Of course we can." Connor flicks through the channels and stops on an action adventure. I move from my position on the floor, where I've been sitting around the coffee table to play Scrabble. Jack joins me on the couch and snuggles up beside me. Connor sits on the chair and smiles, and if I'm not mistaken, his eyes are glazed. I wrap my arm around Jack.

"Ella, thank you for having me. This has been the best night."

I choke back my tears. Something tells me he'll be sitting in my arms the whole night. I don't think he'll make it upstairs.

Chapter 32

I OPEN MY EYES AND search the front room. No sign of Connor or Jack, but I hear their voices in the kitchen. I stand, stretching, and go to them. Pausing in the doorway of the kitchen, I watch the two of them interact. Jack is sitting at the island, his head resting in his hands, watching Connor as he cooks, and from the smell of it, he's cooking pancakes.

"I know I need to go to a new school. Do you think I'll make friends?" Jack asks.

I reach up, putting my hand over my mouth because I'm sad at the thought he thinks he won't make friends. There's a heaving ache in my chest and my heart breaks a little bit more for Jack. He sounds so insecure, and for that, I blame his dad. For not showing him any love or compassion in what has been the most traumatic time of his young life.

I'm not a parent, but to me, a parent should always put their child first. Sadly, I'm finding out this isn't the case for many.

"Of course you will," Connor tells him. "Ella and I are your friends." Connor's eyes meet mine for the first time this morning and there's as much sadness in his as mine.

"Yes, but you're adults."

"Morning," I say, finally stepping into the kitchen. I want to go to Jack, take him in my arms, give him a kiss, and tell him that everything in his life will be okay. He needs reassurance. Instead, I ruffle his hair, flashing him my biggest smile on my way past him, and I give Connor a kiss on his cheek. "It looks as though you've been busy."

"Connor has. I've just sat here and watched."

"So, pancakes this morning?" I open the fridge and take out the milk and fresh orange juice. I set them down and get some glasses.

"My choice. Is that okay?"

"Of course it is. Now, about starting school. I don't want you to worry about it. You will fit in and it will be fun, hanging about with kids your own age."

"I'm not sure I want to. I've not been to school for nearly a year." I stop at his words. "Ella, will I still be able to see you?"

"Yes," I tell him without hesitation, and sit down beside him. "I'll always be here for you."

I take his hand in mine. Jack stares at our joined hands, his shoulders dropping and his back bowed. I hate seeing him sad and uncertain. There are so many changes happening in his life, most of them good, but I can understand his anxiety.

Glancing across the kitchen, I'm met with Connor's sad eyes. He offers me the weakest of smiles. We both feel the same. We're both hurting for Jack.

"Okay, breakfast is ready, you two." Connor says.

"Yay." Jack's voice is full of excitement. Up until last night, I'd only seen small glimpses of Jack the child. Usually, he has a wall built up around him, putting on his brave face; the one he uses every day to deal with the tough and unpredictable world he lives in. But, with us, he can be himself.

The air lifts and we eat breakfast and talk about the day ahead. I have a few things to do before I need to be at the shelter. Michelle said Jack can stay with me until I go there. So, he gets to hang about here all day with Connor and me.

I'm excited about this new project for the charity. There are so many people this new venture can help. And as for Mack, he has a new job. Michelle offered him a job as a maintenance man and he has a permanent bed at the shelter. He was a bit reluctant to take it because he thought that would mean leaving Jack on his own. Mack loves him as much as I do. I'd like to think that maybe, someday, Jack's dad will seek the help he needs and they could build a relationship. Maybe, someday, father and son will get a happy-ever-after.

"These are good," says Jack picking up another pancake.

"They're not bad," I say, teasing Connor.

"You'll pay for that," he says.

Jack watches us. "You two really do love each other." We both nod with a smile. "So, why aren't you married?"

"We will get married," Connor says confidently.

My hand stops in mid-air with my glass of orange juice in my hand, shaking a little.

"When?" Jack asks.

I can't answer that. I'm still too stunned at Connor's last statement. "Soon, I hope," says Connor, smiling at me.

"Well, when you get married can I come?" Jack asks, his voice full of innocence.

"If and when that happens, yes," I say without looking at Connor. He lets out a smug chuckle.

"So, Connor, when are you going to pop the question? Even I know you have a question to ask."

This time, its Connor's mask that falls, but only for a moment. "I don't know about that. I was thinking about just going all cave man, throwing Ella over my shoulders, and telling her she's mine."

Jack laughs. A proper giggle. "You can't do that. Ella deserves more than that. She's special."

"She is and you're right."

I smile at Connor's words. Jack stands. "What are you doing?" I ask, noticing that he's left almost two pancakes on his plate.

"I want to show you something." I nod as he leaves the kitchen. Connor shrugs his shoulders; he doesn't know what Jack's up to either.

"I'd like to show you a picture," Jack says, re-entering the kitchen. "It's my mum."

Jack slides back into the seat next to me with the photograph clutched between his fingers. Nervously, he hands it to me, before eating again.

With the picture in my hand, I lift my head and look for support from Connor. He nods and I allow my eyes to study the picture, my gaze roaming every inch of it, taking every detail in.

Jack with his mum.

Tears fill my eyes and I'm fighting the urge to crumble as I see the love they shared. A mother's love that no one can replace. I had my mum all through my childhood and still miss her every single day, but for Jack to grow up without his mother's love saddens me.

It's a picture on a beach; they're building sandcastles. Jack is watching on with awe as his mother sits back, proudly looking at what they've achieved. I'd say this picture is maybe only two years old.

"Your mum was very beautiful. You look a lot like her," I say.

"She was, and she was my best friend."

"My mum was my best friend." His eyes pop. "She died a few years ago and I still miss her every day, and I'm a grown up."

He puts the pancake down and tears roll down his face. I crumble with him. This time I don't hesitate, and I do what I wanted to do. I offer him my arms of comfort as he cries for everything he's lost.

I sit back down with him in my arms, rocking him back and forth. "I miss her so much." Tears roll down my face and I don't even bother to wipe them away. My concern is for the boy in my arms that I'd happily do anything I could to make his hurt go away.

I hear the scraping of a chair and I don't need to look, because I feel him before I see him. Strong arms engulf us both, trying to protect us and offer comfort. I look up into Connor's eyes and there's something there. Something that makes me believe that everything will be okay.

That Jack will be okay with our help.

"ARE YOU OKAY?" Michelle asks as I walk into the shelter. Jack has my hand in his and I can't bear the thought of leaving him tonight. Although, I'm sure this is going to be easier than leaving him on the streets. I'm just hoping he won't need to be here long.

"Yes." I smile at Jack. "Everything is okay."

After this morning, everything settled down. Jack and Connor watched football while I had some things to do. My dad and Callum dropped by too. So, they had a lads' afternoon, minus the beers.

I spot Mack, busy in the background, "Can I go and help?" Jack asks.

"Of course," I say, and he runs over to Mack, who scoops him up in his arms.

"It was always going to be . . ."

"Don't say it. If you don't say it, I can pretend."

"Okay, well, we still have a lot to do before tonight. The chef is already in the kitchen preparing tonight's meal. Mack is busy rearranging furniture in some of the bedrooms. Oh, and I have some news for you about Stacey and her girls. The council have finally offered her a new house. It's in a nice area, lots of families, and it's all thanks to you."

"Really?"

"Yes, really. She wanted to come along and thank you tonight but didn't want to bring the girls out."

"I'm so pleased for her. She deserves this. She's a great mum."

"She is. Now, we need to get on. I'm worried about tonight."
She looks flustered.

"Michelle, tonight will be fine," I say, urging her to take a
deep breath.

"I know, but I'm so glad we're not having tonight as our grand
opening. If it was, I would be worse than I am now."

"You did the right thing in waiting until all the refurb work
is finished."

"I know. Let's get on with it."

I'VE ALREADY DRIFTED off from what Michelle is saying, sens-
ing him in the room. I lift my eyes and search. It takes a moment,
and then I see him. We hold each other's gaze for a moment. 'I
love you," I mouth as he walks toward me. I wasn't sure if he
would make it tonight; he told me he had a few things to do.

"Hi! I didn't expect to see you."

"Well, tonight's a big night and I couldn't not be here to help
you," he says, pressing a soft kiss on my lips. I glance down at
myself; my t-shirt is dirty. My hair is scraped back from my face
and tied back, and I'm sure I must look as tired as I feel. But, right
now, with the glazed, warm look in Connor's eyes, I feel like the
luckiest woman on the planet.

"Are you here to help or just gawk at me?" There's amusement
in my voice.

"Help and gawk, because, let's face it, there's not a man on
the planet who wouldn't want to trade places with me and be
able to look at you all day long every day of his life."

"Have you and my brother been out drinking?"

He laughs at my question. Everyone is still listening to Michelle as she speaks about who is staying here tonight. She stops
and everyone in the room is clapping and cheering. Michelle has
been working toward tonight, not just for the last few months,

but years. Tonight, she gets to see her hard work and dedication pay off.

Michelle turns to me, taking my hands in hers. "I can't thank you enough, Ella. You have no idea what having you working with the charity has done. You've given us all a sense of purpose. You walked into my office when self doubt about what I wanted to achieve had really kicked in, and I'm eternally grateful." Her eyes are filled with tears and now she's got me going.

"I'm happy to help, and I'm happy for the friendship we have. No more tears. Tonight is about the charity turning a corner. Now, go and see everyone else."

"Thank you." She turns and only manages to few steps before she talks to another member of staff.

I sigh and look around the room. Tonight is more than a good night. Michelle and the team have achieved so much.

Connor is still standing beside me, his wide eyes glazed. "You, Ella McGregor, don't realise how special you are."

I shrug my shoulders then watch as he takes a small box from his pocket. He opens it, drops to his knee, and takes my hand.

I gasp. I'm sure all attention in the room has turned to us. "There's only one woman in the world I want, and she brings me to my knees on a daily basis. She's talented and beautiful. Loving and caring. She's funny and smart. Passionate and loyal. Ella McGregor, will you do me the greatest honour and become my wife?"

A lonely tear trickles down my face and I nod, unable to form words. He slides the ring on my finger and I pull his hands, drawing him back to his feet. "Yes," I say, and he smiles, a smile that reaches up to his dazzling eyes.

There's lots of clapping and cheering around the room. I wrap my arms around him and allow my eyes to search for Jack. He's standing with Mack; both are smiling. Jack is wiping his eyes and Mack puts his arm around him.

Thoughts of this morning's breakfast conversation flood my head. Did Jack's questions spur Connor on, or had he already decided the path our lives would take?

I'm not going to even ask.

Because I love the man in my arms.

Chapter 33

A BEACH WEDDING WOULD HAVE been wonderful, but my day wouldn't have been perfect with two very important people missing; Mack and Jack. There was no way we were getting married without them. Connor and I both felt the same.

So, I'm alone for the first time in weeks, in one of the loch-view suites, staring out of the large windows and taking in all the natural beauty of Loch Lomond. Taking a moment to myself to enjoy the peace and tranquillity before everyone descends upon me and the day whizzes by.

I'm trying not to think about how quickly the day will go; I want to be able to savour it. Enjoy every moment with our closest friends and family.

There's a hazy fog slowly lifting, and I'm hoping it leaves behind a glorious sunny day. Even with the fog, I can still see across the Loch to the castle on the other side. From here, it looks all magical; something straight from a movie. I wonder if the hotel looks the same from the other side. I'm sure it does. I can't see the top of Ben Lomond at the moment, but hopefully, later in the day, it will be visible in the backdrop of pictures.

As I look down at the grounds below, the marquee is being erected for our lunch time ceremony overlooking the Loch.

Who would've thought that I'd be marrying Connor Andrews?

My friend for the last five years is now the most important person in my life. I want to talk to him, even just send him a text, but I won't. I banned all contact from midnight last night until the ceremony takes place this afternoon. I don't think this was one of my better ideas.

Keeping today out of the media hasn't been easy. There has been lots of speculation as to when we would set a date after our engagement was announced recently. We both knew if we wanted to keep it out of the media, it would have to be sooner rather than later. But here we are. So far, so good. No leaks to the media and I'm hoping it will stay that way.

I can now understand why, after a whirlwind romance, Libby and Alex were married five weeks after he proposed to her. And today would not be possible without her and her incredible staff here at the hotel. They have all been superstars. I wouldn't have known where to start.

A light knocking on the suite door has me turning around. I look at the time. Nine a.m. It's too early for Julie; she'll be here at ten and not a minute before. I open the door to find Libby and a member of staff holding flowers. "Well, can we come in?"

"Of course," I say, opening the door wider. After putting the flowers on the table, the member of staff leaves, but Libby stays. I admire the two bouquets. Exquisite. They are just what I had hoped for. Fresh lilies; my favourite, tied with Andrews tartan ribbon. I didn't want anything too fancy, just elegant, and that's what the florist has given me.

"The rest of the flowers that have been delivered look incredible. Outside and inside is going to be stunning. How are you feeling?" Libby asks.

I smile at her reassuring words about the flowers. "Good. A little nervous."

"Nerves are good. I don't know any bride who isn't nervous on their big day, but I bet Connor has got his boxers in a twist."

I laugh because I'm sure she's right. "Can I get you anything? Breakfast?"

"No. I'm not hungry."

"Ella, you should eat."

"I'll order room service when Julie gets here."

"Okay. Do you need me to do anything before I go and check on everything else?"

"No, but I will need you to stop working and join us."

"I'll be changed and looking gorgeous, and in my seat awaiting your arrival."

"You'd better be."

"Don't worry about me. I've told your dad he's not allowed near your room until ten minutes to twelve. Connor and your brother are in the swimming pool at the moment. Your dad is having breakfast with Mr and Mrs Andrews."

I'm glad they're all keeping busy. Connor must've been bored. I bet he's already hit the gym first. "Thank you, Libby. For everything."

"Nonsense. I'm doing my job."

"I think we both know you're doing more than your job."

"Maybe. Right, I'm out of here." She gives me a kiss on the cheek before leaving me on my own again.

I pour myself a glass of water before sitting at the window to enjoy the view and watch a few boats sailing up the Loch. Now the hazy fog is lifting, it is leaving behind a beautiful sunny day. I purposely don't turn on the TV or scroll through my phone or the internet; I don't want to see anything that might turn my mood sour. Today has to be perfect.

Another light knock at the door grabs my attention. "Who is it?" I call out.

"Me." I sigh with relief, hearing Julie's voice. If anyone else had answered, they weren't getting in.

"Look at you," I say, opening the door. Julie's not alone as she enters. She has some help from a porter, and when I see everything she has, I'm not surprised she needed help. Her make-up trolley—because there's nothing else I would call it—a small case, and her dress in a carrier. The porter wheels in her trolley before leaving the room.

"Are you nervous?" she asks.

"Getting there."

"Come here." She puts the carrier with her dress in it over a chair and wraps her arms around me. "Everything will go to plan and you are going to be a stunning bride. Now, I hope you have a bottle of champers. I'll need some to steady my nerves."

"After you've done my make-up."

"I'll have a sip now. You did take your dress from the carrier, didn't you? To let the air around it."

"Yes."

"Okay. I'll go and put mine with yours. Then me and you can have some breakfast, champagne, and get ready for the most important day in your life."

She's right, it is an important day, but there's one person missing. I'd give anything to have my mum here with me, fussing over me and helping me get ready. She'd also ensure Julie and I were behaving. Tears fill my eyes. Would she have approved?

I know the answer to that. Everyone has told me. She always knew we would be together. My parents had a happy marriage filled with love. If Connor and I can have half of what they shared, then we will be very lucky.

JULIE STANDS BEFORE me in her dress. It's a plain ivory dress, a little similar in style to my wedding dress. The buttons on the back of her dress sets it off; they're Andrews tartan. I know Connor is wearing his family tartan and I love that I've been able to incorporate small amounts of tartan into our day. "You look incredible," I say. Elegant, and the jewellery I gave her as a gift earlier is perfect.

"I scrub up not too bad. Now, I'd say it's time to get you into your dress and then you can finally look in the mirror and give me your verdict." Julie covered the floor length mirror with a bed sheet. She said she wanted me to get the full effect. I trust her completely when it comes to my hair and make-up.

Julie helps me into my dress, which we both love. She was with me when I tried it on. Her reaction was priceless; she sat with tears running down her face.

I stand nervously as she fixes the back of my dress before putting my mother's pearl necklace around my neck. I had to have her close to me today, and when my dad offered me the jewellery she wore on her own wedding day, I couldn't say no. I'm honoured.

Julie walks around in front of me and takes a step back. She quickly covers her mouth with one hand and the other rises to wipe her eyes. Oh, no. If she's already teary, this isn't a good sign. "Ella, you are the most beautiful bride I've ever seen. I hope Connor realises how lucky he is to have you."

"I'm the lucky one."

"You ready to have a look?"

I nod.

She pulls the sheet off the mirror and I gasp at my reflection. Julie is quickly on hand with a tissue as I take in my appearance. My dress looks better than I remembered. The cap sleeves sit perfectly on my shoulders. The sweetheart neckline is elegant without being too showy. The natural waistline sits perfectly.

Then I turn to the side to get a decent view of the back. It's completely backless. The sweeping train is what I wanted. I turn back around. My make-up is natural and my curled hair is pinned in an elegant up-style with a few loose curls framing my face.

I touch the pearl necklace and smile a sad smile. "I wish she were here."

"Me too. But I'm sure she's looking down on you today, watching you finally marrying the man she knew carried your heart."

I take a deep breath to steady my nerves and to try and stop myself from crying. "What time do I have . . ."

None, it would appear, with the loud knocking on my door. "That will be your dad, right on time. I'll let him in as I leave. I'll see you downstairs."

I can only nod.

She takes her flowers and I stand in the middle of the room and watch her open the door to my dad. He tells her how beautiful she looks before giving her a kiss. Julie isn't usually bashful or embarrassed, but today, she is.

My dad walks toward me, tears filling his eyes. He's wearing the Andrews family tartan. I was unsure what he would do today. Part of me thought he'd wear the McGregor tartan just to be different.

"For the first time in my life, I'm speechless."

"Can it stay that way?" I joke.

"No. Every single day of your life, you have made me and your mother proud, and today is no different. I wish she was here with us today to see the beautiful woman you've become. You might be getting married, but you'll always be my baby girl." He takes a breath to steady himself. "I love you more than life itself and you are absolutely beautiful today. Perfection."

"I love you too. Thank you for being you," I say with a tear trickling down my face. He hands me a tissue.

"No more tears. Now, come on. Let's go."

He picks up my bouquet, handing it to me, and links his arm with mine. Closing my eyes briefly, I take a deep breath and we leave the bedroom.

Chapter 34

DAD AND I STAND INSIDE the hotel's main entrance, waiting for the go ahead to walk outside. The music is playing and Julie has already gone outside. As our photographer snaps away, I'm suddenly overwhelmed.

My breathing accelerates.

"Take a deep breath. I'm here with you," Dad says.

I turn my head and smile at the man who has loved me unconditionally since the day I was born. A parent's love.

My thoughts drift to Jack. Today is meant to be filled with happiness, not sadness. I know he's here with Mack and Michelle, and I know he's happy for me. For us. For our family. A family that we are praying dearly he will be a huge part of in the coming weeks when Jack's case is discussed.

"No time for second thoughts, sweetheart." Dad knows there are no second thoughts from me. This is the happiest I've been in a long time, and I truly love Connor with all my heart. He completes me. He makes me whole.

"There are no doubts in my head, especially about marrying Connor." We're given the okay by a member of the hotel staff, and we walk slowly down the steps and out into the warm air. The clear blue sky shines like a diamond above us without a cloud in sight.

I gasp, turning the corner, facing the marquee. White rose petals lay on the ground, forming a path. Beautiful potted small trees line the pathway. The scene is completely picturesque, from the lovely warm day to the stunning location.

There's something so effortlessly romantic about an outdoor wedding. The sound of water splashing along the rocky shoreline is faint, but I can hear it through the soft music that's playing. The clear view of the Loch provides a magical setting.

At the moment, I don't see Connor or any of our guests, but all that is about to change as I enter the marquee.

I pause and take another deep breath before entering. All our closest family and friends are here, but my eyes are focused on the scene before me.

Spectacular.

The marquee is completely open at the front with stunning views out across the loch. Connor is standing with Callum and the official, smiling as I walk toward him. Julie is standing at the side and she's already crying. I keep my eyes on Connor's with each step I take toward my future.

I try to take everything in, but I'm sure I'll miss something. The flowers inside are simple and perfect. Rose and lily arrangements all hand-tied with Andrews tartan ribbon line the aisle.

My body shakes. I close my eyes momentarily to steady my growing nerves. My dad squeezes my arm in reassurance. With a deep breath, I open my eyes once again and smile, my gaze on Connor's.

Dad and I stop when I'm by Connor's side. His eyes are brimming with unshed tears. "I love you," he says as the official starts speaking.

I turn and look for Jack; he's sitting in the front row where my dad will join him. Michelle has her arm around him and he's crying as he looks toward me. Mack is sitting beside them, smiling.

"You look incredible," Connor says, drawing my attention back to him.

HE TAKES MY face in his hands. Our lips meet with sweetness and passion as the official declares us husband and wife. Cheering and clapping can be heard around us. "Well, Mrs Andrews, we've done it. You're officially mine to love forever," he whispers as his lips leave mine.

"Do you have what it takes to put up with me forever?" I tease pressing my lips back to his.

"I've always had what it takes."

I smile at his words and lean into him. My eyes drift out across the Loch and beyond to the green hills on the other side and I smile at how perfect this moment feels.

We've made the biggest commitment to each other, surrounded by those closest to us. Some will question why we didn't have a huge elaborate affair. The answer is simple; that's not us. We love our privacy, and today had to be all about that. Yes, we're both classed as high profile personalities and we love that too. But today wasn't about the showbiz couple the world think they know everything about; it was about the real us.

The us only those here get to see.

Today was about the love we share, with everyone here to celebrate.

Do either of us think our wedding won't make tomorrow's headlines? No. I'm sure pictures will be leaked from a guest staying at the hotel. But it doesn't matter.

Connor and I, along with Julie and Callum, sign the paperwork before thanking the official for a beautiful, heartfelt ceremony that was completely unique to us. He offers his warmest congratulations before getting a few pictures with us.

"Well, it's official. You are family," my dad says, shaking

Connor's hand before giving me a kiss. I've surprised myself and I think Connor too, that I've managed to hold myself together. His parents are next, followed by Trevor and Betty.

Our friends are still in their seats and I know I need to speak to them all, but I'm desperate to see and speak to Jack. I tug on Connor's hand as he talks to his mum. "Sorry," I say. His mum smiles when she realises where my attention has gone. To the boy still sitting in the front row, looking lost. I need to go to him.

"Ella!" Jack jumps from his seat and straight into my arms. "You look like a princess. The most beautiful lady I've ever seen. Even prettier than your movies."

I smile at his honest and innocent compliment.

"Miss Ella, Connor, congratulations," Mack says. He looks so much healthier now he's not living on the streets.

"Thanks, Mack. We're so glad you're here with us today," I say, still not letting go of Jack. Poor Connor. I've only been married five minutes and here's someone else getting all my attention.

"Are you okay?" Connor asks.

"Yes, of course I am. I'm surrounded by those I love and I've married my soulmate," I say, taking his hand. His kisses my head and takes Jack by the hand.

"Let's go and speak to our friends. You coming with us?" Connor asks Jack. His eyes light up when he turns and sees the friends we both want to speak to, because Fletcher Adams is standing at the back of the marquee. Yes, he's just the same as any lad his age. Totally daft on football, and he adores Fletcher. It's fair to say Fletcher has a huge soft spot for Jack too.

We talk to everyone before posing for some pictures down by the Loch shoreline. The photographer wanted a few family and group shots. I also requested a few pictures with Jack. Just the three of us. I have a few pictures of us on my phone but these ones taken today mean so much to us. I'm quietly hoping that today marks a new start for us all.

When social services got involved, they had to get in touch with Jack's dad. He wants nothing to do with him. As soon as I was told that, I went straight to the shelter to see Jack. I expected him to be upset, but I was taken aback with his attitude. He didn't want to go back to him. He says if and when his dad ever seeks help then he can be a part of his life, but until then, he wants nothing to do with him.

For such a young boy, he does have a level head.

EARLY EVENING TURNS into nightfall. With our family and friends, we've enjoyed great food, plenty of drinks, and great company. Everyone is staying at the hotel tonight, including Michelle, Mack, and Jack.

"I have a surprise for you," Connor says, as we sit listening to Fletcher telling Jack stories about football.

"What is it?" I ask, wondering what else he's been up to. Michelle smiles and a warm sense of calm spreads through me. I press my hands in a prayer and close my eyes, hopeful that my thoughts are going in the right direction.

Straight to Jack.

"Can I ask everyone to make their way outside to the banks of the Loch?" It's Libby's voice that breaks through the room and has me immediately opening my eyes.

"Why?" I question.

"You'll see."

We make our way outside and I gasp. Fairy lights form a pathway to the Loch. Libby has thought of everything. She has excelled herself today. I have no idea how to thank her for all she's done.

Our group of thirty gathers at the banks of the Loch. Connor slips his arm around my waist. I jump, hearing the first bang as the dark night sky lights up. Warm oranges and silver fill the sky above us.

"I love it," squeals Jack as he grips my dad's hand. He's not the only one who loves it. Music fills the air and the night sky lights up over and over. I lean back, resting my body against Connor's and smile.

Today has been perfect. Exactly the way I had envisioned it in my head.

Connor takes my hand and turns me in his arms.

"Thank for today," I say. "It's been incredible."

"It's not over yet," he whispers, pressing a soft kiss to my lips. I hear the fireworks but they are now firmly in the background as I gaze at my husband. The man who has lit up my life. "I have another surprise for you."

"What?"

"I know you said you didn't want a honeymoon, but I didn't listen to you. We've got some time off. Tomorrow afternoon, we fly out to Bali for two whole weeks. Just us. No distractions. No work commitments."

"I don't know what to say."

"You, my wife, don't have to say anything. I'll do everything in my power to ensure your happiness. We can relax and have fun and enjoy being a family of two, because I can sense that it won't be long until our family extends."

My eyes drift to Jack and I'm hoping he's right. I know there are still obstacles in our way, and neither of us have wanted to get Jack's hopes up because we're scared we might let him down. But Michelle and our social worker have given us nothing but positive vibes.

"Okay. I'll play along nicely then. Only because I love you so much."

"And I love you. Always have and always will," he says before pressing his lips to mine.

Chapter 35

MY HANDS ARE SWEATING AND my knees are jerking. "I'm so nervous," I say as we sit, waiting to be called back into the meeting room.

"You have nothing to nervous about," he tells me, trying to reassure me. "We've done all we can. It's out of our hands now." I know it is, and that's why I'm nervous. The decision isn't mine. Someone else has the power to change lives today, and I hope they realise it.

Nerves are getting the better of me. I don't even think I was this nervous on our wedding day only a few weeks ago. Everything has happened so quickly, and here we are today, waiting to find out if the officials are on our side. If they are, we can go back to the shelter and take Jack home with us.

A door opens. "It's time," Jonathon says, holding the door open and waiting for us. I stand up and smooth down my dress.

I take Connor's hand and we enter the room and sit back around the table with Jonathon. Jack's social worker is smiling, and I'm hoping that's because she knows what is going to happen. The three panel members enter the room and sit down.

"Mr and Mrs Andrews, I understand that you will both be anxious, so I'll give you our decision. We all agree that Jack should be placed with you, and you will be his foster parents. I know your plan is . . ."

Tears fill my eyes and I don't hear anything else the woman says. Connor squeezes my hand and my body sags against his. I close my eyes, thinking about the boy that will have a family of his own. He won't be lost in the system. He'll be loved and cared for more than he'll ever know.

My tears are of happiness and I know we still have a long road ahead of us, because we know fostering Jack is just for a short time. Adoption is the long term plan. We want Jack as a permanent member of our family.

"Ella." Jonathon says my name.

I open my eyes. "She's fine," Connor says, softly rubbing my shoulder.

"Sorry," I say to everyone in the room.

"Don't be. We understand. Today is an emotional day for you," one of the panel members tells me. I sit beside Connor and try to take in everything that is being said, but my mind has already left this building, and it's just waiting for body to catch up. Connor and Jonathon talk, and papers are put before me to sign, which I do in a hurry.

"Can we leave?" I say when everyone stops talking.

"Yes," Jack's social worker says.

"Thank you."

"Ella, Connor, I'll meet you both at the shelter," she says to us.

"Yes, but please can we tell him?"

"Of course."

She leaves before us and we stay behind to speak with Jonathon. He tells us what the next steps will be, but tells us there's no rush and to take one day at a time.

When we leave the room, I stop and face Connor. "We've saved him," I say, crying as he pulls me into his arms.

"We have. Shall we go and tell him?"

"Yes."

I take his hand and we leave the building. My phone rings, and it's my dad.

"You not going to answer that?"

"No. Jack has to be the first to know then I call my dad back, or we can drop in on him on our way home." *Home.* We get to take Jack home today. I'm still in shock. I don't think it will sink in properly until I see him. Hold him in my arms and finally be able to say everything in his life will be okay, because he has us to look after him.

"Won't Jonathon tell him?"

"No. He still has some paperwork to tie up. Let's go."

MICHELLE IS SMILING as we enter the shelter and signals into the games room. I take a deep breath and glance at Connor. "Are you ready?" he asks.

"Yes." We enter the games room and Mack is with Jack, playing pool. His social worker is sitting on the couch, going through her folder.

"Ella, Connor," Jack says with excitement. "You didn't say you were coming today. Ella, why have you been crying?" His tone changes to one of concern as we step toward him.

"Jack, come and sit down," his social worker says. Mack stands by the pool table, quietly watching.

We didn't tell them our meeting was today because we weren't sure what was going to happen. We were open with Jack a few weeks ago about wanting him to come and stay with us. He was so excited, saying, if it happened, he couldn't wait to tell his new friends at school. I know he spoke to not only his social worker, but also the panel members.

Jack's eyes shift from me to Connor then back again. "You've had the meeting, haven't you?"

"Yes. We were all there this morning," Connor tells him.

Jack's eyes fall to the floor and I have to put him out of his misery because he's expecting to hear the worst. "Jack, do you want to go and pack? Because you're coming to live with us," I say.

He looks up, eyes glazed, staring at me. I nod, confirming what I've just said. He rushes at me, throws his arms around my neck, and his tears fall. So many emotions run through my head. Connor's arms wrap around us and we stay huddled together, all of us crying.

Through my tear-filled eyes, I look at Mack. He's still standing by the pool table, although Michelle has joined him. She has her arm around his shoulder. My heart fills with sadness and warmth.

Mack and I have spoken at great length, because I was worried about him. He put my mind at ease by saying Jack needed more than what he could give him. The two of them have a bond that no-one can ever break.

"I'm happy for you," Mack mouths at me.

"Thank you. That means a lot to me."

"This isn't a dream, is it?" Jack asks, pulling out of our hold.

"No, this isn't a dream," says Connor. "Why don't I come and help you pack and we can let Ella stop crying."

"Okay."

They both leave the room.

"Are you okay?" Michelle asks.

"Yes, I never expected to feel so overwhelmed with emotions. Mack?"

"Miss Ella, I'm fine. I'll still see him."

"You will."

"Well, then don't worry about me. I'll go and help him and Connor and tell him I'll see him in a few days. Don't want any tears as you take him home."

"Thanks, Mack."

I pace the room, waiting for them to return, while Michelle and Jack's social worker talk quietly.

Ten minutes later, Connor and Jack appear in the doorway. Jack has his old rucksack over his shoulder, and Connor has a small suitcase. "Are we ready to go home?" Connor asks.

Michelle gives me a cuddle and tells me she'll see me in a few days. "I'm more than ready to go home."

I walk toward them and offer Jack my hand; he doesn't hesitate. Connor takes his other and we leave the shelter.

Chapter 36

"LOOK AROUND YOU, ELLA. AFTER everything that has happened to you, you are still smiling and putting others first. You and Jess have done so much good for not just local communities, but throughout Scotland," says Libby as we stand in the director's box, looking out around the stadium as it starts to fill up with football supporters taking their seats.

"You should be proud of what you have achieved in such a short space of time. You are doing what you set out to do and that is to make a difference." I smile at Jess and attempt not to cry as my eyes fill with tears as her words hit home. I'm not the only one making a difference. My friends and family have and are still helping out.

"Hey, you. We'll have none of those tears today. Not even happy ones," Julie says, wrapping her arm around my shoulder.

Julie may be my best friend, but I honestly don't know how I would've coped without all of them lately. Not just the emotional support I've needed to get me through some tough days, especially concerning Jack, but also the practical support in helping organise today's event.

It's funny how a chance encounter has brought us all together.

Jess has been incredible. After everything she's been through, she shows great strength and character. She's a woman I admire, and now she's also a very good friend. It helps massively that, when it comes to football, she has all the right connections.

And Libby, between her, Alex, and her dad, they have taken care of all marketing and PR for today.

Today's charity match; the football team versus the celebrities. Everyone has been talking about this for weeks. The support we've received has been amazing. Every last penny raised today will be split between the Women's Aid charity that Jess supports and the homeless charity I support. Helping those who need it the most here in Scotland.

To say I'm overwhelmed by the support and generosity for today's match is an understatement. Some of the biggest actors in the world signed up to be part of the celebrity team. The response was incredible. I was inundated with so many requests that I had to turn some people down.

My eyes slowly roam the stadium and it's so busy. There are also a few players from both teams warming up on the football pitch, but I don't see anyone I recognise. Fletcher and Connor must still be inside.

"Come on. You'll get to see all this later when we take our seats, but right now, you two have an interview to do before you get to go and meet with the players," Julie reminds Jess and me.

"Okay, let's do this," I say with enthusiasm.

Jess leads the way through the stadium and I'm so glad she's here because I'd get lost; it's so big. I've learned recently that there is much more to a football stadium than just the grass pitch. We leave Libby and Julie in the players' lounge, where Alex is waiting with a few of Libby's friends and her dad. Jess and I will catch up with them when the game starts; we all have seats together.

I've had butterflies in my stomach since I got up this morning and I'm not sure why. Everything has gone smoothly so far, and I'm sure today will go without a hitch as well. Hopefully, tonight I'll be able to relax at the dinner we've organised for everyone that has taken part or given up their free time over the last few weeks. Tonight is about Jess and me thanking everyone for their help.

Jess opens the door to a lovely room. It looks comfortable and relaxing, almost homely with its natural light, sofas, and a coffee table. Dad, Trevor, Callum, and Stephen the cameraman are waiting on us. There are two banners with both charities' names on.

"Ah, the two gorgeous ladies of the moment. You both look great," my dad says, greeting us as we enter. Callum looks in our direction and smiles when he sees what we're wearing.

Jess is wearing the same football shirt as Fletcher, and I'm wearing the same shirt the celebrities will be wearing. This is all in the name of PR. And we do look good in our football shirts, jeans, and heels.

"Ella, Jess. You look great." Trevor stands and steps toward us. "Stick to everything we've spoken about. Callum knows not to ask anything too personal." My brother laughs and mumbles under his breath. My thoughts go back to the day when he put me on the spot, asking if there was a new man in my life.

"Ignore him. I do," I tell Jess as we take a seat on the sofa and relax.

Stephen and Callum start fussing around the room before my brother takes a seat opposite us and Stephen takes up his position behind the camera. Dad and Trevor stay in the room and it doesn't surprise me.

"Congratulations, Ella and Jess, on working so hard behind the scenes to bring today's event to Glasgow. You both must be so pleased. We all know your reasons for helping the charities chosen; neither of you have hidden your pasts. Jess, how will your charity benefit from funds raised today?"

I smile and turn to face Jess as she answers Callum. I listen in awe at what Women's Aid do, all the help they provide for vulnerable woman and families who find themselves victims of domestic abuse. It will be clear to anyone watching and listening that Jess is passionate about the charity she supports.

Callum asks me the same question and I reply with confidence, telling him about the services my chosen charity provides for, not just for people who find themselves living on the streets, but for families who find themselves living in poor standards of accommodation.

Trevor and my dad smile proudly as they lean against the far wall, watching us. Callum wraps up the interview and I see Trevor check the time on his watch. "Ladies, we should head to the changing rooms now."

"Okay," Jess says.

"I'll see you soon," I say to my dad and Callum. Stephen is going to be down by the pitch, filming some of the game.

"Good luck, although I'm sure neither of you need it," says my dad before we leave. Trevor leads us through the building. The closer we get to the changing rooms, the louder it becomes. The noise level from outside is almost deafening.

We stop in the corridor outside the changing rooms. Jess and I wait while Trevor goes inside to talk to the team managers. Peter is the team manager for Fletcher's team, and his assistant has been training and coaching the celebrity team for the last week, although some of the celebrity players have been training hard in recent months, like Connor.

He was the first to put his name forward. Connor can play football, and from what I've seen recently, he's actually really good, although I don't claim to know much about the sport. "Are you nervous?" Jess asks me.

"About going out there? No. What about you?"

"Yes. I'm not used to all this attention."

"You'll be fine and I'm going to be beside you."

We don't have that much to do; just walk out in front of the players. How hard can that be? The home team's changing room door opens and Fletcher is the first to walk out. He's captain today, and the smile on his face as he looks at his wife is adorable. He nods in greeting to me, but his focus is on Jess.

The other door opens and I can't stop myself from checking Connor out when he is the first out of the door. Yeah, my man could totally be a footballer, going on looks and presence alone.

"Ella, babe, are you okay?" Connor questions me. "You look a bit off colour." I look at Jess she nods in agreement.

"No, I'm . . ." I was going to say fine, but the butterflies in my stomach have turned into a full on spinning cycle. "No, I need to go . . ."

"Come with me." Jess grabs my arm and pulls me along the corridor. I hear Connor and Fletcher talking, but my focus is on getting to where I'm meant to be going, and I'm hoping that's a bathroom so I can be sick. She pushes open the door and I throw myself at the toilet just in time.

"Ella, I thought you weren't nervous," Jess says as I finally stand up.

"I'm not. I have no idea where that came from. I don't even feel unwell." I wash my hands, making sure I still look okay. I catch Jess' reflection in the mirror, watching me. "Come on. If we don't hurry, kick off will be late," I say, leaving the bathroom. Trevor is standing outside, his eyes narrowing as he looks me over. "If you have any gum, it would be appreciated, or some mints?"

He always has something in his pocket. "Here you go. Are you sure you're okay to do this?"

"Of course I am."

He doesn't look convinced, but there's nothing that would stop me from walking out with those teams.

"Fine," Trevor says, shrugging. "Go and do what you need to do."

And I do. Jess and I walk back toward the players who are waiting for us. When I reach Connor, he pulls me into his arms. "Babe, what's wrong? Why are you sick?"

"I'm okay. We don't have time to talk. You, my handsome sexy man, have a game of football to play," I say, pulling back out of his arms.

"I'll let you get away with that because you said nice things about me, but we will talk later. I promise you."

I step in front of Connor and glance over to Jess as we wait to be told to walk out. The noise level picks up, if that's possible. Music plays and the referee signals for us to walk out. Jess and I have practiced this a few times, but I still wasn't prepared for the sight that greets us as we walk onto the pitch. Chanting and cheering fills the stadium, and as I look around, I see everyone is on their feet, clapping.

It's incredible. I've never experienced anything like it.

My stomach is in knots again at the thought of addressing this crowd. Jess and I were asked to say a few words before the game on behalf of the two charities. Jess wasn't so keen, and me being me said, 'Don't worry. I'll do it.' Now though, as I look around the stadium at the sea of people, I'm not so sure.

Hold it together.

Peter, the manager, walks onto the pitch, microphone in his hand, and I know he's headed my way. The players on both teams shake hands and make their way to their own halves of the pitch. Connor and Fletcher stay behind with Jess and me.

Peter speaks to the crowd and silence descends around this great stadium. I don't hear a word because I'm too busy thinking about what I'm meant to be saying, and I don't remember that either.

Peter hands me the microphone, and with a deep breath and a quick glance at my man, who gives me a reassuring smile, I start to speak.

"On behalf of Homeless and Women's Aid, Jess and I would like to thank you all for coming here today to support two very special charities. Domestic abuse and homelessness shouldn't play a part in today's society, but unfortunately, they do. Hopefully, one day in the future, they won't, but until that happens, we have to ensure that those who need help the most receive it. On behalf of the charities, we would like to take this opportunity to thank everyone associated with the club for everything you have done in helping to prepare for today. We'd like to thank the players and the celebrities for giving up their free time to put on what I'm sure will be a great game. Thank you." I hand Peter the microphone, and the crowd claps loudly.

"You were fab," Connor says, kissing me on the cheek. Jess nods in agreement, tears filling her eyes.

"Good luck," I say to Connor and Fletcher. Jess kisses her man before we leave the pitch with Peter.

Today, they are all winners on that pitch. A game will be played, but the result isn't what's important. The important part of today is helping those who need it the most, and I will take great satisfaction in knowing that lives could change for the better.

Chapter 31

"ELLA, ARE YOU SURE YOU'RE okay?" Jess asks as we walk back through the stadium.

"Yes, I'm fine."

I can tell by the look on her face she's not convinced. We stop inside before we make our way to our seats. "Ella, is there a chance you could be . . . ? No. Never mind me. It's none of my business."

"Yes, I could. Well, I think I am. I wanted to do a test with Connor, but after today's game. I already have a test or two in my bag."

She squeals. "Oh, exciting. How late are you?"

"Oh, over two months. I'm not sure of the exact date."

"Bloody hell, Ella."

"Don't! I had put it down to stress, but even during all that crap with Donovan, my periods were still regular. I kept putting it to the back of my mind with how busy we've been with the final preparations for today, but I'm fairly positive Connor and I are having a baby. Please don't say anything to anyone yet. I'm more worried about how Jack will take this news."

"Of course I won't, but I expect a text after you've done the test. And as for Jack, he's a great kid and will be happy for you. How do you think Connor will take it?"

"Honestly, I don't know. We want children of our own, but

we've never really discussed it other than to say we'll have them one day."

"Well, perhaps that one day is now."

"Yes. Come on. Let's watch our men, and after the match you'll have to help me hide the fact that I'm not drinking."

"Consider it done."

We arrive in the stands just as Fletcher's team kicks off. The whole crowd cheers. Julie smiles as I take the seat next to her. Dad, Callum, and Jack are in the seats behind with Trevor. Jess says hello to several people before taking the seat beside me.

I feel guilty for not telling Julie my secret, but I honestly didn't plan on telling Jess. I'll tell Julie as soon as Connor knows.

A baby. Who'd have thought it?

If someone had told me this time last year I would be Mrs Andrews, with Jack living with us, and having a baby, I'd never have believed it. My life has taken a completely different path and I can't help but smile at how happy I am. Everything has finally fallen into place and I can't imagine my life being any better.

Loud hissing around the stadium draws my attention. I look down at the pitch to see Fletcher lying on the ground with Connor standing over him, helping him up. "What did I miss?" I ask Jess.

"Our men are out to put on a show. Connor brought Fletcher down."

"Ouch."

"It's okay. Look at them." I watch as they exchange playful slaps.

The game continues when Fletcher takes a free kick. I try to keep up, but in all fairness, all I see is men running around the grass, chasing a ball. Jess and everyone else gets so emotionally involved in the game, and I know I should, but I'm a tad anxious and still feeling a little sick.

Jess shouting and standing up beside me brings my head back to the game just in time to see Fletcher score the first goal. Why doesn't that surprise me? Callum nudges me from behind, and I stand and clap. Cheering rings loudly around the whole stadium as he celebrates his goal by blowing Jess a kiss.

The noise level drops around the stadium as the game restarts and we all sit back down. Jess smiles lovingly at him, her eyes full of happiness. I settle in my seat and watch the game, trying to ignore the sick feeling in the pit of my stomach.

I never had Connor down for playing football; I always thought he was more of a rugby man, but as I watch him on the pitch, he looks comfortable and relaxed. The game flows from one end of the pitch to the other and back again, and the celebrities look as though they're handling the game well.

The ball gets passed to Connor and I find myself inching forward on my seat as he's close to the goal. Jess grabs my hand; I look at her and she's grinning. Connor lifts his head, looks at the goal, and takes a shot. Jess pulls me quickly to my feet as the goal hits the back of the net in slow motion. Julie hugs me too and the three of us cheer.

"So, that man of yours can score on and off the pitch," Jess whispers, giggling. I shake my head at her and turn back to the pitch as the celebrities celebrate the goal.

"One each. Now, the question is, did Logan let that goal in?" Julie teases.

"No way. Logan doesn't even let the lads score goals during training sessions. I don't believe for one minute he would willingly let Connor score," Jess says.

The game plays out for another few minutes and then the referee blows the whistle for half-time. Everyone around the stadium claps and cheers. Jess takes us inside. I see my dad and Callum talking to a few men so I don't interrupt them.

Jess introduces me to a few of the companies that have sponsored today's match and I thank each of them for what they're doing. Their support is truly appreciated. Whilst Jess seemed uncomfortable about making a speech before the game, now she's more than happy to discuss the charities today's fundraising will help.

I can't hide my smile as she launches into a full spiel, talking about domestic violence and the homeless issues our country has. She is so passionate about the charities; I can hear it in her voice.

Fifteen minutes passes by so quickly, and Julie and Jess lead the way back outside to the stands. The teams are ready to start. We take our seats, the whistle blows, and the game starts at what seems like a much quicker pace than the first half, both teams looking to get the next goal.

We don't have to wait long for that; the celebrities find the back of the net again. Logan kicks at the grass, shouting at his own players. He's not happy, but Fletcher is laughing at him, shrugging his shoulders.

This half is more interesting than the first; more entertaining. I sit back in my chair, smiling, and carry on watching the game. I almost jump from my seat when Fletcher scores another goal.

"Now, this is entertaining," I say.

"Yeah, and I hate to admit it, but I think Julie was right about Logan. They are giving the fans a show."

That they are. The ball is being passed from player to player, and each team has several shots at goal, but both goalkeepers make save after save, much to the annoyance of the fans.

It's great to watch, but I don't think I'll become a huge football fan, although, as I look at Julie, I think she might. She's loving it.

It's funny being here, surrounded by people who accept me for me. They don't want anything from me except the friendship I have to offer. Nothing about my friends feels fake, unlike in L.A. I always felt everyone had an ulterior motive for befriending me. Yes, there are some genuinely amazing people within the industry, like the cast of the soap. They are all incredible; I've never worked with a nicer bunch of people and many of them are here today, supporting the charities. But there are also some real arseholes. I'm not going to dwell on them because they don't deserve my time.

"Go on." I think it's Callum shouting. I turn and see my brother on his feet. "Never mind me," he says. "Look."

I turn to see Connor score another goal, and from what I can tell, it looks like a great goal. The celebrities are winning three goals to two. I'm secretly pleased, especially when I look at the clock. There's only a minute left.

I close my eyes and pray that Connor's goal is the winning goal, and when I hear the final whistle, I open my eyes and stand. Cheering and clapping for the teams fills the air around the stadium. Tears fill my eyes as I take in the enormity of what we've achieved today. I know I'm being over-emotional, but I can't help it.

"Hey, what are those for?" Julie asks, wrapping her arm around my shoulder.

"I don't know."

"As long as they're tears of happiness," Jess takes my hand in hers. "You and me, we make a great team, and I'm so glad we're friends. The sky's the limit for all of us. Now, I think we should make our way inside. You and I have to face the media again. Are you ready for this?"

"Yes." I turn to my dad and make sure he's okay with Jack, who is raving about Connor scoring the winning goal.

"That's the Ella we all know and love."

Everything happens so quickly. One minute we're in the stands, the next we're giving an interview, and now, a club official is leading Jess and me toward the players' lounge where all the players are with family and friends.

I can't wait to see Connor and have his arms around me. I'd love nothing more than to slip away, alone with him so he's with me as we wait for the results of a pregnancy test.

Jess and I are busy chatting when the official stops and opens the door to the lounge.

I look around the room and everyone is standing and clapping. My body trembles and I can do nothing to hide it. "Come on. No tears," Jess says, taking my hand. Connor walks toward us and Jess lets my hand go.

I stop after a few steps and my body sinks into Connor's warm embrace. "Babe, I'm so proud of you," he says, kissing me. My eyes glance around the room and I sigh seeing Jack laughing with some of the players and Callum.

"Seeing them kind of reminds me of us a few years ago," I hear Jess say to Fletcher, but I don't lift my head. I'm too busy trying to compose myself.

"Come on, Ella. There's so many people waiting to meet you and Jess. Are you okay?" he asks, holding me at arm's length and studying me closely.

"I'm fine. It's been an emotional day."

"It's about to get more emotional for you. The club chairman has some news for you and Jess."

A waiter approaches us with glasses of champagne. He hands one to Jess and then offers one to me. "No, thank you. Could I just have some water, please?" The waiter nods and walks away.

I can feel Connor's eyes burning through me.

"There's only a few times a woman refuses champagne. She's either ill or preg . . ." I cringe a little then smile hearing Fletcher. He doesn't get a chance to finish what he's saying as Jess nudges him.

I finally turn to Connor and, dear God, his face is priceless. His grin is from ear to ear. "Babe, do you have something to tell me?"

"Fletcher!" Jess grabs her man by the hand and marches him toward the bar.

"Yes. I think I'm pregnant."

"What do you mean *think*?"

"I wanted to take the test when you're with me."

"Well, let's nip away and get a test. I need to know."

"I have some in my bag."

"So what are we waiting for?"

"What, here and now?"

"Yes." He takes my hand, pulling me quickly toward the bar, and speaks to Fletcher, asking where we can go. Jess is smiling as she looks between us. Fletcher leads us to an empty office; there is a bathroom just outside it.

Taking the test from my bag, I leave Connor in the office and go into the bathroom.

When I open the bathroom door, he stops pacing. He looks so damn adorable right now as he stops and stares at me. God, I really love him. "Well?"

I hand him the stick. "We need to wait two minutes."

"I know we've never got as far as talking about kids except that we both want them one day, but if we're having a baby, all my hopes and dreams have come true," he says, tears filling his eyes. "My hopes and dreams have always been so close, in touching distance, but at the same time, always felt so far out of my reach. Until not so long ago. Having you share my life is not something I'll ever take for granted. There's nothing scripted about the depths of my feelings for you. The love I have for you can't be written. It's pure and comes from the depths of my soul." He looks at the stick and his tears fall, but in this moment, there is nothing that can mask his happiness. He drops the stick, picking me up in his arms, and spins me around. "You have given me the best gift a man can ever get. I love you so much," he says through his tears.

I wrap my arms around his neck and press my lips to his. "I love you, and together, we're facing a new chapter of our lives."

"Well?" We both turn to see Fletcher and Jess standing in the doorway. "I take it from the tears you're joining the fatherhood club?" Fletcher says, stepping into the office.

I nod.

"Ella, congratulations. This is the best news," Jess says, tears filling her eyes. At this rate, none of us will be able to face anyone because we're all crying.

"Thank you, but you two are going to have to keep this to yourselves until we get a chance to tell our family. I want to tell Jack, but we should do that at home."

"Our lips are sealed," Jess says. "We'll give you a minute then you need to be back in the players' lounge with us."

They leave us alone, but I know they're waiting out in the corridor for us.

"Are you happy?" Connor asks.

"Yes. You have brought me so much happiness through some of the darkest times of my life, and this gift, as you put it, is my gift to you. You, Connor Andrews, are an incredible man and you will be an amazing dad. And I'll never take you for granted. You say our love isn't fake and I know that, but you're wrong when you say this couldn't be written. We have in our hands the key to our very own Hollywood blockbuster, because what we share is our happily-ever-after."

"This is us . . . our scripted love."

Epilogue

"MUMMY! MUMMY! DADDY AND JACK are being horrible to me,"
my daughter cries, running into my bedroom. I take several deep
breaths, trying to calm myself as pain shoots through me.

"Cara, what's wrong?" I ask, holding out my hands. She pulls
her body up onto the bed beside me. I run my fingers through
her curly hair before wiping away her tears. Connor better have
a good reason for causing her tears.

She takes a deep breath. "They won't let me play football.
Fletcher is out the front kicking a ball and Daddy said I'm not
allowed to go."

"Sweetheart, you're only four, and playing football on the road
is not allowed." I try to console her with my soothing voice, but
also confirm the rule that she's too young to play out the front.
"You know you play in the back garden."

"But that's not fair," she whines. "I bet when my baby brother
is here, he'll be allowed out the front to play with Jack because
he's a boy."

I try not to laugh. I rub my expanding stomach. "The same
rules will apply to your baby brother, and as for Jack, I'll speak
to him. It will be a long time before your baby brother can play
anywhere. Now, if Mummy gets dressed, can you find my shoes?
And then, how about you and Jack go over and stay with Fletcher

and Jess today? That way you can play with Emily all day."

"Yes." She jumps from the bed, excited, and offers me her hand to help me up. She's so cute. I get dressed, pulling on a pair of leggings, vest top, and a cardigan. "Mummy, these ones?" she asks, holding up my favourite pair of comfortable slip on trainers.

"Yes." I slip my feet into them and stand, taking her hand. "Let's go and find Daddy."

"Yesss!" She squeals with delight.

We walk down the stairs and the front door is open. It's always kept closed because Cara is forever running outside, and usually straight over to Jess and Fletcher's house. I can hear Connor and Fletcher's voices from outside. I pause for a moment as I breathe through another contraction. They're coming more regularly now. I step outside, still holding Cara's hand.

I swear the men are worse than any of our kids.

The two of them are kicking a football about the front drive, with Jack tackling them both. "What the hell are you playing at?" I yell.

I never imagined staying in a small estate like this, but now I can't imagine staying anywhere else. All our neighbours have become our friends and we're still close enough to Callum and my dad. There's a small community here, yet I still have the privacy that I've gotten used to over the years.

Fletcher stands with the ball at his feet as Connor walks toward me. "How are my favourite people today?"

"Not good," I say with a frown, resting my free hand on my bump. "You've made Cara cry." He bends, picking our daughter up, and gives me a kiss. "Daddy's sorry, but you're not allowed out front."

She huffs.

"But, if Daddy and Jack are out front then Cara can play and Daddy can watch her," I say, looking at Connor.

"Really?" she squeals, wriggling in his arms.

"Yes."

Connor stares at me. He knows I've won. He puts Cara down and she runs over to Fletcher. That girl is football daft and it's all his fault.

"Okay. You're right, as always."

"I'm glad you agree."

"How are you feeling?"

"Tired, and I'm more than ready to meet this little one." I put my hands on my stomach just as our son decides to play some football of his own.

Connor puts his hands on top of mine. His face lights up as he feels our son kicking. "Why don't you rest? I'll see if Jess and Fletcher don't mind having Cara and Jack for a bit and I'll make you something to eat, and maybe run you a bath."

"That sounds really nice, but I'd rather you take me to the hospital."

Connor's eyes dart to my stomach and then back to my face. He attempts to speak but nothing comes out. I laugh at him. "What . . . now?" he asks, finding his voice.

"Yes. It's time for us to meet our son."

"Fletch . . . you and Jess okay to have the kids?" he calls out as Jess comes out of her front door. She already knows I've been having contractions; I told her earlier. I didn't want Connor panicking like he did when I went into labour with Cara. He was a nightmare, completely fussing and not giving me a minute's peace the whole eighteen hours.

Jess stands with me as our daughters play with Fletcher and Jack, and Connor runs in and out of our house, looking for God knows what.

"You'll be fine," Jess says. "I'll call your dad because I'm sure Connor's going to forget." We both laugh, knowing what he's going to be like. Although, if he doesn't get a move on, I'll be delivering our son in the middle of our driveway.

He rushes to my side and takes my hands. "Your bag is in the car, isn't it?"

"Yes."

"So, you two are having a right old laugh at me?"

"Us? Never. Cara, Jack," I call over. "Come here a minute." Cara runs over, full of energy. "You be a good girl for Jess today," I tell Cara. "And as for you, don't cause too much trouble," I say to Jack laughing. For a lad his age, he hasn't given us any problems over the years. He's a brilliant kid and a great big brother to Cara.

"Don't you mean be nice to Fletcher?" She is so funny. "Of course I'll be good for Jess and I'll be nice to Fletcher. I won't kick him when we play football."

I bend and give her a kiss because I have no answer to that.

"I'll be good, but I won't promise not to kick Fletcher playing football." I laugh at Jack's honesty. What a boy. When it comes to football, he doesn't allow anything to get in his way. Even Fletcher. "Mum, we'll be fine. I'll look after Cara." Jack gives me a kiss and runs off. Tears fill my eyes at how grown up he is now. Connor gives Cara a kiss then she runs back and starts playing with Jack, Emily, and Fletcher.

"Ella." Connor's voices startles me.

"I'm sure it was just a slip," I say.

"No. He asked me last night if I thought it would be okay if he called you mum," Connor tells me. "Ella, you are his mum in every way possible and I'm sure his mum is watching over you, over us, and thanking God that he's okay."

"You two need to go," Jess says. "The kids will be fine. Get to the hospital, before you have this baby here."

Connor keeps my hand in his as we walk toward the car, but I have to stop as a strong contraction rips through me. "Ella!"

"I'm fine, honest, just excited about meeting our boy." He opens the car door and I pause, looking at him.

"What's wrong?"

"Nothing. I'm just thinking I'm really lucky." I lift my hand to his face, feeling his five o'clock shadow.

"I'm the lucky one."

"We're both lucky," I say, pressing my lips to his. My body quivers at the sweet tenderness of our kiss. The gentle massage of his lips against mine sends currents of desire through my body.

"A simple kiss is never that between us," he says, adjusting his trousers. "Ella, it's not funny. You're in labour."

"Well, at least I know I still turn you on."

"As if there was ever any doubt about that." I climb into the car and wait for him to close the door, but he doesn't. Instead, he kneels down and takes my hand in his again. "Ella, I just want you to know that everything in my life has been worth waiting for. You are worth it and don't ever forget it. I love our scripted love."

I smile with tears filling my eyes because he's using the very same words I said almost five years ago.

"I love you."

The End

Bonus

Connor

I'M DISCOVERING TODAY THAT I don't have a lot of patience. Which is funny, because I've waited five years for Ella to be mine, but she isn't mine. Not really. Not yet. I've battled with my decision since I woke up. There's been plenty of reasons for and not so many against.

I've had to wait all day long until she and Jack left to go to the shelter before I could come here. And now that I'm getting out of the car, my nerves have kicked in.

I know that in today's society, I don't even need to do this, but I have to. Call me old-fashioned, but I have too much respect for Archie not to give him his place.

I walk to the front door, ring the doorbell, and open the door. "Archie," I call out.

"I'm in the kitchen," he replies.

As I walk through the hallway, I can't help but smile at the family pictures on the walls. Ella and Callum are in most of them. Both always smiling and happy. That was what drew me to Ella when I first met her; her gorgeous smile. It could light up a darkened room.

I pause in front of a family picture by the seaside. I wish I had known Sheena for longer. She and Ella had such a close relationship, and even in this picture, Ella must only be about six, I can see the bond between them. I hope our kids have that with Ella.

I'm jumping the gun a bit.

"What are you doing?" Archie's voice startles me and I turn toward him.

"Just looking at this picture."

"This is one of my favourites. Come on through. I've made tea." I follow him into the kitchen. "So, what brings you here tonight?" he asks, pouring tea into two cups.

I ponder his question and try to think of the right words to say, but come up blank. "Archie, you know how much Ella means to me. I love her. Always have and I always will. I'd like your permission to ask for her hand in marriage," I blurt out nervously.

Archie smiles and gives a low chuckle. "Son, do I make you that nervous?"

"No, sir. But this is a big ask."

"Less of the sir. You've already been family to me for a number of years. So, I'll give you my blessing on one condition."

I smile, thrilled that I have his blessing, because it makes life easier, although I would still be asking her even if I didn't have it. "What's the condition?"

"That you treat Ella with the respect she deserves. She's an amazing young woman, very like her mother. If you treat her right, she'll be your best friend, your lover, and companion for life. But fuck up, and you'll be the one paying the price."

"I won't fuck up. I love and care for her too deeply."

"I know you do. Even Sheena knew you two would end up together. How she knew that all those years ago is beyond me. I wish she was here to see it. Ella finally with the man Sheena believed was worthy of her."

"I was thinking that too as I stood looking at the picture in the hallway. I hope our children have the relationship Ella has with you and had with her mum."

"You got something else you want to tell me?"

I think about his words. "God, no. Not yet." I'm not telling him I'm hoping for children in our near future.

"I'm teasing. The day either of my children tells me I'm going to be a granddad, I'll be a happy man. So, when are you going to propose?"

"As soon as possible. I've waited a long time to have her in my life and I would've asked her that very first day I arrived back here."

"So, now you've done what you came here to do, what are your plans for the rest of the evening?"

"I think I'll go and help out at the shelter. I know Mack and Jack will be there."

"So neither of them are sleeping on the streets now?"

"No. They have a bed every night in the new shelter, until . . . There's still a lot of work to be done to bring it up to standards, but it's dry with running water, heating, and lights."

"It sounds like everything is going to plan."

"Yes. I'm proud of what Ella's helped to achieve in a short period of time."

"Me too. Me too. Finish your tea and go to her."

I LEAN AGAINST the doorframe and watch as Ella and Michelle organise everyone and everything in this room. Mesmerised. She's completely unaware of my presence and that means I get to watch her. Everyone she was talking to was captivated by her words. She's always been able to do that, my Ella; hold the attention of an entire room of people, even when she's unaware she's doing it.

I'm completely and utterly hopelessly in love with Ella McGregor.

Always have been. And sure as hell always will be.

Tonight is the first time this room will be used. I know she's anxious about everything going or not going to plan, but she doesn't need to worry. Every single volunteer here tonight wants the same thing. They all have the same objectives. The charity purchased this old building and is slowly transforming it. The room before me is like a huge games room; pool tables, sofas, a TV. Everything in this room is brand new; nothing but the best. Ella approached Alex about looking for other companies that would be willing to make donations. He not only got her the donations she was looking for, but he managed to get companies to donate their time as well, from decorators to kitchen fitters. There has been a lot more interest in the charity since the ad with Ella went live. Only last week, she had a meeting with MPs and the Scottish first minister about the homeless problem in Scotland. I know I said jokingly to her about being an MP, but she could be and she'd be a damn good one.

Mack is moving some furniture and he looks to be struggling. I step toward him. "Here, let me help."

"Thanks, Connor." The two of us position the table where it's meant to be. "Ella didn't mention you'd be here tonight."

"No. I thought I'd surprise her."

He casts his eyes to her and back to me. "I'm glad you're here. She and Michelle both seem stressed. Tom is sick so he couldn't make it tonight."

"Well then, I'd better roll my sleeves up and go and see what needs to be done. What about you? Are you happy to be working?" Michelle has given Mack a job here as an odd job man. He can turn his hand to almost anything.

"You know what? I am. And I'm grateful to your Ella. She's a keeper."

"She is."

"You had better look after her, because if you don't, there will be a lot of people hunting you down, including Jack. He adores her and you, but mostly Ella."

"I hear you. You're the second person to tell me this tonight I'd better look after her."

"Her dad?" I nod. "Well, then you know what you have to do."

"Yes, and there's no time like the present."

I leave Mack and search the room, finding her after a few moments. She is it for me. Always has been and always will be, no matter what life throws our way. Her eyes lift and she sees me for the first time since I arrived. We hold each other's gaze for a moment. I inhale deeply. 'I love you," she mouths as I walk toward her. Her gorgeous smile as she watches me walking closer sets my insides alight.

"Hi! I didn't expect to see you."

"Well, tonight's a big night and I couldn't not be here to help you," I say, pressing a kiss softly on her lips. My heart swells. Her hair is tied back, her t-shirt is dirty, and she looks tired. But, by God, does she look perfect to me.

"Are you here to help or just gawk at me?" I could and would do that all day long given half the chance, because to me, she's perfection.

"Help and gawk, because, let's face it, there's not a man on the planet who wouldn't want to trade places with me and be able to look at you all day long every day of his life."

"Have you and my brother been out drinking?"

I laugh at her. Michelle finishes her speech and turns to Ella, thanking her for everything she's done. They talk for a few minutes, and I'm suddenly feeling nervous as I wait. After a what feel's like forever, Michelle leaves Ella's side.

It's now or never.

I take the box from my pocket, open it, and drop to my knee, keeping her hand in my mine. She gasps and I'm certain everyone in the room stops and is watching us. "There's only one woman in the world I want and she brings me to my knees on a daily basis.

She's talented and beautiful. Loving and caring. She's funny and smart. Passionate and loyal. Ella McGregor, will you do me the greatest honour and become my wife?"

A lonely tear trickles down her face and she nods. I slide the ring on her finger and she pulls my hands, drawing me to my feet. "Yes," she says, and my smile breaks free. All the tension and nerves I felt before I got here have long gone.

There's lots of clapping and cheering. It wasn't my intention to take away from the great work they've done, but as soon as I laid eyes on her when I entered, I knew I had to do it. She wraps her arms around me and my eyes find Mack and Jack. They're standing about ten feet away, grinning from ear to ear. I'm glad they're pleased. Jack is wiping his eyes and Mack puts his arm around him, offering him comfort.

Ella is my life, and I'm hoping that everything will go in our favour when it comes to Jack. I know my wife to be will be devastated if things don't go to plan.

I've always hoped and prayed that my life would head in the right direction. That our paths would bring us together. Right now, in this moment, I'm thankful for everything and everyone in my life. Especially my perfect Ella.

She's my light.

She's my everything.

Books by
KAREN FRANCES

THE CAPTURED SERIES
Family Ties a Captured Series Novella
He's Captured my Heart Book 1
He's Captured my Trust Book 2
He's Captured my Soul Book 3
She's Captured my Love Book 4
Captured by Our Addiction Book 5

A BEAUTIFUL GAME SERIES
Playing the Field, A Beautiful Game Novella
Playing the Game Book 1
Playing to Win Book 2
Saving the Game

Moving On a standalone

SCRIPTED SERIES
Scripted Reality Book 1
Scripted Love Book 2

About the Author

KAREN FRANCES IS THE AUTHOR of ten romance novels and two novellas.

She currently lives just outside Glasgow, Scotland, with her husband, five children and two dogs, although she does dream of living somewhere warm and sunny. Her days are spent helping her husband run their busy family business. She spends some of her free time trying to keep fit and prepare healthy meals for her family, when their busy schedules allow them to sit down at meal times together. The rest of her free time she uses to plot and write and occasionally read.

Karen writes stories that are both believable and full of life. More often than not she loves sending her readers on an emotional journey alongside her characters.

For more information
www.karenfrancesauthor.co.uk

Acknowledgements

WRITING THIS PART OF THE book terrifies me. I'm always scared that I miss someone's name out, someone that has played a huge part in making this book a reality.

So if I do miss anyone, I'm apologising now. I'm sorry.

Through all the ups and downs life throws my way, I'm still blessed with amazing family and friends who support and encourage me. I also have an incredible team who help me bring my stories to life.

Paul and my kids, it's been tougher than usual lately but with all your help and support, I got there in the end. Although if the kids would stop bickering I might make things a little easier. Love you to the moon and back.

My friends and family, you are always there when I need you and I can't imagine not having any of you in my life. Love you all.

Laura, Maxine and not forgetting Suzie, I really would be lost without you. Love you.

April and Leah, thank you for once again reading a very rough draft of Scripted Love and giving me your honest feedback.

Margaret, thanks again for the final read through.

Karen, my editor and friend, I think I'm running out of words for you. Love you.

Kari, as always you are the best.

Christine, you are also the best at what you do.

I've been fortunate and made so many friends on this incredible journey so far, some I've met and others I hope to meet one day.

To all the bloggers and authors that I know and don't know within our amazing community, you all rock.

To all the readers, thank you.

Printed in Great Britain
by Amazon

61825807R00158